THE PAYBACK ASSIGNMENT
"...an exiting and fast paced action thriller that will hold your interest as he takes you from the high society of Los Angeles, into the steaming jungles of Belize and back to the rich and famous in their high-rise apartments. It's not often I support the criminals, but I can relate to the anger and frustrations that both Stark and O'Brien must feel at being ripped off by their unscrupulous employer. I would recommend *Payback Assignment* to everybody who enjoys a good action story."
- Scribblers Reviews

BLOOD AND BONE
"…is an action-packed, sensitively written thriller. Hannibal Jones is a hero whom anyone would want on their side. He and his girlfriend Cindy make one heck of an investigative team. Mr. Camacho creates so many twists and turns that the reader can only hang on until the exciting crescendo. The action spans continents; the characters are chameleons; and the plot is a real corkscrew. A great read from a talented story craftsman!!"
- Midwest Book Review

COLLATERAL DAMAGE
"Nicely worked plot, constant action and likable characters recommend this to larger collections."
- Library Journal Magazine

THE TROUBLESHOOTER
"Austin Camacho, the author of this tale of derring-do, unfolds the story line at the pace of an action movie. He also uses cinematic tricks to establish characters quickly."
- The Easton Star Democrat

DAMAGED GOODS
"… is a fast-paced, thrilling novel that will keep readers frantically reading to the last page."
- Romance Readers Connection

THE
ORION
ASSIGNMENT

by

Austin S. Camacho

Copyright October 2006 by Austin S. Camacho

ISBN 0-9762181-6-X

Cover design by Gerry Brophy

Published by:

Intrigue Publishing
7707 Shadowcreek Terrace
Springfield, VA 22153

Printed in the United States of America
Printed on Recycled Paper

THE
ORION
ASSIGNMENT

Prologue

The priest had just finished the benediction when a rumble like the wrath of God burst in his right ear.

The explosion kicked fist sized bits of his small stone church across the front pew. Screams of panic filled the room, and all but the clergyman ran in a blind panic toward the door. His eyes went first to the crumbling wall, then to old Mrs. O'Casey.

Mrs. O'Casey, who spoke fluent Gaelic and walked with a halting tread on spindly legs to sit right down front every Sunday morning without fail just to his right. The stone wall was shifting, its mortar shattered by the explosive blast. Ancient rock would fall in seconds, crushing Mrs. O'Casey's brittle bones, and she was too shocked to move out of the way.

Ears still ringing from the bomb burst, eyes stung by mortar dust, the barrel-chested priest leaped down to the bench and swept his parishioner up in his arms. Breathing through clenched teeth, he jogged up the center aisle. Cradling the old woman like a child, he burst out into the morning's dampness and sunlight. He managed to stand Mrs. O'Casey up in the arms of two younger women before he dropped to his knees, racked with violent coughs.

*   *   *   *   *

A soccer field's length away, the window of a gray Mercedes limousine slid down, letting a wisp of the fine Irish mist in. The well dressed passenger in the back seat had a thick shock of wavy red hair. He watched the cloud of smoke roll out of the side of the small church building. The left side of the pitiful structure sagged inward. He could just hear the churchgoers, still screaming and running in circles.

A smile lit the red headed man's tan eyes as his window slid up. He tapped his driver's shoulder with his walking stick and the car moved off. His message had been delivered.

*   *   *   *   *

"Are ye all right, Sean?"

"No harm done," the priest said, brushing himself off. "At least not to me." His vestments were filthy, but he removed them with care, revealing a black suit underneath. "At least it looks like everyone got outside okay. But my poor church..."

A man in gray was pulling his hat down over his eyes as he stepped onto the stone path away from the church. Sean's congregation was small these days, and he knew every face in it. This man was a stranger, and strangers were rare in the Irish countryside.

Then Sean turned back to his little church, and walked around the side of the building as if afraid of what he might see. "It looked like it was a small explosion. But, dear Lord in heaven." He stared into a hole wide enough for him to force his broad shoulder through if he wanted to. "What kind of a monster would do such a thing?"

"Ye know full well what kind of monster," Mick Murphy replied. He was a portly man with a big chin and eyes like a ferret's. "You need help, Sean, and if you don't mind me saying so, we both know where you can get it. Go on and get the girl."

"The Lord will provide," the priest said. He watched his parishioners scrambling to the road, many of the women still wailing. His heart sank knowing he was helpless to comfort them or calm their fears.

"Remember the man in the flood, Sean?" Mick asked. "He's hanging on to the roof and a boat comes by. They call for him to jump in and he says `Begone. The Lord

2

will provide'. When he dies on that roof, he ends up facing the Lord in heaven. He says `Lord, I trusted you to provide and you let me die', and the Lord says..."

"Yes," the priest said, "The Lord says `I sent you a boat, you fool.' I remember the story, Mick."

"Well, the Lord has provided you a way if you'll take it, Sean." Both men turned to watch the stained glass window above the hole slide to the ground and explode into shards. The priest's stomach clenched and he fought back tears of anguish or rage. He didn't know which.

"My friend, forget your pride. Go and get the girl. Bring Felicity home."

- 1 -

It was the most glorious Easter ever. A brilliant sun was shining down through cotton ball clouds. The slightest breeze blew in from the lough, carrying the sweet smell of clover. Every person on the narrow street wore a smile of greeting. The little red haired girl stared around like Alice in Wonderland.

She was only six years old, and this was the high point of her young life. Her mother had made her a lovely new pastel blue dress. Father had bought her white shoes and gloves and a darling hat to wear to church. Her deep green eyes sparkled with delight when she looked in the mirror.

They were simple country folk, and the girl couldn't remember going to the city before. Belfast was a teeming metropolis in her eyes. The buildings fascinated her, huddled so close together that they rubbed shoulders. She marveled at the doors, each a different bright color with fan shaped transoms over them. The street was cobblestone, but it had a sidewalk. And it looked like a street lamp stood on every corner. And surely everyone here owned an automobile, there were so many.

The little girl was skipping along, clutching a parent's hand on each side. Every once in a while she tried to swing between them. Father told her she was much too old for that. He wore a new tweed suit and smelled of good wool. Mama smelled like wild flowers.

It was going to be a joyous day. She could imagine everything--the priest greeting them and telling her what a pretty girl she was, her own blushing, and Father telling the priest not to turn her head. It was all just a few minutes away. She could see the tall steeple ahead.

That was when it hit her for the first time. The fear that seemed to crawl out of the ground and up her spine to the nape of her neck. It was the horror she felt when she knew Father was on his way to give her a spanking, but worse. She had no idea what caused it, she only knew she was terrified.

Hair danced all over as she shook her head back and forth. She dragged her feet, trying to pull her parents back. Father asked, "What's gotten into you child?" but she could not answer. Mama said "Felicity Kathleen, you behave like a lady." With a violent wrenching she pulled her hands free from the two holding them.

Father sat down on the hood of a blue Buick with big fins standing at the curb. The girl ran to the nearest shop doorway, flattening herself against the door. She could smell the sweet scent of the baked goods from behind her. Pressing her back against the door put her parents out of sight around the edge of the doorway. She heard mother stamp in her direction. She heard the springs groan as her father pushed to rise from the auto he was leaning on.

Then the world exploded in a deafening blast. There was the sound of shattering glass and metal twisted out of shape. It was so loud she could not hear her own screams. The stench of burning wool and roasting flesh replaced the smell of pies and cakes.

The girl screamed and screamed. The concussion forced her tears back along the sides of her head, into her ears. The horror rose into her throat and she tried to scream it out.

*   *   *   *   *

Felicity O'Brien sat bolt upright, terror stretching her eyes wide. Most of the bulky comforter hung off the side of the bed. Her hair was heavy with the weight of perspiration. Sweat glistened on her taut breasts. A vein pulsed hard in her neck and she gasped for breath.

That dream, that God damned dream was back

again. How many times would she have to relive that tragic day? How many times would she have to watch, helpless and powerless, as her parents died? Must she spend the rest of her life wondering why it had to be them? Why them and not her? If only she had understood the meaning of that awful feeling. If only she had known it was her mysterious ability to sense danger, activated for the first time. It had saved her life many times since then. If only she had recognized it for what it was that day, it could have saved theirs.

Fighting to keep from retching, Felicity stumbled into the bathroom. She got into the shower and turned on the water as hot as she could stand it. Leaning against the wall, she fell into wracking sobs.

If only the nightmare had happened the night before. Raoul had been there, and soothed her with his continental attentions. It would help to have someone to hold onto when the dream came, she thought. But he let himself out before dawn, leaving her to face the terror alone.

She had to pull herself together. She lathered herself with chamomile soap while she administered her self-oriented pep talk. How could she let a dream ravage her mind like this? Everyone knew she had nerves of steel. Was this any way for an infamous, international jewel thief to act?

Ex-jewel thief, she reminded herself, as she toweled herself dry after her shower. Last year this time she was at the height of her trade. Now she was a respectable business woman with a thriving enterprise to run. After a near brush with death, she and her new partner used their savings to set up a corporation on the outskirts of Los Angeles. She retired from crime as he retired from an even more dangerous life.

By seven forty-two a.m. Felicity was dressed for business. She knew the time exactly, despite the fact that she didn't own a watch and not one clock ticked in her penthouse apartment. She was born with the special gift of perfect time sense. Her internal timepiece matched the reliability of any man made chronometer.

Felicity wasn't at all concerned about reaching her eight-thirty appointment on time. She just stepped out the front door, across the central plaza and into an elevator. Five stories below, the doors slid open revealing a wide glass wall. Centered in that wall was a glass door bearing two lines of simple lettering. At about eye level it read, "STARK & O'BRIEN" and below that, in smaller letters, "Security and Crisis Management Consultants." As she opened the door, those words made her smile. In the months since she had ordered the lettering for that door she had taken care of the security side of the business with ease. After all, she had made a career of defeating security measures. Who could know better how to keep people from getting in where they were not wanted?

"Good morning, Ms. O'Brien. Mister Stark is out of town today, and you have an eight-thirty."

"And good morning to you, Miss Fox," Felicity returned as she walked in. She and Morgan hired Sandy Fox away from a big name detective agency, at the very start of "Stark & O'Brien", to be their receptionist and secretary. Despite ash blonde hair and blue eyes behind her high fashion glasses, Fox was not glamorous. Felicity would have described her as cute, of average height and medium build. She wore a neat dark suit. Sandy's look was always appropriate to a business office, something Felicity was not at all confident about herself.

"So Sandy, do I look all right today?"

"You are truly beautiful, ma'am," Sandy said. Felicity was tall, with long, full red hair, piercing green eyes and a perfect body, but that was not what she was asking about.

"Come on. I mean the outfit." Felicity had long since mastered the perfect look to travel in high society or the criminal underground. She also knew how to be nondescript, invisible to passersby. The professional world was still new to her. This day she wore a simple black wool skirt, plain black pumps and a white silk blouse. A gray and green mohair shawl hung draped over her shoulders, tied at the right.

"Oh, yes. The look is all business. So tell me something. How come it makes you look like a movie star?"

Stuck between frustration and embarrassment, Felicity waved a hand at Sandy and muttered, "Go on with you." She headed toward her inner office.

"Oh, that weird guy Paul is waiting in there. He insists on reporting in or something."

Felicity stopped and turned to look back at Sandy. "That weird guy?"

Fox blushed then, as she so often did. "Sorry boss but, geez, that guy gives me the creeps."

"He had the same effect on me when we met," Felicity said, returning to the reception counter and leaning on it. "He's probably the second most dangerous man I've ever met, with his hands or a gun. And when we met he was pointing his gun at me."

"Really?"

"He had been hired to kidnap me and rip me off," Felicity said. "It's a long story. But today he's a valuable member of our little team and if you give him a chance he kind of grows on you."

While Fox blushed even deeper, Felicity moved on into her office and sat behind her custom made desk. It was shaped like a paisley print amoeba, the fat end on her right. Its top was white Italian marble, resting on steel polished to a mirror finish. The legs seemed to grow straight up out of the plush white carpet. The entire office had been designed and decorated to say, "success."

"So, Paul, what's on for today?" The tall man with ice blue eyes stood in front of her desk with no expression at all on his face.

"I have a courier assignment that will take me to the East Coast today," Paul said in his accent-free voice. "Unless you have something else, Miss O'Brien."

"Will you please relax," she said, pulling a folder from her desk drawer. She planned to review the proposal she would present at eight-thirty. "You've done a fine job from the beginning and I trust you know what you ought to be doing. Lord, you're an employee not a slave."

"Sorry, Miss. I caused you some inconvenience last year..."

Felicity interrupted him. "Inconvenience? Well, that's one way to put stranding a girl in the South American jungle. But you got the drop on me, and that's not an easy thing to do."

"Yes, ma'am, but after you and Mister Stark saved my life..."

"I've asked you never to mention that again. You're a professional. When you tried to hurt me back then you were doing a job. Just like you will today, I'm quite sure."

"Yes, ma'am. I should begin. Good day." Paul wafted out of the room without a sound. He was good, which is why they hired him. He recognized their professionalism, which was why he worked for them. That, and his imagined debt.

She reflected back on the first days of their thriving business. Marlene Seagrave, a New York businesswoman, recommended them to several industrialists. It was the least she could do. Morgan and Felicity saved her life too, after her husband tried to have them killed. Paul worked as an enforcer for Mr. Seagrave then, but Morgan and Felicity rescued him and Mrs. Seagrave from a blazing building. This earned Paul's loyalty and several referrals from Mrs. Seagrave.

Many other early clients were wealthy individuals whom Felicity knew were recent robbery victims. She knew this, because she had committed those robberies.

From there, business grew by word of mouth.

Today's job involved a chemical plant. She had already spent hours designing a comprehensive security plan, to theft-proof the factory as much as possible. She used third generation electronics, combined with state of the art surveillance equipment and her own years of experience in surreptitious entry.

This particular contract was one of their most lucrative, since it included an executive personal security plan devised by Morgan Stark, her partner. He had built an excellent reputation for expertise in arranging for the safety of key personnel in a short time. He designed their schedules, offices and cars to reduce the terrorist threat. Years as a mercenary soldier made him an expert in such matters.

While she thought, she stared at the diamond shaped étagère on the left wall. She bought this glass-shelved case because of its uniqueness, but now it seemed everybody had one. She wondered if she should keep it.

The annoying buzz of her intercom snapped her back to reality.

"Miss O'Brien, there's a Father Sullivan on the line. He insists on speaking with you now." In those five seconds, she went from julep cool to flustered. How did he find her? What did he want? Why was he calling her now?

"Hello," she found herself saying into the telephone receiver.

"I know you're busy and can't talk now," said the voice from the other end. "I just needed t'be sure it was really you and you were in. I'll be coming up there in five minutes. We'll talk then. Bye bye." She struggled to mumble good-bye. God how she had missed that thick brogue.

The next few minutes seemed like hours. She found herself pulling up her hose, smoothing down her skirt and pacing. Pacing? Where were the iron nerves she

10

had when walking a high wire?

Then Ms. Fox opened the door and in he walked in his tweed suit and white collar, with his nose broken from his early days and a big smile under bright blue eyes. They embraced and all those memories came rushing back at her. Mental pictures of a youth spent in the Catholic Church flew past her mind's eye, a whirling kaleidoscope of images from her years being raised by this man built like a bulldog with salt and pepper hair.

"By gosh, girl, are you trying to crack me ribs?"

"I'm sorry Uncle Sean," Felicity said, her face beaming. "I've just missed you so much."

"Have you now, girl? Then why is it you've never called or written?"

After a brief awkward silence, she said, "Well, why don't we go up to my apartment? I can cancel my appointments, and there's so much to catch up on."

"Felicity, me dear, the reason I came to your office is because I'm here on business. I want to hire you to do a job for me."

"You came all the way from Ireland to see me...to hire me?" Felicity looked around in confusion and realized they were still standing in the middle of the room. She motioned Sean toward a chair and moved her left hip onto her desk. He continued to stand, slid his hands into his pockets, and spoke in a flat professional tone.

"We've got a bit of a problem back home. A security matter you see. Threats. Vandalism. Finally, last week, a small bomb set off in me church. I hear you're in the business of keeping these things from happening."

"Oh Uncle Sean, are you sure these aren't just random acts? I mean, why would anyone want to hurt you or your church?" She began to build a smile, but her uncle's stony stare froze it in midair.

"I'll tell you why. I speak out against the violence up north. Against the hatred. Against the `Provisional Irish Republican Army' and the Sinn Fein. It's not a popular stand with some."

"But that's all over," Felicity said. "There's a cease fire on. The Provos, the IRA, have quieted down now. They've all disarmed, for goodness sake. Let's face it, bombing churches is a little out of fashion, even up in Ulster." Her logic bounced off her uncle's face, which was set hard as carved granite.

"You're serious, aren't you?" she asked. With slow, halting steps she paced to the far end of the room, gaining time to think. When she turned she was shaking her head. "Uncle Sean, I'll gladly help you, but I don't want to do business with you."

"Nonsense! I need your professional help. Don't you think the church can raise your fee?"

"Don't be ridiculous!" Her words snapped out like the end of a lash through teeth set in a stubborn grimace. "If you insist on handling your problem in a businesslike manner, then I would have to consult with my associate, who's out of town at this time."

"That would be fine. I'll be back tomorrow at four."

"No," she cried when Sean reached for the doorknob. "Please. Come up and stay at my place."

"I have accommodations, thank you. And I'd like to see some of your lovely city while I'm here."

"You stubborn old..." she began, then regained control. "All right. Just tell me where you're staying. We could meet for dinner or something. I'll pick you up tomorrow evening. We'll sit in my apartment, we'll make our business arrangements and then maybe we can talk a little. Please? Okay?" She ended her plea with a hug and a peck on his cheek. The older man put his arm around her slim waist. He smelled of tweed and leather.

"All right, child. I'll come to your home tomorrow if you really insist."

"Uncle," she grinned, giving him a squeeze, "I really insist."

- 2 -

Felicity O'Brien was a connoisseur of fine cars. She had driven all the Italian greats: Maserati, Ferrari, Lamborghini. She owned a Lotus Elan Coupe, a Datsun 350 ZX Turbo, a Mazda RX-7, a vintage Jaguar XKE and the latest edition Corvette ZR-1. As a driver of some of the slickest sports cars ever designed, she hated the borrowed Jeep she was driving. The clutch was hard, the gear box stiff, the steering unresponsive. The seat was a spring loaded granite slab. Her teeth rattled with each bump. Lord, she hated cross country driving.

But that dusty old Jeep was all the blinking sod of a rancher had. He was reluctant to lend it to her, but Felicity was persuasive and even convinced the man to point in the direction Morgan had gone just hours before.

It had been a short flight to the sheep ranch. Ms. Fox had given her Morgan's location. She said he had spent the last three days on that ranch and that he had gone there to do some hunting. Felicity knew that he liked to go off by himself every so often, to live off the land and perhaps experiment with some new field equipment. This time it was labeled a business trip, for which it appeared he would receive some small fee.

Armed with that information she had rushed home and changed into jeans and leather boots. Then she hurried to a small airstrip, hired a private plane and charged off to that remote locale.

Ten minutes of desolation bumped past before she started feeling a subtle mental tug to her left. A slow smile spread over her face as she wrestled the wheel over. She was becoming accustomed to the peculiar psychic link she and Morgan shared.

She had been able to sense when danger threatened her since she was very young. But then, just months before had she met Morgan, and found that he had the same bizarre warning instinct. It didn't take long to discover that they were on the same "wavelength" somehow. Not only could she sense his distress, but if she relaxed enough, she could feel his very location. Even now, the weird tingle in her scalp guided her to her partner and best friend.

As she rattled on over rolling grassy land, her mind flashed back over the last year. They met in a South American jungle. She had stolen a rare piece of jewelry for a man named Seagrave. He double-crossed her and ordered his men to leave her stranded in that tropical forest. As it turned out, Seagrave had done the same to Morgan. In the days that followed, Felicity and Morgan saved each other's lives, fought and bled together, and became closer than either of them had ever been to anyone.

It was in those first few days, long before either of them considered going straight, that they learned about their mental link. At moments of intense emotional reaction they could somehow feel each other's sensations. This, as it turned out, made sex impossible. But as their relationship evolved that fact became irrelevant. Felicity supposed that she loved Morgan as much as she would a brother if she had one. But she trusted him much more.

Dragging her mind back to the present she stopped about fifty yards away from him, pulling the Jeep up beside a motorcycle parked among the dunes. The ground there was like a calm but rolling sea somehow frozen solid. Morgan lay prone against a sandy swell, his head and rifle stretched over the crest. A desert camouflage uniform covered his muscular, brown-skinned body. His kinky hair was cut short. A large tumbleweed lay to the left of his head, and a wide, squat cactus bush stood on his right. His six foot two inch frame was frozen in absolute stillness.

She could feel the tranquility of the scene, just as she could smell the sweet cactus blossoms and fresh crisp air. The total silence gave her the feeling of a diorama, set up in a museum for the viewer's amusement. Perhaps Morgan was staring, fixed on some faraway target. If his concentration was strong enough, maybe she could even sneak up on him.

When she wanted to, Felicity could move with absolute silence. It was a cat burglar prerequisite. Not even a professional mercenary of Morgan's experience could hear her approach.

Of course, he did not need to hear her.

"Freeze, Red." Morgan's sharp voice snapped out, low but intense, when she got within twelve feet of him. His right arm swung back, his index finger jabbing right at her face. He remained still except for that one arm. When his finger returned to its original position, curled around a trigger, his stillness resumed.

Seven seconds later she was startled by a crack like earthbound thunder. The echo flashed out to the horizon and back, and Morgan stopped holding his breath. He waved Felicity forward and pulled his Remington model 700 back to reload the bolt action weapon. In a moment she stretched out beside him, feeling the comforting warmth of the sand and the annoying scratch of the short, sparse grass. She didn't bother with a greeting beyond her smile and a brief nod.

"So, what are you shooting at?"

"Coyotes," Morgan said. "The sheep rancher's having a problem with coyotes. I saw an opportunity to test this new round I'm experimenting with."

"He's paying you for this?"

Morgan waved the question away. "Every one of those pelts is worth a good hundred dollars. The coyotes will pay for the trip."

"A new round? I thought you told me that rifle fired twenty-twos."

"Sure," Morgan replied, settling behind his Leopold variable power scope. "Twenty-two two-fifty caliber. I reamed the chamber out to take a larger case. I use the six millimeter Remington case and neck it down to take the twenty-two cartridge."

"Of course," Felicity said with a smirk. "That's just what I'd do. So much better for, well, must be better for something."

"Sniper work," Morgan said. "Coyote hunting is a lot like sniper work. I don't know if you pay that much attention to my side of the business, but I've got a couple of subcontractors working as counter-snipers in Iraq."

"Counter snipers?"

"When some insurgent takes a shot at our civilian contract force, we hit back, but with precision. For them, I wanted a cartridge that would shoot a bullet fast and flat. It's got to have a lot of power. And it shouldn't make a big mess of the target or in this case, damage the pelt. Here, take a look." He handed her a pair of binoculars. "Today I'm using forty-six grains of powder behind a fifty-two grain hollow point bullet."

"Right." From her viewpoint, Morgan was speaking meaningless gibberish now. He was in his own world, a world of soldiers and hunters. All she could see through the binoculars were two...well, dogs, maybe two feet high or so, with beautiful fur in a light brown, almost yellow color. The Steiner glasses brought her face to face with these animals across the plains. They were looking around in confusion, sometimes looking down at their fallen comrade.

A loud crack on her left made her jump again. In her binoculars, she saw the larger coyote stiffen and fall onto its side. His partner's ears perked and he backed away.

"Right through the lungs," Morgan said, grinning and cocking his fist back, "at three hundred fifty yards." He could judge distances with incredible accuracy, as she well knew. Silence returned and she went back to viewing the distant coyote, pacing back and forth with that light tread that made some animals appear to float across the ground. She knew this beast was raiding some rancher's sheep. Yet, this whole scenario bothered her. No, the truth was, it was Morgan who bothered her. Rifles, she thought, were a way to make killing impersonal and remote. Yet he made it as personal as possible. He modified his rifle, hand loaded and even designed the ammunition to bring these animals down.

"Morgan, I need to talk to you."

"In a minute, Red," Morgan said, getting a good sight picture on the third coyote.

"I'm looking at a job I'm not sure we should take."

"Not now, Red," Morgan hissed through clenched teeth, tightening his cheek weld to the walnut butt stock.

"Morgan, please don't shoot him."

"What?" Morgan stared at Felicity as if he doubted his hearing.

"He's so pretty. And you've already proven twice that you can do it. And my uncle who I haven't seen in seven years wants to hire us."

"What?" Morgan asked again, sounding like an eavesdropper, falling behind the conversation.

"I want to hug him and ask him how things are back home, not do business with him."

"You might have to do business with him as an excuse to visit home," Morgan offered.

"And why do you hunt, anyway?"

"Huh?" Morgan was kneeling up now, as if maybe reading her lips would aid his comprehension.

"I mean, you don't need it for food, like those poor beasts."

He seemed to seize on that point, as if finally she had asked a question he could answer. "Red, hunting is the best way to improve your hearing. To sharpen your eyesight. To acquire stealth." He paused to think.

"Besides, it's fun."

"You should try being the hunted. It does all the same things for you. Nothing could match the rush of walking through a crowd of police with a pocket full of hot diamonds. Uncle Sean is meeting me tomorrow evening. Please come back tonight. I can't deal with him alone."

Morgan sat up, laid his rifle down and rested a hand on her shoulder. "This thing's really got you shook up, hasn't it? Of course I'll come back. We'll work out your family problems together." He gave her a hug, and felt her gratitude as she returned it.

Morgan saluted the lone coyote who howled, perhaps in return. As the animal trotted off, Morgan headed for his bike. His partner needed him, and that was enough reason to leave right away. He would send the farmer back for the two valuable pelts.

While Felicity settled into the Jeep, he slung his rifle across his back and straddled the five hundred cc Yamaha waiting for him. His bike was not over-chromed but it was a pure off road racer built for speed. From his saddlebag he pulled leather gloves. The black helmet he lifted from the ground had a one way visor. When he slid it over his face, he was unidentifiable. He kicked the bike into life, circled Felicity's Jeep once and moved out next to her.

His mind was reeling. He couldn't begin to understand why a visiting uncle with a business proposition would be such a traumatic event. So much about this girl, his partner and best friend, was still a mystery to him. He knew she had left her homeland before she reached twenty and never looked back. He believed she sent money home during her impressive career as a most daring and successful jewel and art thief. He knew her parents died when she was a child, but she never talked about what she had done between then and her appearance on the continental crime scene. And he would never ask. She always came across as a total loner. Was it possible she missed this uncle, or felt guilty about leaving? Maybe they parted on bad terms.

His front tire hit a clump of dirt that almost toppled him. He realized it bounced him much harder than it should have. A glance at his speedometer told him he had pushed his machine over ninety miles per hour in his reverie. An unconscious lapse back to his bike racing days, he thought, as he doubled back to rejoin the Jeep.

- 3 -

Father Sean Sullivan left his motel room, easing down the steps from the landing outside. It certainly was not like any hostelry he ever stayed at in Eire. He found these rooms cold and impersonal. The management was standoffish, the blankets scratchy and thin, and if you wanted breakfast you could very well walk out and find it yourself.

The priest wore rich brown wool trousers and big brown shoes with laces. He held a big bowled briar pipe clenched tight in his teeth. The sleeves of his hand knit turtleneck sweater were pushed up over muscular, hairy forearms.

He didn't need a sweater against the rain here. It came down hard enough, but it seemed to turn to steam as soon as it touched the pavement. The mist, as thick here as at home, had an entirely different texture. It seemed dirty, as if it was mixed with factory smoke and car exhaust.

Sean stood with hands thrust deep in his pockets, staring into the rain, just under the porch-like covering outside the manager's office. Would his ride come in a big limousine to impress his guest? Or worse, in one of those dangerous little sports cars? What kind of man would his little Felicity be sending round for him? These days she was living in a world of big fancy offices and thousand dollar suits of clothes, showing off her body, like a real American. How far she had wandered from her roots.

Sean pulled his hat brim low over his weathered face, hiding his long eyebrows. A vehicle approached through the shimmering sheer curtain of the rain. It screeched to a halt in front of the priest. He did not know it was for him until the plastic windowed door of the Jeep CJ-7 popped open and a deep voice with no detectable accent sprang out.

"Father Sullivan?"

After a beat of hesitation he answered, "Yes," and stooped to see into the Jeep.

"Get in. It's wet out there."

Within a second of Sean getting under the cloth top, Morgan popped the clutch and the small sport Jeep dived forward into the night.

This would be Felicity's business partner, of course, the expert in crisis management. Sean was not quite sure what he expected but this certainly wasn't it. Not this big, broad shouldered black man in jeans and leather boots. He wore a black tee shirt with a gold map of Vietnam overlaid with red letters reading "Next time let us win." It wasn't prejudice but lack of familiarity that caused his slight hesitation when the long fingered brown hand thrust toward him. When he took it, the handshake proved firm, warm and dry.

"So...Father? Sullivan? Sean?"

"Father will be fine," Sean said. "And you must be Mister Stark, Felicity's partner."

"Morgan will be fine."

"So you're partners as I understand it, but just what do you do in this business?" Sean asked. "Felicity provides security for people?"

"Yeah, Felicity handles most of the domestic stuff. I've got a small team doing security work in Iraq right now, and another one training Pakistanis in night flying and airborne assault tactics to combat foreign and local fighters in the tribal areas of Pakistan near the Afghan border."

They drove in silence for a time, with Sean's attention moving from the road to the driver and back again. Just as the priest was getting comfortable, Morgan spoke without turning his head. "You know, Father, Felicity's real glad to see you, but it's funny. She's more nervous than I've ever seen her. She's concerned about your approval. I don't know. She says you're her uncle, but she acts more like you were her father...Father."

"Well, you certainly get right down to the point, don't you lad?" Sean said as Morgan down shifted and pushed the Jeep into a smooth slide around a corner. "Well Felicity's real father was my brother-in-law. But he and my sister were killed when Felicity was still a wee child, and that left me her only living relative. They lived up in Ulster, you know. I went up and brought Felicity down to Glendalough."

"Correct me if I'm wrong, but they don't usually let priests raise kids, do they?" He seemed to drive with total disregard for speed limits, yet he had total control of the Jeep.

"Course not," Sean said, refilling his pipe from a pouch in his pocket. "I placed her with the Daly's, a fine couple. Married four years at the time and still childless. They so wanted a little girl, and they lived right by the church. The child was in shock for a while but I figured she'd adjust with God's help.

"Then poor Paddy Daly lost his job and he started drinking. I tried to...I did my best with him, but he wandered away from The Church. Then one day he just...wandered away."

Morgan sat through the following silence without prodding for more. Sean wondered if the other man could guess at the guilt he felt. He was a priest who could not stop one of his flock from sliding away from the Church. And that one was his niece's chosen guardian.

Smoke filled the Jeep like stale memories. Morgan unzipped his window to let some slip out. Sean cleared his throat and continued.

"I was Felicity's father figure mostly. Mrs. Daly, bless her heart, she tried to be a good mother to her, to steer her little fire haired vixen in the right direction. The girl was a constant reader and good in school. Her mind was incredibly quick, yet there was something odd about her. Like there was something inside her no one could touch."

Morgan interrupted with a curse as a light turned red in front of them. He stopped just in time. The jolt made Sean realize how much he had dominated the conversation, and wonder what it was about this hard driving black man that made it so easy for him to babble on like this.

"By gosh, I never meant to fill your ears with so much mush, lad."

"Why not?" Morgan asked with an easy grin. "I care about her and I want to know. Not just about my partner's childhood, but her relationship with you, too." He popped the clutch as the light turned green and Sean literally held onto his hat.

"My relationship with Felicity doesn't go very far. She was on the heavy side as a child, and yet she seemed to always be with a boy. Much too young, I'd say. Just couldn't control her in that regard. I never stopped trying though, and the constant arguing just drove us apart. Then, when she was seventeen, she just up and left. She took a change of clothes and ten pounds and the gold crucifix I'd given her. There was a rumor she'd gone off to live with the wanderers out west."

"Wanderers?" Morgan asked.

"Tribes of, well, Irish Gypsies I guess you'd call them. Drunkards. Beggars. Some people say they're just a bunch of thieves and con artists."

"Funny what you hear," Morgan said, with a knowing smile. He turned the Jeep down the ramp into a parking garage. He screeched to a halt in a designated slot, yanked the emergency brake, and turned to his passenger for the rest of the story.

"Well, no one heard from the girl for nigh on three years after that," Sean said, opening his door. "Three long, tough years. The town had some bad times. The mill shut down. Do these go inside?"

"Yeah," Morgan replied. He hefted a grocery bag and

did not stop Sean from taking the other.

By the time they reached the elevator, Sean's face reflected Morgan's easy smile. Sean figured that this young fellow had to be the easiest man to like that he had ever met. Irishmen aside, of course.

"So, three years passed..." Morgan prodded as the elevator rose.

"Yes, they did. Then the checks started coming in. Every month. Sometimes, quite substantial. Actually, cashier's checks, made out to the church. Never any kind of address. A lot of times, they were in different languages and I wouldn't know how much it was until I got them to the bank."

"But you knew where it was from," Morgan said, more a statement than a question.

"I figured she didn't want me to know what she was doing, or where she was. But I used the money to help the poor and such. I only found her here by luck. Wonder what she was doing before this."

"Guess we'll let her tell you herself," Morgan replied. They went to the door of one of the two penthouse apartments. Morgan pushed the doorbell. Sean looked around at the multicolored flowers behind them. The rainbow petals looked like hawks' beaks opened for an attack. They held his attention, even as he heard the door open.

"They're called bird of paradise plants, Uncle Sean."

Sean spun to see his niece in the doorway, and it all came rushing back. The plump little girl was trim and tall now, but she bound her hair in the same emerald ribbon she used as a seven year old. She wore her wool knit pullover as she had worn them in her youth, sleeves pushed up, almost to her elbows. Her maroon corduroy slacks were much too tight, just like back then. And like the old days, she was barefoot.

"Well, come in and put those bags down. Have a seat, for goodness sake."

"I'll take the groceries," Morgan said. "Why don't you

get us some coffee?"

Sean Sullivan had never been in a place like this. The sunken living room, surrounded by a broad marble platform, appeared to be as wide as his entire cottage, and almost as long. Across the room, an oak table with three chairs sat up on this platform.

Three steps down he sank into deep pile carpet, rose colored like the walls. Then he sank into the end seat of the light tan velour sofa, scorning the matching easy chairs at either side of the couch.

"Here we are," Felicity said, sitting two large mugs of coffee on the oak cube which served as a coffee table. "Like the view?"

"I'm impressed, girl. The ocean is lovely at night." Sean turned to stare out the back wall, made up of three foot wide, floor to ceiling glass panels.

"So, dear uncle, how ever did you find me?"

"No magic lass, just luck. You remember Mick Murphy at the paper? He's still putting out his little local news, you know. Well, he's got this service now. Some computer thingie that types out the news from UPI. They put all kinds of stuff on there, filler he calls it, so they can keep it running all day. Mmmm! You make a good cup of coffee, girl.

"Anyway, one day he sees your name on the paper and he wonders if this Felicity O'Brien in New York City could be our own long lost Felicity. He writes a letter and he gets a picture from some big New York paper. The story's about two people who saved a couple of others in a big fire. The pictures are you and your partner here, eh.."

"Morgan, Uncle Sean. My partner and best friend."

"Yeah. By the way," Sean twisted around, raised his voice, "what are ye doing up there, lad?"

"I was putting these sandwiches together. Here." Morgan came out of the kitchen, sat on the floor in front of the cube table and set three huge sandwiches and a plate of fries on it. The sandwiches were thick Italian loaves split lengthwise, heaped with roast beef and a little lettuce. Course ground mustard coated the meat on one side.

"Felicity wanted to take you to some four star restaurant for some French sounding stuff, but I figured you'd rather have something less formal. Me, I don't eat anything I can't pronounce."

"Thank you, lad," Sean said through a mouthful. "This feels like coming home."

"So anyway, how'd you trace us from New York to here?"

Sean chuckled. "Felicity did that herself. Old Mick corresponded with the New York paper. A reporter wrote and told him how the girl had talked a blue streak. She had an apartment in New York he said, but her main home was in Los Angeles. From there, we just called up information. We didn't find a home number, but her name is on the business."

"Well, I'm impressed," Morgan said, laughing through a hunk of sandwich. He pulled mustard from the corner of his mouth as he pulled his thoughts together. "But you didn't go through all those changes just to say 'hi' to your long lost niece. She mentioned some kind of...a problem?"

"Aye lad," Sean replied, emptying his coffee mug. "When I found out you did security work, I figured you could help me protect the church from the toughs who've been threatening it."

Felicity shifted on the couch, frowning toward Sean. "Uncle Sean, I'll be glad to come and do all I can, but we've got to be realistic. You don't live in a security compound, you know. No alarm can stop a thrown pipe bomb, for instance. Besides, that kind of personal security is really Morgan's specialty, but he's booked to go to Paris for an arms convention of some type."

"It's not that important, Red. We ought to just go to your old home town as a sort of vacation. I've never seen Southern Ireland."

"The Irish Republic, lad," Sean said, correcting him.

"Whatever. And we don't even have to charge for our services as security advisors. It's a church, right? We can call it a charitable donation of services. Then we can write the whole trip off our taxes. It's perfect. Now how about bringing us a couple of bottles of brew from the bar, Red?"

"Sure, and I'll be glad to," Felicity said, rising. Her accent was back, full force. Sean imagined that once back in country she would sound like she had never left. He waited until he was sure she was out of earshot before turning back to Morgan.

"She's changed a lot," he said. "So sure of herself, and so proud. And she lets people call her Red now, does she?"

"Not people," Morgan said in low, conspiratorial tones. "Just me."

"Really?"

"It's not so odd. You're the only person who calls me lad. And yes, Felicity is all grown up. She's really quite a respectable business woman, you know."

"Yes," Sean said. "Now. But what of the time in between?"

Felicity's return cut that conversation short. Sean was delighted to find a Guinness stout pressed into his hand. For the next hour and forty-five minutes, conversation bounced around the three of them. Morgan talked about odd jobs he held in the past. Sean went on about how different Ireland was from what he consistently described as "this crazy country". Felicity laughed a lot, and spoke about her childhood, most of which sounded pleasant enough.

At length, Morgan stood up to make his apologies. The empty bottle score stood at two for Felicity, three for Morgan and four for Sean. Felicity's eyes widened when Morgan said his good-byes and made an abrupt move for the door. She bounced up to follow him out.

"You don't have to leave, you know."

"I figure you'd like...you needed some time alone." Morgan said, opening the door.

"What do I do? I mean..."

"Look, have you told him anything about your life before? I mean, before there was a Stark and O'Brien." Morgan asked.

Felicity blanched. "Of course not!"

"Is that fair?" Morgan asked. "I know. You think he'll disapprove. But think it through. All he knows right now is that you made some big bucks and you're not proud of it. The man's a priest but he's not stupid. What do you suppose he thinks?" He paused to watch Felicity bite her lip, and then shrug her shoulders. "For all he knows, you could've been a hired killer, or a drug dealer. More likely he thinks you've been whoring." Felicity's mouth dropped open. "Well, how do pretty girls usually make big money fast? Look, you've got to tell him the truth. I've done all I could but now...now it's up to you."

Morgan headed for the elevator. Felicity stood with her back to her door until he stepped in. Then as the doors started closing she called out.

"Morgan." He stopped the hissing doors with his hand.

"Yeah?"

"Thanks," she said. "Just...thanks." Then she turned, took a deep breath, and went back into her apartment.

- 4 -

How many plane trips had Morgan taken in his life? No way could he count them. He guessed he had visited maybe twenty-five different countries in his lifetime. But he could not remember when a flight had made him feel this way.

The airplane was nothing special. He sat in a window seat on the wide-bodied Boeing 747. Felicity sat beside him, with Sean in the aisle seat.

The service differed a little from what you got on airlines in America. The hostesses' smiles seemed more sincere, and somehow warmer on Aer Lingus. Even the passengers seemed friendlier. There was nothing here to make him uncomfortable.

He didn't realize what was happening until he saw the big green island approaching out the window. He was getting a low level signal from his instincts. Normally he would get a sharp tingle whenever he was in immediate danger, like when someone pointed a gun at him. That danger sense had saved his life uncounted times in the past. But this felt like a slow dull ache compared to the brisk jolt he was accustomed to experiencing. And then he remembered the only other time he felt this way.

It was on that very first plane ride. The United States Army drove him from New York City to Fort Dix, New Jersey for basic training. At that time, those two states contained all of the world he had seen. Weeks later he lifted off for Vietnam on his very first airplane trip.

It was also the first time his danger sense alerted him this way. It was this very same low level disturbance. The eerie feeling that he was heading into a danger much greater than anything he had ever known. Since then he had become a mercenary soldier, and pursued several other dangerous occupations because after his time in Southeast Asia, risk became a drug to him.

As the landing gear touched the runway he realized that there had to be much more to Sean's problem than he had told them about. This would somehow turn out to be his deadliest job. He glanced at Felicity, but her smile gave no hint she felt any such emotions.

It was late afternoon when they disembarked, and all took a deep breath of the crisp clean air. Morgan and Sean shared the luggage during a brisk walk to the parking lot. The priest opened the trunk of a ten year old green Volvo. While loading in the suitcases, Morgan could feel the light mist close in around him. It was not quite a fog, yet it dampened him, almost like sea spray. Felicity looked at him, grinning.

"I know," she said. "It's that soft Irish weather. Isn't it glorious? I've missed it so." The three travelers climbed into the big auto and Sean moved out at what seemed to Morgan to be a crawl. He was glad to be a passenger there, happy to avoid adjusting to driving on the wrong side of the road. Despite the cool of the evening, he rolled down his window to avoid the stuffiness of a car left standing for several days. Sean and Felicity followed suit.

"So now we ride into the sticks where Felicity grew up?" Morgan asked.

"Actually we're north of Dublin," Felicity said, wearing what Morgan could only describe as a dreamy expression. "Uncle Sean's parish is about thirty miles south of the capital, so we get to drive right through the glorious big town.

Despite his broad travel experience, Morgan did find Dublin colorful, like the world's biggest small town. Even in Africa, he had never before seen a national capital without a single skyscraper. He enjoyed every minute of the hour's slow drive. Sights common to Sean and familiar to Felicity were beautiful and wondrous to him. They tooled south through Dublin with its glorious squares and greens. The Georgian buildings had a

Disneyland feel to them with their doors painted in wild colors under fan shaped transoms. The pace seemed so relaxed, and strangers waved and smiled as they cruised by. These had to be the friendliest people on earth, he thought.

The big car moved out of Dublin on the coast road through towns with names like Dun Laoghaire and Loughlinstown. They passed through a lovely little Victorian seaside resort called Bray. All the way, the rocky shoreline was right there on their left.

"To your right stand the Wicklow Mountains." Felicity said in a tour guide voice. "The very garden of Ireland."

Morgan smiled, but was unimpressed. After hiking in the shadow of Kilimanjaro, skiing one of the Alps and climbing another, these "mountains" looked more like rolling hills to him. At the town of Wicklow they turned west and drove into them. Deep green forests covered the hillsides. Between the hills they saw the golden gorse, the tall purple heather, and the occasional small field dotted with grazing sheep. Morgan knew they were nearing Felicity's old home when she started narrating again.

"Call this place Glendalough, they do. The name literally means 'the valley between the lakes'. The only way into our little valley by car is right through Laragh. Over there, that's the remains of a sixth century monastery. Local folk have pretty much left it alone for hundreds of years."

The fir trees on the slopes ran right down to the ruins of the cathedral and seven churches. A round tower, thirty-three meters high dominated the ruins. Beyond them, the car pulled in behind another house of worship which appeared slightly newer. Morgan had seen pictures of this type of barrel-vaulted church in books about "Old Ireland." They always seemed to have this kind of high pitched roof too.

One wall of this building showed signs of recent construction. A good size cottage stood behind the church. It was modest, but clean and well maintained. Sean shut off the engine, got out of the car and stretched. Morgan slid out of the passenger side, pulling Felicity after him.

"Is this it?"

"This is Uncle Sean's home." Felicity said through a smile.

"Where's the town?"

Felicity chuckled. "Well, I guess there's hardly a village here. Uncle Sean's parish really amounts to a group of farms and a few isolated thatched cottages. I guess it's pretty rural."

"Really?"

"Don't worry," Felicity said. "We'll go back to Wicklow and take rooms at a boarding house."

"Nonsense," Sean said around the raised trunk lid. "I'll not hear of it. You'll be staying right here and no argument. You, lass, can have your old room. Morgan can have my room and I'll take the couch."

"Don't give up your bed for me," Morgan said, following Sean into the house with the luggage. The priest lowered his bags to the floor in a very deliberate manner and turned to make eye contact with Morgan.

"You'll not sleep in any other bed in this house, lad."

Morgan missed a beat before he realized what Sean meant, but Felicity caught the implication right away.

"Uncle Sean I'm insulted. Morgan and I don't sleep together, at home or away. If that was the case, I certainly would not sleep here. I'd never sleep with a man in your home."

"All I meant was that I'd be quite comfortable on the couch," Morgan said. "And I can speak for myself, Red."

"Well, it was a natural enough mistake," Sean said. "You can still be taking the bed."

"No!" Morgan said. "That's not negotiable. I get the sofa or we stay elsewhere." He plopped down on the couch as if to confirm his hold on his territory.

"What a silly thing to argue about," Felicity said,

ruffling the priest's hair, then rubbing her hand across Morgan's close cropped curls. "Why don't we all get a shower, then go down to the crossroads for a late supper?" Both men nodded and said "You first" at the same time.

As Felicity took over the bathroom, Morgan looked around at the basic bachelor furniture. The end table and coffee table looked handmade. The floor was wide planks with no carpet.

"Well, you may as well get comfortable," Sean said. Morgan slid off his blazer, revealing the new custom made double shoulder holster he had slipped into in an airport restroom as soon as they landed. A nine millimeter Browning Hi-power automatic was nestled under his left arm. A sheath for his seven inch bladed Randall number one fighting knife hung under his right arm. The priest did not seem startled at the arrangement, just curious.

"I don't think I've ever seen a rig quite like that one."

"It's new." Morgan slid his arm out of the right side loop. "I used to carry the knife in a belt sheath at the small of my back. I figured I was tempting a back injury in the event of a fall so I had a company I've worked with before concoct this deal. It's comfortable and fast. But I figure I can leave it here this evening. I don't figure I'll need weapons to have supper with a priest."

- 5 -

The place was called "Paddy's" although no sign hung above the door. With its few small windows, this public house was the kind of place that made you feel like you were inside, being held within something. It was warm, both in temperature and atmosphere. The bar spanned one long side of the building. The bartender, Paddy himself, wore a white apron and a white shirt with rolled up sleeves. Every stool held a patron. The cast of characters, perhaps eighty percent male, was loud but jovial. Most of them smoked homemade cigarettes rolled needle thin.

Sean walked over to his traditional booth at the end by the big stone fireplace. Paddy came out from behind the bar before the priest could sit down.

"Paddy, you might not recognize her," Sean said, "but this is my long lost niece, Felicity, back home after too long a stay overseas. This gentleman is her business partner and friend Morgan. Now how about some supper for three weary travelers?"

Introducing them to Paddy was much like introducing them to the house. Many of the men present remembered Felicity and in the rush of loud conversations that followed, a few embarrassing comments flew about how well she had developed. A few of the patrons were hesitant about Morgan, but he found that it took little more than a big smile and a strong handshake to win them over. Morgan had changed into a natural color cotton pullover, canvas khaki pants and moccasins. He was pleased that he had guessed the local dress code pretty well and fit right in. Felicity wore a denim yarn cardigan and light blue mountain pants. A little over done, Morgan thought. Sean had also changed, but the basics were the same.

A plump but attractive woman soon carried a tray to their table. It held three large bowls of stew, biscuits, two quarts of stout, and a pint for Felicity. Morgan was surprised that she didn't react to inequality.

"This is Maureen," Sean said, making it a grand announcement. "Paddy's wife of twelve years and the worst flirt in the county. She's got a gift for reading people. Once told me I was made of peat and clover. Can you imagine?"

"How about Morgan here?" Felicity asked. "What's he made of?"

Maureen put a hand on the back of Morgan's arm and gave it a gentle squeeze. "Muscle," she said, smiling at Sean. Then she turned her smile on Morgan. "Muscle, and ice for all his smiling. And coiled springs. I'd want this one at me back in a fight. Or maybe at me front, eh?"

"Go on with you now," the priest said. He pushed her off, but in a playful manner. Morgan grinned and, after casting a wink at Maureen, tasted his food. The stew was basic and good. It was more potato than meat, but it had cooked long and grown hearty.

Felicity glanced at her partner, envying his evident enjoyment of a home cooked meal. She had longed for the taste of home herself, but now that she had it, it tasted bland. Salt and pepper were the limits of spice there. She had cultivated her palate on fine French cuisine. This food was basic, strong and steady, like the people there. And boring. Perhaps Thomas Wolfe was right. You can't go home again.

The men ate with gusto and Sean was just lighting his after dinner pipe when a newcomer entered, to loud greetings from the bar.

"There walks Max Grogan," Sean said. "Running dog to that devil-on-earth, Ian O'Ryan."

"O'Ryan?" Morgan asked. "Not Ian O'Ryan the motorcycle racer?"

"The very same," the priest answered. "Cycle racer and hate monger. This one's his gamekeeper. Gamekeeper to the scum who brings the evil from up north down to Wicklow county."

When Grogan shambled over to the table, Felicity's eyes flared wide and she sucked air between her teeth. This guy was big. Big shoulders, big head, big hands. Barrel chest under a sweater it must have taken someone all winter to knit. Thin brown hair hung to his long eyebrows as he looked down at Sean. Across the table, she felt Morgan bracing for battle. She knew if it came to a fight, he would have to go all out and take this fellow out quick.

"Ye've no call to be bad mouthin' me boss," Grogan said, in a brogue even thicker than Sean's.

"The man's no good and even you know it, you big dumb clod," the priest said. Grogan's jaw clenched, his shoulder muscles rippled, and a fist like a ten pound ham closed and began to rise, ready to strike.

"Well, mighty peculiar company for a priest to be keeping. A girl young enough to be his daughter and a nigger."

Morgan stood very slowly, resting a hand on Grogan's wrist. At his full height of six feet two inches, Morgan was still a couple of inches shorter than Grogan. He looked up into the big Irishman's dull eyes with a tired half smile.

"Let's not ruin a nice day," Morgan said. "How about we go over to the bar and I stand you a quart of stout?"

"No man buys for Grogan except the man who can whip him. You figure that's you?"

Tension froze Felicity into silence. Of course, she knew Morgan did figure he was the man who could whip Grogan, but she hoped he understood that to say so now was a losing move. This was not about physical ability. It was about face: Morgan's, Grogan's, and her uncle's. Morgan could whip this man, perhaps even survive the reaction of a room full of his friends, but the bad blood would last forever. He needed another option.

The corner of Felicity's mouth curled into a small smile when she saw Morgan sit down and slam his right elbow down on the table with his hand raised and open. "Let's find out, big man," Morgan said. Grogan broke into a broad smile and stretched out his arms, then pulled up a chair. When his elbow hit the table, dishes rattled and glasses jumped. He slapped his hand into Morgan's, smothering it completely.

"Winner buys," Morgan said.

"This won't take long," Grogan said. The two men locked eyes and smiled.

"Father?" Morgan said without losing eye contact. "If you could start us off?"

"All right then. One...two...three...go!"

Felicity could only grin at Morgan's brilliance. Her uncle had set him up, and she wasn't happy about that, but Morgan had managed to turn a potential pitched battle into a contest for the right to buy the beer. He had created a win-win situation. Whoever won, they would drink together afterward. They would respect each other. It would all end with everyone as friends.

Paddy's patrons gathered around, sharing an air of excitement, and Felicity could guess their thoughts. They wanted to see Grogan thump the black man's arm down on the table. After all, was he not the strongest man in the county? His arm looked twice as big as the stranger's, but the other man looked pretty strong too. Money began to change hands, being stacked on the table. Felicity nudged her uncle, prodding him in a stage whisper.

"Well? Where's your heart Uncle Sean? You've got to put some money on Morgan."

Nodding, Sean pulled out a sizeable pile of small bills. "This says Felicity's partner puts Grogan's arm down. The better man will win."

After blessing her uncle with a grateful smile, Felicity sat at the far end of the table and stared into Morgan's face. Judging by his appearance, he was oblivious to the wagering. His arm was slanting backward, bit by bit. At that point he and Grogan were both grimacing. Grogan grunted with the effort.

She feared Grogan might just be stronger, but she knew Morgan had the advantage of concentration. Grogan roared, using rage for energy. Morgan stayed relaxed. She had seen it before, only once or twice. He was reaching for that deep state of total pinpoint focus on his center, just as she did during yoga practice. It was the true source of power, she knew. Once he reached his steady state, he focused all his strength up into his right arm. The movement was slow and gradual, but as she watched and grinned his arm righted itself. Then he smiled into Grogan's twisted face. Morgan forced the giant fist toward the tabletop, and for the first time the outcome of the contest was in doubt.

That was when one of the drunks, seeing his hard earned ten pounds slipping away, shouted "no!" and dived forward, reaching for the back of Grogan's hand. He barely made contact, but it was just enough to push both arms back the other way. And that was when all hell broke loose.

"I don't need no help from the likes of you," Grogan screamed. He stood up, snatched up his would-be helper by his shirt with his left hand and slammed him against the wall. Another drinker dived at Grogan's back. Morgan stopped the sneak attack with a side stamp kick to the solar plexus. Behind him, another man aimed a bottle at Morgan's head.

"Aw shite," Felicity said as she backhanded Morgan's attacker with her beer mug. "It's a brawl now."

Bar brawls were an environment with which Morgan was familiar. He knew that in such close quarters all he had to do was to keep his arms pumping and his head moving. A series of short jabs mowed down the fighters in front of him. His elbow thrusts kept them off his back.

Grogan was smashing in all directions with his huge fists, downing all comers. He was no good at dodging or ducking. On the other hand, he didn't seem to mind being hit. When the crowd got too thick, he seized one poor drunken man, lifted him overhead by the neck and one leg, and tossed him down, felling three others.

One big Irishman landed a solid right on Morgan's jaw. When he looked up into the man's grinning face, Morgan saw no anger or rage. He realized that this man and everyone else in the place looked as if they were enjoying the action.

But Morgan didn't fight for fun. Before the attacker's follow-up left could find its mark, Morgan put three lightening fast punches into his midsection. Then, with a loud shout he delivered a crushing flying side stamp that lifted the brawler into the air and put him into two others with enough force to smash them to the floor.

When he spun around madness shone in his eyes. Three fighters still stood, but they were backing away. Paddy and Maureen stayed behind the bar, not speaking or even moving any more. Felicity and her uncle eased out from under their table. Grogan stood in classic boxer's stance, but he too seemed uncertain. Morgan dropped his hands, mumbled, "I don't need this," and walked out the door.

* * * * *

Two hundred yards out on the heath, Felicity caught up with her partner. He was staring up into the clear night sky. When she reached him he spoke without lowering his eyes.

"Full moon. It figures."

Felicity stood silent beside him. There was an odd comfort in sharing the stars and the quiet. A moment later, Sean caught up to them.

"Paddy's hasn't seen a donnybrook like that in years, lad. What a fighter. Are you sure you're not Irish?" His tone made it clear he wanted to keep the mood light, but Morgan's grim face should have told him that was impossible.

"You set me up, `Father'," Morgan said. "I think it's time you told us why we're really here. What's the real job, old man?"

"Real job, Uncle Sean?" Felicity asked after a short pause.

Morgan looked down from the sky to glare into Felicity's eyes. "You don't think he got us all the way over here because of some vague threats and what amounts to vandalism at his church, do you? Me, I think it's this O'Ryan guy."

"Is this true, Uncle?" Felicity asked. "You came after me for a personal vendetta?"

"You don't know him, girl," Sean said. "The man's a terrorist he is, a terrorist who hides down here after he kills up north."

"Terrorist," Morgan repeated, his voice thick with irony. "Isn't that what the big army always calls the little army?"

"Uncle Sean, you couldn't have thought I'd chase this man away for you," Felicity said.

Sean looked a little embarrassed. "It wasn't you I wanted, Felicity, but your man."

"Of course," Morgan said, raising his eyes and one palm to heaven. "You found out about my past as a mercenary. That's why you weren't surprised at the weapons I carried. You were looking for a solider. You want to know what I think? I think this O'Ryan guy is threatening your power base here. I think maybe he's stealing your followers and you wanted me to get him out of the way."

"It's not like that, son. I am a priest, after all."

"Sure," Morgan said, beginning to pace in a small circle in front of the other two. "And that priest gig is all about power. Every priest has absolute power over his people. Especially here. What, do you think, I'm ignorant? Like I don't know what a big deal it is in Ireland to give a son to the church? How many priests you figure there are in this country, Father?"

"The church provides guidance for every member of its flock."

"And how many guides does that take in Ireland? How many priests?"

"Well...maybe twenty thousand or so," Sean replied.

"Twenty thousand! In a country of maybe three and a half million. That's, what, let's see, a religious leader for every hundred and seventy-five people or so, right? It's just a power trip."

"Hold on, Morgan," Felicity stepped between the two men. "We don't know the whole story. You're not being fair. Why don't we go back and have another drink? We can discuss this in detail tomorrow, like adults."

"I'm for it," Sean said. "Well, lad?"

Morgan just stood there in the dark, with hands on hips, looking at the ground, shaking his head. At a signal from Felicity, the priest turned and walked toward the pub. She moved over and put her arm through Morgan's. After a slight tug, he began walking with her. His mouth was set in a straight line of resignation, like a man facing a battle he knows he can't win. A soft wind whirled around their bodies, brushing back the grass and flowers. Once they were walking across the gorse, Felicity spoke.

"You know, I've never seen you fighting, I mean full out like that. You're pretty awesome."

"Yeah, well nature boy back there must have donated his fair share of broken noses and jaws too." Morgan replied.

"You mean Maxie Grogan? He is a strappin' lad and that's for sure. Cute too."

"What?" Morgan looked at her as if she had lost her mind.

"The big dope's got kind of a baby face, considering his life. He's the end of a long, noble line, you know.

41

The product of countless generations of peasant fishermen."

"If you ask me, he's the product of too much inbreeding," Morgan muttered, almost under his breath.

- 6 -

When Morgan and Felicity walked into Paddy's pub things were almost as they were when they first entered. Furniture was back in its original position, spilled potables were cleaned up, and the patrons had resumed their original diversions. Felicity moved off, wallet in hand, to cover damage done during the fight. Paddy and Maureen were smiling. In fact everyone in the whole place seemed to be smiling, as warm and friendly as when they ordered supper.

Max Grogan turned on his bar stool, looking at Morgan like an unpleasant bit of unfinished business. The only thing Morgan could do was walk right up to Grogan, look him in the eye, and wait for him to speak first. The room seemed to hold its breath during the brief pause while Grogan stared hard, as if trying to measure the extent of Morgan's threat. However, Morgan had drawn his aura in, offering no emotional reflection. He presented no menace for Grogan to read.

"Can I buy you a stout?" Grogan asked.

"I did work up a thirst after my supper," Morgan replied. "Why don't you buy this round? I'll buy the next. We'll see who passes out first."

Morgan sensed no danger before Grogan's huge hand whumped him on the back, putting his chest into the bar. "Well said," Max roared. "Quart of Guinness up here for me new friend and his friends, and the devil take the hindmost." Morgan was sure that the friendly gesture would raise a bruise, but he didn't care. He had saved the big man's face without losing any of his own.

Being a good bartender, Paddy poured their cups half full from the small tap. He let them rest and settle while he served another customer, then topped them each twice. When a big mug landed in front of him, Morgan took a deep pull. It was warm, thick, and malty.

"I'll tell you something, Max," Morgan said, wiping froth from his mouth. "I've had light beer, dark beer, ale and malt liquor all over the world. I got to admit, Guinness Stout is the pinnacle of the brewer's art."

"You mean they get this stuff over in the states?" Grogan asked.

"Well, yeah, but unless you've had it fresh from the tap, in country, you haven't really tasted it."

"Thanks for standing me the drink, handsome," Felicity said, sipping foam from the top of her mug. She slid onto the stool on Grogan's left, opposite Morgan. "My Uncle Sean's off moping in the corner, but I'm grateful for the both of us."

"Your uncle?"

"Yes, of course," she said, offering her hand. "We haven't been introduced. I'm Felicity O'Brien. Your fighting partner there is my business partner, Morgan Stark. He learned to fight like that in Vietnam and parts east."

"Business partner, eh?"

"Sure. Are you here alone?" she asked with that sparkling smile that can make a man forget his own name.

"Well, maybe not." Grogan covered Felicity's hand and wrist with one massive paw.

While they talked and drank, Morgan examined Grogan, trying to see what his partner could find so attractive in this hulk. His ears were jug handles. His skin was a mass of freckles so dense that at first glance he appeared red faced. His eyes were set deep and wide, with huge bushy eyebrows above them. His face was somehow weathered, but with no lines around the eyes or on his forehead. His smile was big enough, easy and sincere. A smile most people would trust. He probably had a simple view of life and lacked the intelligence to feel either ambition or dissatisfaction.

In a corner, someone started singing. Morgan didn't

recognize the song, but he was sure it was an old Irish folk ballad. A minute later someone drew a harmonica out of their pocket and joined in, accompanying the song. A few old timers started stamping their boots on the wooden floor, slapping their thighs in counter time to the music. It got faster, and a Jew's harp picked up the rhythm. Paddy pulled out a banjo, and all of a sudden, everyone was on the floor. Grogan was twirling Felicity to a dance that Morgan figured she was born knowing. He was watching her feet flashing across the floor when he felt a warm hand on his arm.

"Come on, big boy," Maureen said, nodding her head toward the center of the room. "Give a girl a twirl, why don't you?"

"I think I'll sit this one out, ma'am. You can do better." Morgan smiled into her confused face before letting his eyes drift back to the dancing crowd. The truth was that he could execute the most complex karate kata, perform a gymnastic tumbling floor routine and walk a high wire, but one thing he could not do was dance. He just never had that type of coordination.

Besides, he didn't like folk music much.

Felicity collapsed on her stool ahead of her dance partner. Her cheeks were filled with color, her hair loose and flowing. Morgan could see her as ten years younger. One thing he loved about this girl was her ability to feel, and show, complete and total happiness. He wondered when and where he lost it.

"Having fun?" Morgan asked.

"He's putty in me hands," she whispered back. "By the end of the night I'll know all there is to know about his mysterious boss, this Mister O'Ryan. Then we can discuss the situation."

"Good girl," Morgan said, patting her shoulder. He withdrew his arm just in time, before Grogan crashed into the space between them. The dance was over for now.

"That's more work than plowing a field, my friend,"

Max said. Then he turned to the redhead, watching her ample bosom heave as she tried to catch her breath. "This could turn out to be a night I'll never forget."

That moment in time was frozen for the two occupants of the pub who shared a psychic rapport. For that one stop-action instant Morgan's senses probed his environment, but he could see that Felicity had zeroed in on the source of the danger alarm they were getting a split second before he did.

"The door!" she shouted, pointing, but Morgan was already moving. In seeming slow motion, they saw the black spherical object float into the pub through the open door. A hand grenade was falling toward the floor. Morgan launched himself into the air toward the steel ball. The grenade bounced on the hardwood floor once, twice. Morgan's right hand wrapped around the spheroid as he flowed into a shoulder roll. His right arm whipped around, flipping the grenade back out the door. He dropped flat on the floor, eyes clamped shut.

Grogan grabbed Felicity's arm in a rough grip, threw her to the floor, and smothered her with his body. The explosion rattled glasses and shattered the pub's front windows. The building shook and Morgan's ears popped.

Before the sound died down, he was on his feet. He sprinted straight toward the door with his eyes still clamped shut. Outside he opened his eyes again, but to little use. The world was black, the sun having set while they were inside. As his eyes adjusted to the dark he could see a still body forty yards up the road. The courageous grenadier, Morgan assumed. Not much past the corpse, on the other side of the road, a Citroen's lights popped on. Morgan saw a flash next to the car. As he dived left, he heard the TV western sound of a bullet ricocheting off the cobblestone road.

Morgan slapped his left side in impotent frustration and cursed himself for leaving his weapons behind. On the run, he could have counted on hitting the car, perhaps putting a nine millimeter slug into the gas tank. Since he loaded the tips of his hollowpoints with fulminate of mercury, a single hit would give enough explosive pop to ignite the gasoline in the tank. If he had his gun. As it was, he could do nothing except watch the killers roll away. After a moment of silent rage, he turned and leaned in the doorway.

"Father Sullivan. You might want to come out here and give this guy his last rites. Then we need to get back to your place and have us a little conference."

*   *   *   *   *

They made the short ride back to Sean's cottage in silence. Felicity didn't want to believe the apparent truth, and she knew that Morgan felt the same, but the evidence was obvious. Sean's windshield was cracked and the right side windows were out. If he was the target of this attack, then his enemies were indeed serious. The previous bomb must have been a warning. The only question was whether he had traced his problem to the right place.

When the big black car pulled up beside the house, Felicity nudged Morgan.

"There's someone in the house."

"How do you know that?" Sean asked

"I just know. Someone's in there."

"Yeah," Morgan said, "And my gun is in there."

Their eyes met for just a moment, before Felicity said, "Your play."

"Give me three minutes. Open the door and hit the lights."

They all got out of the car. Felicity never even heard Morgan move out for the back of the house. He was just gone. Once he was out of sight, she pulled her uncle to the door, making more noise than usual.

As the seconds ticked off in her head, she reflected that Morgan had given himself more time than he needed. When she opened the front door, he would come in the back window. He had no way to know the priest never locked his door or windows.

Just before she opened the door, Felicity prodded Sean's arm and said, "Now give us room, Uncle Sean." Then, at the designated second she slammed the door open, flipped on the lights and screamed. Her voice covered the sound of Morgan's body hitting the floor, going into a forward roll. When his feet hit the floor he thrust himself forward.

For a brief instant Felicity was staring down the muzzle of Morgan's automatic in the hands of a gray man. His hair was gray, as were his coat, his suit, his tie. He was medium height, medium build and medium weight.

All this she took in just as Morgan's crossed forearms smashed into the gunman from behind. The gray man fell forward on his face with Morgan's chin in the small of his back. Stretching out his left arm, Morgan grabbed a hand full of gray hair, snapping the man's head back. Morgan's right arm fell like an axe. The edge of his hand chopped into the gray coated upper arm. The gun skittered across the floor and Felicity scooped it up.

Morgan forced their uninvited guest to his feet and slammed him into the wall, face first. Patting him down yielded a wallet and a thirty-eight caliber Webley service revolver. Then Morgan tossed their unwanted visitor onto the couch. He flipped the wallet to Sean and pointed the revolver at his captive. Felicity returned Morgan's gun to its holster and traded his rig for the Webley. Morgan stripped off his sweater and strapped on his weapons while Felicity pointed the Webley at its owner's face.

"Now, stupid, let's talk," Felicity said. "We'll start with the easy stuff. Who are you?"

"You may call me Mister Grey. I am..."

"From London," Sean said, staring at the man's identification. "From the Central Intelligence Division."

"Saints preserve us," Felicity said, covering her face with one hand. "He's C.I.D. Why on God's earth are you here?"

"To talk to you about your uncle's problem," Grey answered, his accent betraying a hint of Manchester. "The source, by the way, of the hand grenade I barely missed warning you about."

"You're saying that grenade had a specific target?" Felicity asked.

"Oh yes," Grey stood and straightened his clothes, "I was observing at a discrete distance. I didn't know our man intended such direct action, especially with one of his own inside. But yes, Father Sullivan was most definitely the intended target. The man I've been observing seems to have given up on intimidating him."

"I see," Morgan said, holding his pistol on Grey. "You're here about the, er, terrorist."

"You sound skeptical, Mister Stark." Grey reached inside his sport coat, ignoring Morgan's gun, and pulled out a comb. "You apparently think we follow every Irish tough and Tommy around for a lark. Or perhaps that we keep tabs on every citizen of the realm, as I understand they do in the States." He straightened his hair as best he could without a mirror. "Well let me inform you about this joke of yours. Let me educate you about the deadliest man in the Republic of Ireland and Ulster. Let me tell you a bit about Ian Michael O'Ryan."

- 7 -

The small group gathered in the kitchen. A fire crackled in the hearth to knock the chill out of the house. Felicity had brewed coffee, black and strong. Its aroma added sweetness to the smell of the burning peat

Mister Grey sat at one end of the table, the center of attention. Felicity perched on a counter by the sink, looking down at him. Morgan sat in a chair at the other end of the table with his heels hooked on the bar between the chair's legs. His cup hung between his knees, held with both hands. Sean stood beside the sink, running a hand through his hair. It was getting past his bedtime.

"So you're saying this Ian O'Ryan really is some sort of an Irish terrorist?" Morgan voiced the question to Grey.

"Not an Irish terrorist, son. *The* Irish terrorist." Grey emphasized "the" as if O'Ryan were the only one. "We can find trouble with his name on it back more than three decades."

"Can we have this from the beginning?" Felicity asked. "I want the history, and I want to know how this character ties in with Uncle Sean."

"I can give you history," Grey said, lighting his meerschaum lined pipe. "I've chased this fellow so long I know his story by heart."

"So?" Felicity waved her hand as if to say, "Go on."

"So, Ian Michael O'Ryan was born July twenty-third, nineteen fifty-two, out here on the heath in Wicklow County."

"On the cusp of Cancer and Leo," Felicity said. "That would give him a pretty interesting character."

"I suppose so, young lady," Grey said, sipping his

coffee, "If you believe in that sort of thing. Anyway, his mother died in childbirth and his father soon after. Some say of a broken heart. He's kept his youth a pretty good secret. But we know that somehow he wandered up into Ulster. He was quite young when he tied up with the newly formed Provisional Irish Republican Army. We know he was in on the action at the start of the war. We believe he took part in the violence in nineteen sixty-eight."

"Let's not call it a war," Morgan said. "I've seen war and that ain't it. But are you saying this guy was shooting or blowing people up when he was fourteen or fifteen?"

"That's precisely what I'm saying. And by the way, between British soldiers and the Irish so-called freedom fighters we've had well over fifty-seven hundred documented casualties since sixty-eight, killed and wounded. Put that into perspective with your country's adventure into Iraq. And that's not counting more than eighteen hundred innocent civilians killed. Where I come from, we call that a war."

"My parents were among the first of those casualties," Felicity said, tight lipped. "A car bomb. No reason. Just bad luck. Go on, Mister Grey."

"Yes, well he became more and more important as a `hands on' man in the blow-'em-up business. Soon he was juggling a double life. He made a name for himself as a champion grand prix motorcycle racer in the early seventies. He's famous for winning at any cost. After a second opponent met a violent end during a race, his black Harley Davidson was dubbed `the widow maker'.

Still, he's a very charismatic man, and here, like everywhere else, a winner is a hero. He attended fox hunts all through the seventies and again acquired a winning reputation. All this time he was recruiting and training for the IRA. I think he just enjoyed the bomb bit.

In nineteen eighty his hunts moved to Africa. He bagged every legal big game and some that weren't.

And he picked up a nickname. As sort of a pun, actually, he began calling himself Orion the hunter, spelling it O-R-I-O-N you see. Like the mythological hunter."

"He begins to sound a bit mythological," Felicity said. "A bit larger than life."

"Well, he was a god to the Provos. He kept killing and killing and not getting caught. And his reputation as a hunter and a racer attracted more and more young men to the cause.

Now you know Sinn Fein and the more legitimate groups they support get a lot of their money from donations in the States. Some of the others deal drugs, work the protection racket and such. Not O'Ryan. While he was hunting in Africa he made contact with the Middle East terror groups. Started picking up funding for the IRA there."

"Must be tough now," Morgan interrupted. "Whatever funding that isn't staying in the Middle East seems to be headed for the Pacific Rim or into Africa. And now, with Arafat gone and Sinn Fein calling a cease fire, it's a hard life for the terrorist who ain't Muslim."

"Perhaps, but he's a rebel, often working independent of his IRA brothers," Grey said. "And he seems to have hooked up with Bin Laden's boys through a connection in Spain, and you know those lads couldn't care less about any cease fire. We believe they're financing him now. Anyway, when he turned fifty he appears to have decided to move up into management. He returned to his home county and bought a country estate. Does everything long distance now. Recruits here. We believe he smuggles weapons into the Republic and funnels them up into Ulster."

"So he's a hero around here, probably because he spreads money around," Morgan said. "Meanwhile he's financed by some arm of al Qaeda to spread terror in the north."

"Well, financed by the Russians at first, years ago,

and later the Cubans through a Syrian or Libyan connection, more likely. But yes, the Talaban appear to feed his budget today. Whoever's paying his bills doesn't like this cease fire one bit. We expect he's been holding back, but with army patrols stopped and Her Majesty's forces being withdrawn from Northern Ireland, we anticipate he'll make a big move. In fact, my information is he's expecting another weapons shipment very soon."

"One well timed riot or wave of killings would shatter the peace process," Felicity said, almost to herself. "He could bring it all down."

"Maybe." Grey allowed himself a small smile. "Maybe, but we think he's living a bit too well and may have over spent or over gambled. He might be in danger of being accused of misusing his sponsor's money."

"Well, thanks for the background briefing," Morgan said, "but none of that explains why you followed me around, or why you're telling me all this."

"It wasn't you I wanted, but the girl."

"What?" Felicity paused in the middle of pouring a second cup of coffee. "How could you know I was even coming here?"

"Oh, we didn't. We just got lucky." Grey stood removed his coat, since the house was warming up. "You see, we've been watching the situation here for some time. O'Ryan's money and lifestyle have made him very influential in these parts. Young men flock to him. Father Sullivan's been resisting that influence. We thought there might be violence and we hoped O'Ryan would slip up. Then during our surveillance, your uncle got you over here."

"I take it you don't really have anything on O'Ryan legally." Morgan held out his cup and accepted a refill from Felicity.

"You got it, boyo." Grey stirred more sugar into his coffee. "He's dead crafty. We can't prove any terrorist activity. But when the young lady entered the picture, I saw a chance to stop him, indirectly."

"And just what is it you think I can do for you?" Felicity asked. "I'm a security expert, not a policeman."

"Well our information leads us to believe that you have certain special talents," Gray flicked a brief glance toward Sean, "perhaps best discussed in confidence?"

"I have no secrets from my partner," Felicity said with a smile, "or from my uncle, now. Morgan?"

"I trust Father Sullivan," Morgan said. "Maybe I should have a little sooner."

"Thanks, lad," Sean said.

"Well then, here it is," Grey said. "We understand that you, Miss O'Brien, have been involved in some highly daring and successful thefts in the past several years. Our information is that you mostly collected expensive jewelry, but also some rather special artwork appears to have changed hands, thanks to you."

"Can you prove it?" Felicity asked.

"Of course not," Grey said, waving a hand at the notion. "We could no more convict you of a crime than we could Ian O'Ryan. Nor would we want to. On the contrary, we want you to commit one."

"Ah," Morgan said, grinning and nodding his head. "I've been dense here, but the light finally dawns."

"Well I still don't get it," Felicity said, dropping to the floor and walking to the fireplace. She tossed a log on and stirred it with a poker.

"Stop me if I go wrong," Morgan said to Grey. "O'Ryan's juggling funds, right? He's robbing Peter to pay Paul, so to speak, to keep up his flamboyant lifestyle for the public. He also has to maintain the appearance of full time terrorist for his private audience. He's been managing but he's short of dough. If he was to suffer a sudden financial loss, his backers would never believe he was ripped off. They'd assume he swindled them. Embezzlement in those circles usually brings swift retribution."

"Exactly, sir, and well put," Grey said, pointing his

pipe's stem at Morgan. "If the terrorists from the Middle East were to eliminate him themselves it would do more than just rid us of this one evil man. It would destroy his reputation and prevent a martyr reaction. Do you think you can help us in this?"

"It's not my call," Morgan said. He leaned back, looking at his partner. He could guess the conflict in Felicity's mind. She would want to strike at the force which caused her parents' death, however indirectly. She would want to make her only known living relative happy and this would make her a heroine in her uncle eyes. On the other hand, after her experience with Adrian Seagrave months before, she hated the idea of working for anyone else. Besides, she bristled at the thought of helping the police no matter the cause.

Felicity paced the kitchen now, looking at the three men in turn. Her face was blank, expressionless. The solution to her dilemma seemed obvious to Morgan, but it was not his place to speak. He new she needed to arrive at it on her own. When she looked at him next, her expression remained unchanged but he recognized the sparkle in her eye and knew she had hit upon it. Then she stopped and focused on the stranger from the C.I.D.

"First, Mister Grey, are you authorized to make decisions in this matter?" Felicity asked.

"I have absolute authority."

"Good. Now, let's say some money were to leave O'Ryan's control. Where does it go?" she asked.

"I suppose the funds stay with whomever is in possession of them when they leave O'Ryan's control."

"That's the right answer," Felicity said, pacing again. "Now, a person would have to be dead crackers to officially inform an agent of Her Majesty's government of their intention to commit a crime which may take place, in part, on British soil, eh?"

"Agreed."

"Good. Now, one more thing," Felicity said. "You

mentioned information you had about my past. I
assume we're talking about official records. Your
government records will have to be updated, to officially
recognize that I'm retired from all criminal activity." It
was not a request, a demand.

After a thoughtful pause, Gray said, "I can see to that.
In fact, I'm fairly certain that after a thorough update,
there may be no record at all of past suspicions."

That brought a smile to Felicity's face, but she was
not finished. "And I must not be interfered with, or even
observed by any agent of your government for the next
thirty days."

"Miss, we have a very effective intelligence machine
which could..."

"I have no connection with any intelligence service.
Why would your organization be in contact with me, if I
have no illegal intentions? Besides, even if I were doing
anything unusual, I have always worked alone. I repeat,
there must be no interference or observation."

"It would be physically dangerous for anyone to do
so," Morgan added in a low monotone.

"Message received," Grey grimaced, rubbing his back
for emphasis.

Grey and Felicity locked eyes in a way which, in
ancient times, would have been more significant than a
signed contract. Then she reached out to shake his
hand, bringing an abrupt end to their conversation.

"Well, Mister Grey, I suppose you'd better be going,"
she said. "I believe our business is concluded." She
walked him to the door and helped him with his coat. As
she opened the door, she blessed him with one of her
patented smiles.

"Off the record, sir, it does seem that good Saint
Patrick did an incomplete job of it those long years ago.
So yes, for my uncle's sake, I will help to get this one
last snake out of Ireland."

-8-

In the total stillness of dawn, Sean stepped out of his bedroom door on tiptoe. He figured his house guests would still be asleep. After all, he had heard his niece pacing in the kitchen long after he went to bed. He knew the two of them had been up late making their plans for how, in the next few days, they would take everything O'Ryan had away from him.

Sean always got up early, but he didn't know if his house guests were early risers too so he dressed as quietly as possible. But when he stepped into the living room at dawn he found a vacant couch. The sheets and blanket were folded in a very precise, military manner, with the pillow on top of them. His first suspicion proved wrong. Felicity's door stood open and that room was also empty.

Curious, Sean opened the front door and looked out. The air was crisp, perhaps fifty-five or sixty degrees. On his right, Morgan was on hands and toes, back straight, facing away from the door. He wore a gray sweat suit and running shoes. Felicity's voice said "Go," and the black man's arms started pumping out perfect push-ups.

Felicity, to the left of the door, wore similar attire to Morgan's. Her body was rigid as she stood with her hands together at her chest in an attitude of prayer. Her hands moved upward in slow motion until she was stretching for the sky, then in one fluid movement she bent forward until her palms rested on the ground. Still her knees were locked and her feet had not moved. Her forehead touched her knees, then those knees flexed, her left foot stretched back and her back arched until she looked skyward.

This strange mystique fascinated Sean. He never

imagined the girl was so limber. Her flexibility seemed in direct counterpoint to the power of Morgan's rhythmic rising and dropping.

As he watched, Felicity extended her other leg until it too was straight and she was in push-up position. At first he thought she was suspended there but soon he could see her dropping in an extreme slow motion push-up. Just before her breasts touched the ground she stopped and lowered her head to touch the earth with her forehead.

The priest stepped out for a better view as Felicity's arms straightened. Soon her back was arched, her face turned skyward. Then she seemed to reverse her position, until her hips were thrust skyward with her body in an inverted "V". Her feet stayed flat on the ground. After a brief pause, she moved her left leg forward, planting her foot two inches behind her left palm. The leg then straightened and the other slid forward, bringing her full circle to the first bent over position. Once more her head touched her knees.

When she stretched up Felicity filled her lungs. Then her arms went out to her sides. The tension was evident when she pulled her hands back in to the prayer position, pushing the air out of her lungs.

"Lovely," Sean said, clapping his hands. "Like ballet."

"Thanks." Felicity had just then become aware of him. "It's just some basic yoga. I need to stretch in the morning."

"What about him?" Sean asked, hooking a thumb in Morgan's direction.

"He wanted me to time him for two minutes."

"Oh yes," Sean grinned. "Felicity O'Brien, the human stopwatch."

A few seconds later she said "Stop," and Morgan dropped to his knees, taking in deep breaths of the humid air. Sean walked over and bent down, hands on knees.

"Well? How many lad?"

"Eighty-four," Morgan said, still gasping for breath. "I'm getting old." He flipped over and Felicity sat at his feet. She lifted her left foot onto her right thigh, then her right foot onto her left thigh. Morgan hooked his feet under her legs and lay back, his arms crossed so his hands rested on his shoulders. Felicity said "Go," again and he pulled his upper body into a vertical position. His back remained straight as he did the crunches, rising and falling like some steam powered piston.

"Do you do this every day?" Sean asked.

"Only when we're not near a health club," Felicity said. "Well, I usually do my yoga routine every day. I'll do gymnastics three times a week if the equipment's available. Morgan usually lifts weights the same days I'm in the gym. On the off days we run together. I think he practices the karate stuff every day."

"Not Sunday." Morgan grunted the words between his teeth at the top of a sit-up.

"Oh yes," Felicity said. You'll be happy to know we both rest on Sunday."

"Why do it to yourself?"

"Well," she hesitated for a moment, then asked, "Do you still read the Bible and pray?"

"Of course. Every day."

"Why?" she asked.

"Because I keep on getting closer to God, child. Like you should be doing."

"Well, that's your business," she said. "My business is protecting people and sometimes that can be a rough business. You don't get to be the best at anything if you don't keep working at it. Besides, I like to stay in shape. You'll see when I do my routine in a bit. Coming up on the end Morgan. And...stop."

"How many this time?" Sean could not resist asking.

"Ninety-three," Morgan replied. "Enough for one day." When he stood and moved to the side, Sean could see that he wasn't finished. He wasn't sure what was coming but it occurred to him that it might require more focus than simple calisthenics.

"Does either of you mind me watching?" Sean asked.

"It's your house, Uncle Sean," Felicity said.

"I most likely won't even know you're there once I'm into the kata."

Still, Sean kept quiet while leaning against the door. Morgan did most of what he called a kata in one place. It was no more than a choreographed series of movements: punches, kicks, and blocks. Meanwhile, Felicity moved around the lawn in a series of balancing maneuvers and running tumbling passes, complete with somersaults and flips. Sean had not been to a circus in a lot of years, but this was much of how he remembered it. And the two went on for a good deal longer than he expected them to. At some silent signal Morgan switched to stretching and Felicity's activity became slow pacing.

"Stopping for a breather?" he asked.

"Actually, we'll run for a couple of miles now," Felicity told her uncle. "Two miles is just enough to get your heart going. Do you suppose you could have some coffee ready when we get back?"

"Sure, and some of those sticky buns Mrs. Cassidy brought by yesterday. And maybe an egg cream, like you used to like."

"Egg cream?" Morgan asked. "Like with seltzer and chocolate syrup like I used to get when I was a kid?"

"That's New York," Felicity said. "Here, it's breakfast. Trust me, you'll love it. Thanks, Uncle Sean."

"Glad to, girl, but how'll you know when two miles go by out here. There's not much for landmarks."

"Morgan will tell me. He's as good with distances and directions as I am with time."

"You do make a pair, don't you?" Sean said, shaking his head. Felicity called another start and they took off at what Sean considered a sprint.

* * * * *

"When it's done right, like this, an egg cream is like angels on the tongue," Felicity said. Egg creams, as Morgan learned, really involved eggs in Ireland. His plate was covered by thin potato cakes slit open and filled with creamy coddled eggs, and fried brown in butter. This was a tasty breakfast and, even better, the coffee was good and strong and the warm sticky buns were delicious.

After eight or nine minutes of running, he and Felicity had showered and pulled on casual clothing. Now the three of them were sitting around the fireplace. To Morgan, it felt like being with family.

"So, do you have plans for the day?" Sean asked.

"Not really," Felicity said, shoveling her food with a passion Morgan was not accustomed to. "I would like to take some time after breakfast to go into detail about our approach to taking O'Ryan's money. I don't want you to have any unpleasant surprises, Uncle."

Morgan watched Sean's face, waiting for him to ask what that meant, but a knock on the door drew everyone's attention. Sean got up to open it but then stepped back, as if he was greeted by an unpleasant sight. In less than a second Morgan moved across the room to get a view of the door. He was taken aback and amused to find Max Grogan standing there, cap in hand, holding the reins to two fine horses.

"Well, this is a bit of a surprise," Sean said. "I don't see your face hardly enough at mass, Max Grogan. Have you suddenly been taken with a midweek need for the holy spirit then?"

"I know I've strayed, Father," Max said, his head lowered. "I promise you I'll be there this Sunday. This morning, however, I've come to call upon your niece, with your kind permission. I thought she might enjoy to take a morning ride with me."

"I'd love to take a morning ride, Maxie." Felicity had appeared at the door, her face beaming. "Only, right now we're having our breakfast and, well, I want to spend a little time with my Uncle Sean." She waited just long enough to see his face fall before adding, "I'd sure be grateful if you'd stop back after lunch. Say...one o'clock?"

The overgrown little boy's face lit up and he mumbled "Sure and I'll be glad to." Looking flustered, he tried to back away but he became tangled in the horses' reins. Felicity closed the door and bounced back to the living room.

"I didn't think he'd move so fast," she told Morgan. "We'll go over plans quickly, so I can get into town and back. I'll need riding clothes and some skirts and dresses, the kind he'll like."

Morgan kept his voice low. "I think you'd better say something to Father Sullivan. You know, to prepare him."

"You know, I'm thinking we're way too formal," Sean said. "Son, you saved me life and the lives of all I hold dear. And I've seen enough to know you're a decent man and you're like a big brother to Felicity. Why don't you call me Uncle Sean?"

"Sure," Morgan said, smiling. "And thanks."

"Now, what is it I need preparing for?" Sean asked. He looked at Felicity who stayed quiet for a moment, composing her thoughts. Morgan hoped she'd go easy, but saw that she decided on a tough approach.

"Uncle Sean, what I heard last night convinced me this O'Ryan character is really dangerous. Morgan tells me the loyalists killed more people than the Provos, the two years before the cease fire. If O'Ryan sets it all off again, they'll all be back to setting up massacres."

"And if he starts it, the rest of the IRA might decide to join in," Morgan added. "I know that publicly there was a big disarmament but believe me, those boys have got enough light weapons and explosives stowed away to equip a couple of combat divisions."

"You don't have to sell me," Sean said. "What's your

point?"

"Dear uncle, you haven't been able to beat this devil with angel tactics. Well, Morgan and I can do it, but not by playing like angels. Some of our actions might be as bad as his, but we'll put an end to O'Ryan's power here. Okay?" Sean nodded his head, but still looked unsure.

"To stop O'Ryan, I'll need to get into his home. He's built himself a Georgian mansion by one of the lakes. And I'll have to use Max to get into the house. He lives on the estate. Once I'm in, I can probably handle the whole thing while Max is asleep."

"You're planning to sleep with him," Sean said. It was not a question.

"It's not like I'm sacrificing myself. I may well have, anyway. I kind of like the boy. And it's the easiest way in. It's infinitely safer than trying to defeat whatever security O'Ryan's got."

Morgan suspected that whether or not she liked Grogan didn't matter. Even if she found Grogan repulsive she might still use the same plan as the most rational way to accomplish her goal. Just the same, he hated to see the priest avert his eyes in shame.

"You said something about Paris last night," Morgan said, in an effort to shift the subject.

"Yes. When is that weapons expo you were talking about?"

"The Paris Air Show you mean? Let's see...is it Thursday today?" Morgan shook his head. "I still have a small touch of jet lag. Yes, the show starts a week from tomorrow."

"Good. I want you to go."

"What?" Morgan's eyes widened. "Why?"

"Taking O'Ryan's money is only half the battle. If he's shipping guns in he can sell them to raise more cash. I want you to meet with Raoul Goulait. He'll be there for his own business reasons. He's a professional smuggler and a very close friend of mine."

"Lord have mercy," Sean muttered, walking away.

Felicity ignored him.

"I think Raoul can find out when any illegal shipment might be headed this way. We can stop that shipment and cut off his last chance of squaring things with his bosses."

"Since you know him, wouldn't it be better if you went?"

"It won't work," Felicity said. "I'll be making my move Friday night. It'll take me a week to get myself invited in for the evening."

"A week? Losing your touch?"

"No. It's just that the Irish sexual appetite is, eh..."Felicity fished for words, "shall we say, a bit low key?"

A cry of "Lord forgive us" came from the kitchen.

"I'll need your help too, Uncle Sean," Felicity called.

"And just who must I cheat, rob or kill?" Sean asked, walking back into the front room.

"Don't be silly." Felicity gave him her charmer's smile and threw her arms around his neck. "What I do need you to do is to take some of my money and open bank accounts in four different banks. The accounts will be in my business' name and I'll set it up so you can sign. We'll need them for the money. Don't worry, we'll give you a chance to rob and cheat later. Now, will you please take me to town so I can be pretty for my date?" She pecked his cheek, and Morgan laughed seeing him melt just as he himself had under similar conditions in the past.

- 9 -

The spot Felicity pointed out for their late afternoon picnic was covered with a bed of clover, but lay just a few feet from the line where the green surrendered to the purple heather.

"It's perfect!" Max said, putting down their picnic basket. In the past week, he had declared everything she said or did to be perfect.

That first day they rode for hours. She astonished him by showing how well she sat a horse. With subtle questions and keen observations she easily learned his tastes and preferences in women and set about becoming his perfect match. She wore her hair down, and never wore pants except while riding. She shied away from makeup, except a touch of lipstick. She did start wearing nail polish, a color he thought very feminine. She figured it was probably his mother's shade.

They took long walks, dined together at Paddy's and drank a lot of stout. As promised, Max attended mass with her, sitting right up front to make sure Sean knew he was there. That was the only time all week Max saw Morgan. They spoke briefly after mass, while Sean was greeting other parishioners.

"I wanted to say I appreciate the fact that you trust me with the girl," Max had said. "I wouldn't have been surprised if you came along on our dates."

"You guys need your space," Morgan had answered. "And I have other business."

"I figured. I've heard that Father O'Brien doesn't appear in public these days without you being in plain sight. I hear you wear a jacket or blazer every day, and everyone you meet suspects they know what's hanging under it."

"Really?" Morgan kept his smile light. "Well, they're right, you know. You got a lot of friends around here, right? You can help them stay out of trouble."

"How's that?"

Just make it clear to everybody that Sean is now my adopted uncle. And make it just as clear that if anyone were to try to hurt Sean, well, I would not wait for the Lord's vengeance. I would personally consign that individual to the lowest pits of hell. Can you carry that message for me?"

But that conversation on Sunday was overshadowed by far more pleasant chats. Wednesday, Max took Felicity fishing and Thursday they went up to Bray so she could play tourist. All week he made tentative passes at her, stealing an occasional kiss or even trying to touch her. She parried his approaches but by keeping her rejections gentle she made it clear that she was interested. Still she was a lady and he would have to show some patience.

Thursday night he took her to a movie show in Wicklow, and there in the dark he got up the courage to put his arm around her. When he bent to her face she accepted his attentions, returning a most passionate kiss. In their embrace she could feel his boyish heart pounding.

Friday morning she drove with her uncle to Dublin to put Morgan on a plane for the continent. When she left for her picnic that afternoon, she told her uncle this was the day she would be in late. He grunted and nodded his head. He accepted, but she knew that was not the same as saying he approved.

So Friday afternoon Max spread a checked tablecloth on the clover for them to sit on. Felicity opened the large woven basket she had stuffed that morning with sandwiches and slices of a cake she had baked. She wore a sky blue shirtdress with the top two buttons open. A breeze fluttered the long skirt when she stretched out on her side to pour iced tea for them.

Grogan sat quite close to her. She could see he was trying to be romantic.

"You have the loveliest big green eyes," Max said, staring at her cleavage.

"Why, thank you, kind sir."

"And the most beautiful smile," Grogan continued. Following his gaze, she wondered if indeed her legs were smiling when the wind flipped her dress, exposing her long thighs.

"Look at that blue sky," Max said, daring to place his rough hand on her knee. "The heather blowing. What a day. Where will it end?"

"Well," Felicity replied, moving his hand to the tablecloth between them with a firm but gentle grip, "I'd like it to end with a long drive around the lake. Then, maybe," she stroked the back of his hand, "maybe with a late snack at your place."

*   *   *   *   *

As Felicity pulled away from Dublin Airport, Morgan experienced a wave of déjà vu. It wasn't a hot LZ. No one was shooting around this landing zone and yet, he felt very alone. Walking through the crowd he was very aware that all of his hardware was secured in his carryon bag and that people sometimes die in Dublin for no good reason.

More than twelve million travelers passed through Dublin's single terminal every year, and Morgan thought that most of them were there that day. In this environment the Irish behaved much like other Europeans, jostling and bumping one another without comment or apology. The density of the crowd also reinforced Morgan's notion that the Irish were halfway between the British and their other European cousins. That was because the stench of body odor in close quarters was only about half what it would have been in Paris or Frankfort or any other airport on the continent.

Morgan spent nearly thirty minutes displaying his passport, identification and various licenses before surrendering his checked luggage. Even the Irish girls at the counters couldn't make that process pleasant. But once it was over Morgan had plenty of time to kill so he decided to settle in one of the airport's many taverns for a pint.

He sat at a small, two-person table trying to relax, just listening to the mix of accents and occasional alternate language. Dublin was a fairly busy crossroads and its three runways handled just about every airline on earth, except British Airways of course. But a certain amount of tension would remain, despite the effects of the dark, rich stout. He judged airport security as excellent, but there were an awful lot of people crammed into a confined space and they came from everywhere. This made it a target rich environment for terrorists and it was just good sense to maintain your awareness in such circumstances.

So when Morgan's senses alerted him to a possible threat from behind he did not react, at least not in any way an observer would notice. But his feet slid under his chair so that he was on the balls of his feet, and he leaned toward his mug raising part of his weight from his seat.

Through hearing and instinct Morgan tracked the figure walking up behind him. The stranger stepped around to his side, eyed him with raw hostility, and lowered himself into the other seat. Morgan had kept his eyes low, staring into his dark brew, but how he raised them to the face of his new seatmate.

"Do I know you?"

"I don't think so," the stranger said. "But I know who you are. You're the boy what's been following around after Father Sullivan these past few days."

The stranger bore the ruddy, freckled face of a native. His hair was home cut and unruly. His crooked teeth, flannel shirt and Brogan shoes spoke of a man bred in the countryside who only entered the city when he had to. This was no chance meeting of travelers.

"Yeah, I been following Sean," Morgan said. "To keep him safe. Got a feeling you been following around too, but maybe with a different objective."

The stranger rested a fist on the table and raised an eyebrow. "You don't understand our struggle, boy. The priest keeps a lot of people from seeing the truth. He keeps people from assisting their brothers in the struggle against the murdering Anglicans."

"Your struggle?" Morgan snorted and emptied his mug before continuing. "First of all, as a merc I seen the same tribal bullshit all over Africa, then in Eastern Europe and it's been going on for centuries in the Middle East. All the hate don't solve nothing, it's just there, part of the environment. So you can talk all the shit you want to about your idiotic struggle. But if you call me boy one more time, I'm gonna have to kick your big Irish ass."

The crowd around him seemed awfully quiet and Morgan realized that he had gotten a lot louder than he intended. Passersby had stopped to stare at him. Their faces were not kind. They may not mean him harm, but they certainly wouldn't help him if trouble started. After a deep breath, he got to his feet.

"Nice talking to you, buddy, but I got a plane to catch."

Morgan strode away from the bar hoping to disappear into the crowded concourse. He walked the airport at random, but the feeling of danger followed him. As he strolled past the duty free shops that feeling spread. He stopped at a newsstand and picked up a copy of the Irish Times. The stranger walked past him just as Morgan was leaving the newsstand. Morgan moved down two doors and stopped. Staring into the broad shop windows he was able to scan the crowd flowing past. One fellow to his right was paying too much attention to Morgan. Another watcher, pretending to consider a liquor purchase, was a bit more subtle. A fourth man entered the shop and turned to stare openly at Morgan through the plate glass. He was a broad, tall bruiser of a farm boy. But then, they all were.

Morgan considered his options to be limited. He had no weapons with which to threaten his followers, but he doubted they would allow him to board his flight. A brawl in the airport would probably result in his being held for questioning at the very least, which would keep him from taking off on time. He might be able to avoid the troublemakers altogether if he moved straight for the boarding area, but their frustration could send them straight to Sean Sullivan while Morgan was away. He needed to engage them, but without drawing public attention.

The men's room was not quite as busy as the concourse, but Morgan knew this was a temporary situation that would change when the next wave of planes landed. There was no door to insure privacy, just a passage that wound left, then hard right to the long column of stalls. Beyond that was a separate long tiled space holding urinals on one side and a row of sinks on the other.

Morgan knew he would have a moment inside. They would want to be sure he wasn't laying a trap, and they'd post a man at the entrance to turn other men away. That was okay. He took the opportunity to make use of the facilities.

By the time the stranger entered the men's room Morgan was drying his hands under the hot air machine. All the other patrons had left, leaving him alone with the humidity and the smell of urine.

"About time you showed up," Morgan said. "And you brought two of your friends I see."

"You didn't think I'd come alone, did you?" the stranger asked, smirking as he sauntered forward. His two friends entered behind him, fists already curled.

"Of course not," Morgan said while rolling his

newspaper up. "I'm kind of glad, because I need to send a message to all your happy little terrorist pals, and I want you in one piece to deliver it. So. Who's first?"

The tallest of the three men stepped forward, his fists raised, his steps echoing in the tile hall.

"You are a big one," Morgan said, moving his feet a bit apart but not advancing. "You're taller than me, and you got a longer reach. How could I ever…"

Morgan stopped talking when he sensed that his opponent was about to swing. Less than a second before the big fist moved toward him, Morgan leaned forward, snapping his right arm forward, holding the newspaper like a spear. Its edge struck the big man's face and Morgan gave it a slight twist before his arm snapped back. The big man's hands flew to his face. Morgan stabbed again, this time into the man's solar plexus. The stunned fighter staggered back, his body sagging as he dropped to his knees. As his hands dropped to his stomach he revealed a neat circle of blood inscribed around his left eye. Morgan tossed the newspaper aside and focused his attention on the second fighter.

"Those paper cuts are the worst, ain't they? Okay, now you."

After only a moment's hesitation, the second man lunged forward, arms spread as if he would wrestle Morgan to the ground. Morgan maintained a bored expression as he sidestepped the clumsy lunge. One foot stayed out to trip his attacker and he grabbed the front of the man's shirt. A sharp yank down smacked the man's forehead into the edge of the sink. The sound of the impact bounced around the room, followed by the slap of his body hitting the floor. Morgan stepped over him toward the stranger who had first sat with him, who was backing away.

"Now you're ready to understand the message I want to send back with you," Morgan said. The stranger started to turn but Morgan quickly captured his right arm and twisted it up behind his back. Ignoring the howl of pain, Morgan steered the man back into the room and slammed his face into the wall between two urinals.

"Now you can lose the arm, or you can hold still and promise to do as I say."

Through gasps of pain the stranger managed to say, "Whatever you want."

"Good," Morgan said, pressing the man hard into the tile wall. "Now you don't need to report any of this to your boss. I imagine that would be pretty embarrassing. But you *do* need to tell all your friends and neighbors who might have liked the bombing of the church or who might have been involved with the grenade tossed into a certain public house not long ago. You need to tell them everything that happened here today. Right?"

"Yeah. Yeah. I'll tell them."

Morgan twisted the arm up another inch. "Good. And you make sure they all understand that I don't need a gun or a knife to kill any of you bastards. They need to know that if anything bad happens to Sean Sullivan while I'm gone the police won't mean shit to me, the IRA won't me shit to me. I'll just find the son of a bitch who did it and destroy him in place. No discussion. No mercy. Just an ugly death. Are we clear?"

The stranger nodded his head with such vigor that Morgan had to let him go and watch him sink to the floor, clutching his arm. Nodding, he stepped toward the hall. He wasn't even breathing hard as he walked up behind the muscular man standing at the entrance with his arms folded. An older man was approaching the men's room but the guardian shook his head. Morgan slapped the man lightly on the shoulder and jerked a thumb toward the inside.

"Hey, we're done inside. You can let people in now. And your friends in there could use some help. They don't look so good."

Morgan smiled as he headed toward his gate. He was more confident that Sean would not be bothered in his absence, he had not worked up a sweat, and most importantly, he would board his plane on time.

* * * * *

"Wait till you see this place," Max said as he drove his aging Citroen down the long gravel driveway. They had indeed taken a long lakeside drive, with Felicity cuddled into Grogan's massive side all the way. They found a remote place to park, high school style, facing the sunset.

She found herself enjoying the part she was playing. She was coming to like this big, simple country boy quite a bit. In his innocence she found a sincerity that seemed to be missing in the cosmopolitan circles in which she usually traveled. She felt a little guilty about using him, which she would nonetheless do without hesitation. She was glad she would at least be able to give him something in return that night.

As the car turned the final curve on the drive, the mansion took Felicity's attention. It was an authentic reproduction of an old style Georgian mansion. In front of the house, the driveway split to circle a flagstone-edged pond and came together to flow on through the ten-foot wide gap in the hedge wall. A life size female nude statue stood atop a marble column rising out of the pond. The hedge she figured for a good six feet in height.

She got out of the car next to a large swinging sign while Grogan went off to park. The sign read "ORION HOUSE" in large Gothic letters. Between the two words was a painting of a Herculean figure in ancient Greek attire, holding a huge club over his head. His left hand held a short sword. The mythological hunter had red curly hair. She figured she was looking at the owner's self image.

The house itself was breathtaking. She tried to take the entire rambling structure in by mentally cataloging it.

It was all brick and three stories tall, at least the central portion. There were nine windows across the top two levels. On the ground floor, the center was dominated by a semicircular landing, which surrounded the door and one window on each side of it. The landing had its own semicircular roof supported by a half dozen Doric columns.

The windows on the first two floors were easily six feet tall. The third floor windows were about half that size. A stone fence ran along the edge of the flat roof. Four large chimneys sprang from the roof at even intervals.

She took two steps back to take in more. A square tower projected forward at each end of the main house. Beyond these, level with the main portion of the building, a wing projected out to each side. These had their own porches, running their full length, terminating in another semicircular landing. The porches were each supported by three pairs of columns about five feet apart. With the terminal landing, the wings were about thirty feet or so long. That would make the house a hundred and twenty feet across.

For the first time, she realized how conceited her enemy must be. How many hundreds of thousands of pounds must have gone into this gargantuan edifice in tribute to his enormous ego? Perhaps it wasn't just for his public image. Maybe he believed he was Orion, the mythical hunter.

"Isn't it the most amazing thing you've ever seen?" Grogan asked from behind her. "I feel like the luckiest man alive to live and work here."

Despite the apparent traditional design of the house, a keypad hung above the bright bronze doorknob. Grogan stood close to it and punched five buttons in order. The huge oak door swung open without a sound. Reaching back, he took Felicity's hand and guided her into the house. Victorian furniture decorated the large reception area. Max steered left and they started down the long hallway. They walked on parquet floors, between walls paneled with cedar.

"Know how I got this job?" Grogan asked when they stopped at the last door on the right.

"Do tell me." She hung on his arm, beaming up at him.

"Well, I was coming in from plowing the fields on me pa's farm," Max said, unlocking the door. "There stands this redheaded bloke in fox hunting clothes. He says to me `you Max Grogan' and I says `yessir'. He says `I hear tell how you're the biggest man in the county' and I says `'strewth, I'm the biggest I know of." Max stepped into his room and hung his jacket and cap on a coat rack in the corner. "He says to me `my name's Ian O'Ryan and now I'm the biggest man in the county. But as you're the tallest and widest, I want you as me gamekeeper.' How's that for a wild piece of luck, eh?"

"What more could you ask for?" Felicity said. She smiled, but a quick look around told her there was a lot more a loyal employee could ask for. Max's room was about twelve by eighteen feet, furnished with the simplest appointments. The floor was bare boards. There was a basic wooden bed, a dresser, a tall wooden wardrobe, a desk and a coat rack by the door. She walked in, looked around, and faced Max with a big smile.

"Maxie, is there a place where a girl could, eh, freshen up?"

"By gosh, I didn't think," Grogan said, blushing. "There's a W.C. two doors down on this side. You go on and I'll ring for tea." He reached for the simple phone on his simple desk.

*　*　*　*　*

Max's description proved to be most inadequate. This was no "water closet." It was bigger than the "slave's quarters" Grogan lived in. The toilet and bidet occupied their own little alcove to one side. The marble counter held two large sinks. The mirror above them was at least three feet high and six feet long. She felt no need to explore the sunken tub at the far end.

The real reason for the trip, aside from "freshening up", was for Felicity to unstrap the tiny camera from her inner thigh. The camera, no bigger than a pack of chewing gum, traveled in a black leather case about the size of a checkbook. Two Velcro bands held the case to her long leg, just below her crotch.

The case also held a tiny set of lock picks and a length of piano wire. With the picks she could enter any door. She would use the wire if she went upstairs. She always strung a wire across the stairs when she went up them during a burglary. If a residence guard surprised her, she could flee down the stairs, remembering her trip wire's location. She could count on her pursuer to fall, giving her time to escape.

She concealed the small case in a cabinet under the sink. Then she prepared herself to go back to the small room and enjoy the evening.

She opened Grogan's door ten minutes after she left. The lights were out, but three candles glowed on the desk. They surrounded a silver tea service and a small vase of wild flowers. Max, sitting on the bed, motioned her toward the chair. Her heart went out to him, seeing that he was trying his best, and she had no desire to make it difficult for him.

"Oh Max, it's so pretty," she said, in a low, seductive tone. "And so formal. I'm flattered, I really am, but I'm a big girl. We both know I didn't come all the way out here for tea. You look as if you don't know what to do next. You big lug, don't try to tell me I'm the first lass you've had in here."

Max looked down at his hands hanging between his knees. "Oh, I've had lasses here. Lasses. Women. Dollies. But never a lady before. I mean, you're not even drunk."

She knew this was a time to stifle the laughter trying to burst out of her. She stepped forward, stood over him and said, "Maybe I can help." When Max looked up, Felicity had finished unbuttoning her dress and slipped the sleeves off. She stood naked to the waist, her body offering clear evidence that a bra was indeed unnecessary equipment. He stood up, wrapping one arm around her waist, cupping one erect breast in his other hand. As that rough palm slid across her left nipple, Felicity felt herself melting. When Max lifted her to his bed with hardly an effort, she knew she would enjoy bringing this big country man pleasure in a way he had never known before.

- 10 -

"It's the world's greatest arms bazaar, and I can't think of a nicer pirate to be here with."

The lady's name was Claudette Christophe and she wore Morgan on her arm like an expensive fur as they strolled along a short row of hedges. On their right was a row of Paris chateaus, set up like cafes, with multicolored umbrellas standing over the tables. On their left, more than two hundred and thirty working combat aircraft awaited inspection. The airplanes and helicopters were strewn across acres of runway like toys left behind by a haphazard giant. Visitors wandered about in this circus atmosphere, many in the uniforms of the world's armed forces. Bombs, missiles, and automatic weapons stood row on row within easy view of the "chalets" lining the main runway. This was the Paris Air Show. For ten days every other year it is the weaponry and war machine capital of the world.

Tall and willowy, Claudette Christophe had a dark chocolate complexion and eyes that shined like polished ebony. She was a little thinner than the American ideal but Morgan always favored tight hips and upturned breasts, voting for quality over quantity. Her hair was jet black, straight and full. Her teeth were perfect and almost too white to look at, but her smile forced you to pay attention. Her cheekbones were high, and if not for the accent, most people would have difficulty placing her. Nothing, however, sounds like the lilting melodic language that is the French the Haitians speak.

Morgan slowed his pace to watch her walk for a few steps. She wore tall white boots that flashed with each step, thanks to the slit that reached almost to the waistband of her long, sky blue skirt. Her hat and vest were also the height of Paris fashion. Claudette was made for this kind of carnival atmosphere, but Morgan reflected that the outfit she chose for that day was quite different from the jeans, black leather boots and wool sweater she had on when she met him at the airport.

She had been waiting there, the day before when he had climbed off the jet at Orly Airport just before one o'clock. The crowd was thicker than Maureen's stew and everyone seemed to be talking at once, in a wide variety of languages. He had stepped into the waiting area, pushed his way through the forest of rudeness and fallen into her arms.

"So happy to see you, mon chere," Claudette said. "But why are you looking so grim? Don't you like what you see?" She backed up to display her trim figure.

"Nothing wrong I can see," Morgan said. "I guess after Dublin, the noise level here is kind of deafening."

"I think I have the solution to that problem," she whispered in his ear, "but it will cost you a kiss."

Morgan was happy to pay the required toll in return for escape from the noise. Claudette's solution was to take him away from Paris' major airport as quickly as possible. They rode in her black BMW to a quiet cafe at the southern edge of Paris and enjoyed a light lunch while Morgan readjusted to the grime, the noise and the hustle of the "City of Lights." At the same time, he was readjusting to the joy of this woman's company.

Morgan had known Claudette since his days as a corporate bodyguard. He was still wandering in those days, but she had already found her calling as an industrial spy. They met as respectful rivals. Later they became lovers. After that, they became close friends.

After lunch they walked the three blocks to Claudette's apartment to pull the shades for the afternoon and remind themselves what made them such perfect partners in the past. Years before Morgan had learned that Claudette gave of herself in a free and open way, more than any other woman he had ever slept with. Her body told him that this was no one-sided exchange. At a quiet moment she had once told him out loud that no man she had met could keep her in the throes of ecstasy for as long as he did. He chose to believe her, not that this alone was enough to bring him back to Paris now and again. Even more important than their physical compatibility was the fact that she was not at all possessive. This was so important because Morgan was not yet ready to settle down. These two things, sexual compatibility and lack of possessiveness, constituted a sporadic match made in heaven.

Claudette had collapsed onto his chest for the final time, panting and glistening with sweat, when she got around to asking him, "What brings you to town, lover? Are you here for the air show?"

"Basically," he answered, pulling a sheet up over them. "I'm working on a private project. Got to meet a man and get some information."

"Is it confidential?"

"Not really," he said. "How about you? You free-lancing the air show? Now that we've got the preliminaries out of the way, I ought to know what ground rules we're playing under."

"Don't you trust me?" Claudette asked, nibbling his shoulder. "Actually I've got a pretty sweet setup this trip. First, I'm working for General Dynamics as a consultant."

"Meaning spy, right? You attend the trade shows to gather information. You keep the company up on what the competition is doing, and who's buying what from whom."

"You'd be surprised what a stuffy old exec might tell a pretty girl," she said. "You should know that I'm also being paid by the Chinese. I arrange sales between them and the U.S. Very tricky right now."

"A glorified gunrunner," Morgan said, stroking her back. "Just like the guy I'm here to see."

"So why don't you tell me, darling?" She smiled into

his eyes, her body relaxing under his touch.

"No reason." He pushed a pillow up against the headboard so he could sit up. "His name's Raoul Goulait. He might know when a certain shipment of weapons gets shipped."

"You're meeting a man to find that out? A man? Have you forgotten that information is my business? I traffic in gossip for a living." She pressed her face into his body, kissing his stomach. "And I know this man Goulait. He is a premiere smuggler with a lot of experience behind him. Whoever put you on to him is pretty deep in the underworld."

"My new business partner." He said, returning to rubbing Claudette's back.

"Mmmm, that feels good. Your partner, eh? What's his name?"

"Felicity."

"A woman?" she rose up to stare up at him. "Well she can't be as much fun as I am. Should I be jealous?"

"No. We don't sleep together."

"She must be an idiot." Claudette nipped at his muscular stomach. "But I bet she's the reason you're here. Whose shipment are you trying to hijack?"

"Hijack? Did I say hijack?"

"Please," Claudette said, her eyes rolling. "At least show me that much respect." She bit a little harder into his chest.

"Ow! All right! Some guy named Ian O'Ryan if you must know." His response was light and playful, but as he dropped the name, he felt his bed partner stiffen, as if an icy breeze had just blown through the room. "Oh, you know him."

"Oh, Yes, I know him. The man's got Papa Doc's eyes and a black Irish heart. You should stay away from him."

"On the contrary," Morgan said with a grin. "I'd like to meet the man. Could you introduce us sometime?"

"You stay away from him." Claudette's eyes were

pleading. "He goes right off the scale on my danger meter."

"Don't worry. I can take care of myself. Let's forget all this for a while. Here, get dressed and we'll go check out the show."

*   *   *   *   *

This is how Morgan came to be browsing about the great arms bazaar late in the afternoon with this beautiful industrial spy on his arm. Le Bourget airport is not a major attraction most of the time. Hanging onto the northern edge of Paris, it is often overlooked by sightseers and tourists. However, it is world famous in certain government circles for one biennial event.

At General Dynamics' plush chalet Claudette introduced him to her company contact. The corporate executive could spare them little time, as he was busy wining and dining potential customers. Representatives from more than thirty nations were browsing there and with more than a thousand exhibitors present at the show, competition was fierce. And General Dynamics had a lot of ground to make up.

Americans had shunned the previous Paris Air Show, in the wake of the 9/11 attack and the launch of the Global War on Terror. Two years ago, the Pentagon had sharply scaled back its fighter jet demonstrations and sent no officers of a higher rank than colonel. In deference to the Defense Department, American aerospace companies and military contractors cut back their presence as well. But this year Morgan had read that a hundred and twenty-five American generals and admirals were in attendance, and the civilian companies were also back in force, vying for the international defense dollars. As Morgan had learned during his mercenary career, war was a growth industry as reliable as real estate.

Tracking Claudette at a distance, he decided to

mingle with the crowd. He fit right in, in navy slacks and blazer. From the buffet he selected a light red wine, some pate, a small steak, various cheeses and some unrecognized pastry. Then he moved to a quiet corner to sit and watch the high tech hustlers in action.

Claudette flowed through the milling throng like a barracuda amongst a school of carp. Her smile dripped honey and the most self assured executives melted under her gaze. How easy it must be for her, he thought, to wrest the petty secrets of industry from these poor fish. After a few minutes, she wandered over to him, carrying a diagram of some sort.

"I thought you might enjoy the show on the roof," she said, and led him to a flight of stairs. After the short climb they saw that the terrace area at the front edge of the roof was lined with chairs, all occupied by spectators. A crowd milled about with their faces turned skyward. Even with sunglasses on it was painful to stare up into the bright, cloudless sky.

"That dot approaching in the sky is Boeing's latest F-15 Eagle," Claudette said. This is the demonstration flight everyone's been waiting for. For years they've been in competition with the French, you know. Now they've got Dassault Aviation SA Rafale, which is even better than the Rafale C of a few years back. They're the main competition, although the RAF's fielded the Jaguar. Plus, there's the Eurojet EJ200 going after the NATO market. But we're not worried. When Boeing lands that fat Singapore sale, we will get our share as a subcontractor."

Morgan checked the diagram of the choreography of the flight. Even on paper, the pilot's ability impressed him. He watched in honest awe as the F-15 roared into vertical climbs, thundered through screaming power dives, and, with glowing afterburners, carved loops into the clouds. He knew for a certainty that this was the most maneuverable and sophisticated jet aircraft in the world, and that the European pilots in their brand new machines would have to raise hell to beat this show.

"There he is," Claudette hissed in his ear, and it took him a moment to realize the significance of that statement. He tore his eyes from the sky and began scanning the crowd. His gaze settled on one figure facing away from him. This man was about six feet tall, a full two inches shorter than Morgan, yet he would weigh about the same, two hundred and ten pounds. Curly red hair hung about the man's head and neck like a mane. His broad shoulders strained against the confines of his safari jacket. He stood with his booted feet placed wide apart. Like everyone else, he held a program, but his left hand hung in a tight fist at his side. The fist seemed to be the natural shape for his hand.

The man radiated pure animal vitality like no one Morgan had ever encountered. This had to be Ian O'Ryan, and Morgan was elated. While Felicity was invading his home, Morgan had made first contact with the enemy.

The stranger tensed for just a second as if he felt he was being stared at. Then his entire body made a slow turn and he locked eyes with Morgan. After a slight pause, Morgan broke into a bright smile and raised his glass in a nominal toast.

"You're not going over there?" Claudette said through clenched teeth.

"Are you kidding? I've got to get to know this guy. Any man who can scare you..."

"He's a killer," Claudette whispered.

"I'm not? Besides, there must be a couple of thousand police and heavily armed private security guards on the grounds. Nobody'd start anything here." Giving Claudette a confident wink, he moved toward his target, traveling several feet before he realized that Claudette had stayed behind. When he reached his quarry he stretched a hand forward.

"Hello. I don't believe we've met. I'm Morgan Stark."

"O'Ryan," the man replied, shaking Morgan's hand

with a power that would have made a lesser man wince. During the handshake Morgan watched his eyes. O'Ryan's florid face was handsome, despite teeth almost too big for his mouth. His great bushy red eyebrows arched. The eyes below them were light brown with flecks of red in them, as if so much power was roiling inside him it threatened to burst out through his eyes and sear whoever they focused on.

"You seem to be able to appreciate these jets," Morgan said, keeping his voice casual as he freed his hand. "Who do you represent?"

"Just here as a tourist, I am," O'Ryan replied in a thick lazy brogue. "And although the big planes and missiles are fascinating, I find hand to hand weapons more interesting."

"Really? I was here looking for some personal things myself. Maybe you could help me." O'Ryan looked as if he was about to ask why, then reconsidered. Morgan hoped the man's curiosity was peaked. With luck he would play along long enough to find out what this crazy black man was up to.

"Why don't we head over to the pavilions?" O'Ryan said. "Some of the small arms companies have booths set up. You might see something there that interests you."

From the corner of his eye, Morgan saw the horror on Claudette's face as he and Ian O'Ryan walked out of the chalet like old friends. They entered the nearest pavilion, a huge hangar converted into a showroom, holding three or four dozen exhibitors. O'Ryan steered him to the noisiest spot he could find. One small American company advertised its machine guns using a bank of a dozen television screens. Each video monitor extoled this one submachine gun's virtues. It was a loud, blasting assault on the senses and in the middle of this, O'Ryan turned to poke Morgan's chest.

"I'll bet you're licensed to carry weapons, even here," O'Ryan said. Denial seemed pointless to Morgan, considering the trouble he had gone through to get authorization through his security business. He replied with a nod.

"Let me take a look at what you're carrying now," O'Ryan said. Still smiling, Morgan moved close and handed over his nine millimeter Browning Hi-power and the Randall Number One fighting knife with its seven inch blade. O'Ryan looked at the pistol's walnut grip and checked its weight and balance. He rubbed the knife's black micarta handle, admired the brass guard and tested its shaving-sharp edge. Then he handed them back with appropriate respect.

"These are very personal weapons indeed," O'Ryan said. "They say a great deal about you. I would assume you've used them both for their ultimate purpose."

"I'm a soldier by profession," Morgan said. "An independent operative. I had the feeling you might be, too."

"Me?" O'Ryan chuckled. He was the only man Morgan had ever met who had a sinister laugh. He heard them on television and in movies all the time, but this was his first sinister laugh in real life. "I'm just a hunter," O'Ryan said. "And a racer. In fact, I'll be competing in the Belgian Grand Prix in a couple of weeks."

"Race cars?"

"Oh no, my friend," O'Ryan said. "Motorcycles. Nothing between me and the wind. Or the other riders, eh?"

"I see you're the type who likes to handle things up close and personal. Did you come to the show looking for new weapons? I'm after a sniper rifle myself."

"As I said, I'm a hunter," O'Ryan reminded him. "I'm looking for hunting arms. Such as...ah, here we are." O'Ryan had led them to the Mossberg exhibit and was reaching for one of the demonstrator models. The representative seemed to recognize him and smiled as the Irishman picked up the sleek weapon at hand.

"This one is a beauty. Mossberg's model 712 Auto. Four shot, twelve gage, twenty-eight inch barrel, seven and a half pounds weight."

"You've done your homework," Morgan said, picking up another display model. "Light, fast, easy handling. What about the elevator?"

Sighting down the barrel, O'Ryan looked up, apparently surprised by the question. "Stainless steel. I see you know something of shotguns. Why did you attach yourself to me, Mister Stark?"

"You stood out in the crowd and I liked your style. Two extractors?"

"Yes," O'Ryan answered, keeping his eyes on the gun. "I don't believe you. I think maybe you're connected with the British police."

"Right. I bet I sure look British. And sound like it. Can you hit anything with that thing?"

"I'm the best there is with this type of long arm," O'Ryan said, swinging the gun as if he were tracking a flock of geese.

"Well, maybe second best." Morgan turned to aim a conspiratorial wink toward the demonstrator.

"Really?" O'Ryan lowered his weapon to lock eyes with Morgan. "And who's to be my better, eh? You?"

Morgan's answer was a nod and a smile.

"You're an arrogant man, my friend. You claim to be American? Well than I have one thousand American dollars in my pocket that says I cannot be defeated."

"Yeah?" Morgan asked. "And how we going to prove it? A showdown at twenty paces?"

"Well, there's the rapid fire demonstration this evening," the Mossberg representative said, speaking for the first time. "The Scots have set up a Starshot competition out on the center field. Should be great fun to watch, and you can sign up for it right here, if you wish."

"That sounds to me like a lovely way to spend the evening," O'Ryan said. A smile split his face, flashing big, even teeth.

"Wouldn't miss it." Morgan maintained his jovial tone, but he was not pleased that it proved so easy and convenient for O'Ryan to call his bluff.

"I'll need two of these," O'Ryan told the company representative. "One for my friend here and one for me. On my bill, please. We must be equally equipped if I am to teach this arrogant cobber how to shoot."

- 11 -

At two a.m., Felicity O'Brien's eyes popped open. Her internal alarm clock never failed her, so even without Max Grogan's heavy snoring she would have been awake.

Lifting her head from the thatch of hair on his chest, she turned a smile on her bed partner. He had been passionate, there was no doubting that. Or perhaps earnest was a better word. He had tried his best. She had not reached her ultimate release in her first rough encounter with Max, but she made all the appropriate noises and gave him all she could. A couple of hours later they tried again and this time she found the satisfaction she had missed before. Max showed genuine delight at having brought her real pleasure.

Overall, however, she had to admit to herself that, like the local food, she now found the attentions of the local men rather bland. Not enough spice. Her sexual palate had been cultivated on more continental cuisine. She just had to face the unfortunate fact that Irish lovers resembled their diet, mainly meat and potatoes. In contrast, French lovers seemed like pastry men to her. They were light, and sweet, and a little flaky. And Germans she found to be like their chocolate cakes, heavy, thick, and dense. Ireland, perhaps significantly, did not have its own hallmark dessert. Men like Max were potato men, solid, filling, but somehow lacking in flavor.

But, hell, his intentions were good. She had come to really like the big lug. Still, she had a job to do.

She slid out of bed and dressed in seconds. Her first stop would be the bathroom for her camera. Then she would search the palatial building, room by room if necessary, for O'Ryan's private office.

The wing she was in appeared to be the servants' sleeping quarters. She started searching on the ground floor in the center of the house and got luckier than she expected. Right there, off the main dining hall, she found her objective.

Even in the dark she realized she was stepping from one world into another. The dining room was done in baroque decor, all white and gold, with a harpsichord in one corner. Stucco work imitating the Georgian period decorated the upper part of the walls. In harsh contrast, the office beside it was cold and contemporary in steel and black enamel.

The lock on the door was a joke to someone with her ability. The lack of security might have meant that O'Ryan had complete trust in all his employees. More likely it implied that no cash or negotiable securities were kept here. All the better, in her mind. What she wanted would interest few local thieves.

As further evidence of his confidence, a small combination safe stood in plain sight against the wall behind the desk. Opening it required no more than for her to put her ear to the lock while turning the knob. It was child's play for a woman of her skills. Inside she found a large photo album, bank records and a small stack of pound notes which she assumed was his petty cash fund. After taking a second to memorize the position of the contents, she removed everything but the cash. It would not do to take anything O'Ryan would miss. Such a discovery might not go well for Max.

What she was after would be in the bank records. Not the book of personal checks, which would be missed, but some deposit slips. Almost no one keeps track of them. Like in the States, these were preprinted but not numbered. Two from each account would do. O'Ryan kept his money in three different banks. One was local, one in Northern Ireland, and the other in London.

Notes lay scattered across his desk. Felicity thought some of them could prove important. She closed the door and turned on the desk lamp. Yes, these notes mentioned an important shipment. Maybe useless, but it would be better to be safe. She took the camera from its pack and clicked over every piece of paper on the desk. Each sheet she moved she replaced in its exact original position.

The bank records and check books went back into the safe with equal care. Felicity lifted the photo album to replace it also but, as an afterthought, she took a look inside. The only pictures inside were on thin yellowed paper. O'Ryan was using the album as a newspaper clippings scrapbook. If they were what she suspected, they might be good incriminating leverage if things got sticky later. She photographed the first few pages, and then replaced the album in the safe. She slipped her camera back into the portfolio with the deposit slips. Once her carrying pack was on her thigh, she slipped out of the room, locking the door behind her.

She planned to slip past the dining room and out the door at the end of the far wing. However, as she passed the next room its ornate door drew her attention. A small brass plate above the transom labeled the room "The Gallery."

The room was secured, but again the lock offered little challenge to Felicity. Thinking about the well known effects of curiosity on cats and other creatures, she eased the door open. It was indeed a gallery of some sort. She should have hurried to leave, but she thought she had plenty of time before anyone in the building would awaken. Her curiosity was peaked by speculation of the kind of collection a man like O'Ryan might have. She couldn't resist exploring the room.

She stepped inside, closing the door without making a sound. When she flipped up the light switch, three gigantic double tiered chandeliers flooded the room with brilliance. She caught her breath.

The long gallery was decorated in Pompeian style. It

was such a perfect representation of the style of the period that if not for the electric lights she could have believed that the room was designed two hundred years ago. Two cabinets filled with curios stood against one wall. The hand worked wood and glass cabinets were separated by a statue of a lovely toga clad woman standing on a three foot pedestal. The statue was at least eight feet tall from floor to head. The walls of the alcove behind it displayed fine and delicate carving.

Above the cabinet and statue stood a marble cornice, much like a mantelpiece, but covered with intricate engraving. A painting imitating the period hung above the cornice. The painting, in the shape of a hemisphere, seemed to depict several people milling about in horror as Mount Vesuvius erupted in the background.

Along the rest of that wall, on either side of the statue and cabinets, a low platform projected from the wall. This held a row of life size marble busts, four on each side. They stood about a meter apart.

Was all this a reflection of O'Ryan, or simply a show to overawe his rustic visitors? If the former, what did a fascination with lost Pompeii say about the man?

Two tall bookcases stood against the far wall, separated by a small fireplace. Above it, a large oil painting depicted another imaginary Pompeii scene. The other long wall held two narrow tables displaying gold, silver and carved jade objet d'art.

She was admiring a golden, jewel encrusted chalice when her internal alarm went off. It figured that this room would be guarded, and someone was coming toward it now. The approaching footsteps would have gone unheard by almost anyone else. She sprinted to the switch to kill the lights, but what next? There were no closets, no drapes, hardly any furniture it seemed, no hiding place. Desperation gripped her heart as she did a slow pan around the room looking for any kind of concealment.

Two minutes later, a key turned a heavy dead bolt

and the door to the Pompeii gallery swung slowly open.

- 12 -

The night was as black as the bottom of an abandoned mine, the air clean, and crisp as a gunshot. The dry grass covering the field crackled under O'Ryan's booted feet. With an arrogant stride he approached the firing line, twenty meters from the semicircular target area. He was backlit, the same floodlight illuminating his form and making the tubular steel frame beyond him glow.

The target grid was shaped like half a dart board, twenty-six meters across. Each target area in the top row was labeled with yellow iridescent numbers. From left to right they were three, one, two and four. The row below was marked seven, five, six and eight. The four targets nearest the ground, closest to the "bull's-eye", were numbered eleven, nine, ten and twelve. The blackness beyond made the spaces between the red florescent lines of the "dart board" seem solid.

Morgan, standing with several other shooters several meters behind O'Ryan, admired the Irishman's concentration. The silence and tension were enough to unnerve anyone. There was an occasional murmur from the crowd, hushed comments from people who recognized O'Ryan the racer, O'Ryan the hunter. A buzz of recognition rose from the press as well, and Morgan heard one or two remarks about O'Ryan the suspected IRA leader, made in still quieter tones.

Yet, O'Ryan focused on the four traps in the ground in front of the target grid. His gun was mounted, and he stood leaning a little to the right for the best view of the target and the traps.

"This game is too fast for me," Claudette commented. She clung to Morgan's arm. "No one's made it `round the clock' yet."

"No one's got more than seventy points so far," Morgan replied. "Those four bottom targets are too quick for the average trap shooter."

"Think you can do it?"

"I've got a hidden advantage." He winked at Claudette. Then he examined O'Ryan's body English and wondered if he also had an instinctive edge.

All eyes were on Ian O'Ryan and the air was electric with anticipation. Without a warning the first florescent clay target flew almost straight up into the air. O'Ryan tracked it as accurately as radar locked onto a target, seeming to pull his shotgun's trigger at the same time as the launch. In front of the number one space, the clay pigeon exploded.

"That's one point," Morgan whispered.

The second target flew and O'Ryan caught it dead center of the number two area.

"Two more points," Morgan said. "That's three so far."

The third target popped up and this time, O'Ryan missed it. Clay pigeons five and six flew straight into the Irishman's shotgun blasts. Then number seven came out. O'Ryan caught it, but in the higher number three space. No score.

"Each shot is worth the number of points in its target area," Morgan said. "He's weak on the left, and he knows it. If he misses the other left hand spot it'll cost him eleven points. Then I can beat him."

O'Ryan's stance was rock solid. He swung his shotgun's barrel all the way to the right to shatter the clay bird in the number eight space, and swung back anticipating the next target. He squeezed the trigger before the disc flew and nailed the number nine target, then the ten, which was nearly next to it. Bending further forward, holding his gun sideways, he blasted the number eleven target just before it flew out of the designated area.

"Damn," Morgan said.

Ian O'Ryan had no trouble catching the clay pigeon in

number twelve. Then the two extras were thrown, worth five points each. The shooter chooses where he hits them, and the Irish marksman burst them in the one and two spaces. He turned and walked to Morgan's position, arrogance covering him like a cloak.

"I believe that a seventy-eight puts me in the lead my American friend. Tell your associates in The Company that I don't miss much. Especially those who come up behind me."

"The Company?" Morgan said, amused. "Now you think I'm CIA.? Look pal, I've been a full service independent operative for too long to hook up with those amateurs."

"Well, you're the last shooter. Let's see if you're as good as you say."

"Just get your dollars ready," Morgan said in a terse, grim tone. After giving Claudette a quick kiss he turned on his heel and strode for the firing line. He slipped hearing protection like headphones over his head and shook his arms out to loosen them. Before mounting his gun he glanced over his shoulder. He met O'Ryan's confident stare. Then he saw the Irishman turn to smile at Claudette.

Morgan's pulse quickened as he watched her step backward a few feet, then turn and almost run away. He did not think she was in any real danger, but it grated on his nerves to see her threatened, even if the threat was subtle. He took three deep breaths, faced forward, and began tuning out the entire world except the target area.

His focus was not even on the target grid, standing like the top half of a huge dart board sunk deep in the dry ground. As he brought the new shotgun to his shoulder his senses were forming a link with the four hidden traps imbedded in the earth in front of the target. They were the source of the targets that would soon fly through, or more accurately in front of, the target grid's various zones.

At that moment, he was very happy he possessed an

unexplained sixth sense that alerted him to danger. He had read a lot on the subject in the last few months, since he discovered another person, Felicity, with the same sense. He had always thought his five senses combined to alert him on some subconscious level, but he now suspected he possessed a true form of extrasensory perception. He figured if he relaxed and let his instincts guide his aim, perhaps this bizarre sense would tell him in advance when a clay pigeon would fly.

As if in slow motion, he watched the first clay target leap into the air, and shattered it in zone one with little effort, not reacting to the muted blast. The second flew, then the third and the fourth. Each one he blasted with ease. Five was lower and faster, but he pulled the trigger at the right time to hit it in the zone. The gun's stock punched into his shoulder, but it was a comfortable and familiar pressure.

While he reloaded he glanced at O'Ryan. The Irishman smiled back. He had hit one target O'Ryan missed, but the toughest ones were still to come.

He leaned far over to the right to sweep onto number six and kept swinging so that he blasted number seven well inside the target zone. Then he was swinging right. As lead shot crashed into number nine, he thought to himself that he had caught both clays his opponent missed. Now he had a shot. He could beat him.

In the same microsecond that thought was born in his mind, another part of his brain recognized it as the distraction of overconfidence. The bottom row of target grids was much too fast to be forgiving. An instant's hesitation caused the next blast to be high. He hit the clay, but above the ten space. No score.

Forget it, he told himself. *Move on. Swing onto the next target.* The clay pigeon exploded in the number seven spot, and the final disc shattered well inside grid twelve a few seconds later. He kept squeezing the trigger with gentle pressure and potted the last two flying targets with almost casual ease. Only when the blast died away and the clay shards lay on the ground did he turn to face O'Ryan. They had tied.

The big Irishman was walking toward Morgan, but the black man was looking past him. He was scanning the area for Claudette, but it seemed that she had not waited around for the finish.

"Well, my friend, now we shall stand side by side." O'Ryan's too-big teeth shone in a death's head grin. "The tie breaker game is called `one hundred and out'. You know the game?"

"I think so. Why don't you refresh my memory?" The gentle breeze stopped dead as Morgan spoke and at that moment the world population shrank to two for this pair of combatants. Their eyes locked for a moment. Then O'Ryan turned and shouted to the crowd behind them.

"First I choose three targets. Eight, ten and twelve." He turned and mounted his weapon. Clay targets flew in the order called, one right after the other. O'Ryan shattered them in order.

"Each target is worth the number of points corresponding to its position. The total of eight, ten and twelve is thirty, which I now deduct from my score. I have seventy to go, and the first man to get to zero and then break a pair, wins. Of course, as I have hit all three targets I shoot again."

While the stocky Irishman reloaded, a man wearing a press badge eased up to Morgan's side. His windblown hair gave him a wild, flighty look.

"Do you know this man?" he asked in a neutral British accent.

"Just met. Why?"

"A word of advice," the reporter said.

"Yes?"

"Lose."

"What?" Morgan stared. "Why?"

"Mister O'Ryan is not a good loser," the reporter said in a confidential tone. "I mean, he don't lose often, and them what beats him, well, sometimes they disappears."

Then he was gone, and O'Ryan called for the same three targets. Again they flew, and again he dispatched them with three quick blasts. He turned, smiled at Morgan, smiled at the onlookers and shouted, "Again!"

"Can you be lucky three times in a row?" Morgan asked just before the first clay leaped into the sky. Flying lead pellets smashed number eight. Another clay bird died in the ten spot but the twelve came up faster than O'Ryan could react and he undershot it.

"I have twenty-two to go, me Yankee friend," he said, backing away from the mark. "Now, will you take an easy combination and risk having to shoot all day, or will you be daring and take higher numbers like us grown-ups? You do realize, don't you lad, that my next turn will be the last?" O'Ryan was playing to the audience, and his brogue was coming out with his viciousness.

Morgan's response was calm and assured. "Judgment is the game. I'll call six, eight and ten." He had called an easier combination not worth as many points. He hoped that with consistent shooting he could continue on and take the match in one turn.

The six was a medium easy shot. For the ten, he just dropped his point of aim a couple degrees. An easy swing to the right brought him on line for the eight. The first set was gone in seconds. During reload he glanced over at O'Ryan but his opponent was focused on the targets. Would he feel beaten if Morgan won this way?

Morgan set himself for the second wave. Bending forward was beginning to bother his lower back a little and as he tracked and blasted clay number six he received a short message from his right shoulder. After the eight and ten he realized that a padded jacket would be an asset. But he was down to fifty-two points and he was confident he could win.

A third time clay targets flew into the black void. In the six box lead scattered fragments of a clay bird. He waited and caught the ten just as it left the ground, but he barely caught the third fugitive at the upper edge of the eight space.

His score was down to twenty-eight, but he was getting physical reminders that he was not a regular shotgun hunter. His right shoulder was sore as hell, and at this rate he would have to do this twice more. An extra opportunity to miss and give that Irish murderer the one chance he needed to laugh in Morgan's face.

His mind wandered to the reporter for a second. He may have been a concerned citizen, but Morgan suspected he was a shill sent by O'Ryan in an attempt to unnerve him. If so, he could not allow him to think it worked.

He knew what he was talking himself into.

Some days, your common sense has no choice but to compromise with your ego.

"Let's not drag this out," he said into the hunter's florid face. "I'm changing my numbers. I call nine, ten and eleven." In return, he received a stare of disbelief. Targets shot through the bottom zones with incredible speed and now he was going for three of them in rapid succession, including the one space that had been O'Ryan's nemesis.

He had just a moment to reach to his center to achieve perfect calm and a kind of relaxed tension. All his senses beamed in on a spot inches from the ground, a spot through which the first target would fly. He had to be ahead of it. He wondered, just for an instant, if he had made a stupid mistake.

He felt a feather touch of sensation on the back of his neck and knew it was time. Even he was surprised when he fired a split second before the first clay cleared the trap. He was already aiming at the middle of the ten zone when the number nine pigeon exploded. He fired on the next clay disc, and before the buckshot hit it he was swinging hard to the left. *Faster*, he told himself. His back screamed as he pivoted left and down on the flash of movement in the darkness, like a target acquisition computer, and squeezed the trigger.

He felt the punch into his shoulder which told him the gun's butt had not been fully seated. Across the bead sight at the tip of his barrel, he saw the clay burst apart in front of the glowing yellow eleven in the corner of the grid.

After three deep breaths, he called for the closeout double. With an arrogance born from the union of ego and skill, he fired from the hip, and caught them in zones one and two. There was a smattering of applause when he returned to O'Ryan's position.

"Good shooting," O'Ryan said through clenched teeth. He held out his hand, which was full of American bills. "Especially for a soldier. And you said you're not a hunter, did you not?"

"Oh I hunt," Morgan said, putting his hand into O'Ryan's to accept his bet winnings. "But I only hunt terrorists. Know any?"

Ian O'Ryan locked his short thick fingers around Morgan's and what the crowd saw as a courteous handshake threatened to break bones in Morgan's hand. O'Ryan was applying crushing pressure and he had caught Morgan off guard. It seemed too childish an attack to consider.

"Terrorists are always hunted, even though it is they who are the hunters." O'Ryan glared into his new enemy's eyes.

Morgan did not allow the pain or the anger he felt to cross his face. Instead, he took a small step toward O'Ryan and moved his left hand forward in a casual manner. Out of sight of the onlookers he ground the knuckle of his middle finger into the back of O'Ryan's hand.

"Now be a good loser and let it go," Morgan said, maintaining a cheerful smile. "I don't want to have to hurt you in front of all these people."

O'Ryan emitted a muted growl and their clasped

hands sprang apart. Money fluttered to the ground but neither man moved to collect it.

"One day, boy." O'Ryan spat the words out. "One day you'll forget to look over your shoulder. That's the day I will be there."

"I look forward to you getting that close," Morgan answered. "I like to look a man in the eye when I break him."

As Morgan walked away, he heard Ian O'Ryan say under his breath, "Don't sleep too soundly, boy."

- 13 -

Patrick O'Neill led the young maid into the long Pompeii gallery with a flourish. He was on night guard duty this time, and the end of the shift was not far off. The girl had never been allowed in the gallery but she had heard stories. Patrick had tried for several days to convince her to share his bed. Last night she decided she might just give him what he wanted, if he would take her to see this room that was always locked.

The instant the light came on, the simple maid was captivated. There was beauty there she had never experienced, except in an occasional book. She drank in the deep richness of the paintings, the smooth detail of the busts and sculptures, the sparkling majesty of the jeweled pieces. This was indeed a rainbow's end of loveliness and being able to say she had seen it was a cachet well worth the price of admission.

While she indulged in this beauty, O'Neill was busy clearing a place on the long table for collecting that price. He moved one item at a time, careful to remember where each one was. By the time he made enough space, the maid was coming to him with a new glow on her face. He was impatient and she saw no reason to delay. In seconds she was leaning back against the table and he was hiking up her skirts.

* * * * *

Enveloped in a sea of blackness, Felicity listened to the young couple's grunts and groans. She hung suspended in the fireplace, no more than five feet above the floor. Her bare feet were pressed against the wall in front of her. The rough brick of the opposite wall scraped her back sparking flashes of pain.

The stale air she breathed was thick with dust, not soot. If she reached above her head she could touch the bricks blocking off the flu over this fireplace that was no longer used. Her body was wedged into a space no more than thirty inches square. Years of yoga training and burglar experience prepared her to ward off claustrophobia. With a conscious effort she forced her muscles to relax, except for those really needed to hold her in position. She created a calm center within herself, and then expanded it until it held her entire being. One small piece of her awareness was left to follow the activity out in the room.

*　　*　　*　　*　　*

Colleen O'Hara, upstairs maid of Orion House, had proved herself to be well worth waiting for. She bucked her ample hips one last time, draining the last of Patrick's love essence from him, and released a contented sigh. She preferred these hurried meetings to having a man in for an evening. For one thing, a different setting made it all the more exciting. Also, she didn't face the hassle of having to shoo a boy out of her room.

Two minutes later she and Patrick were returning the articles on the table to their original positions. Three minutes later they were closing the door behind them.

*　　*　　*　　*　　*

Four minutes after the lock clicked closed, Felicity lowered her toes to the floor. One thigh was cramping but despite the pain she moved across the floor without a sound to retrieve her shoes from behind the toga covered statue. She had thrown them there on her hurried way to the only hiding place in the room.

It would not do to be seen now, begrimed by her hidey-hole, but she doubted anyone was abroad at this hour. Her hearing and her instincts told her the hallway was empty. She slipped out of the room, losing no speed for all her stealth, and moved like a living shadow to the front door.

Crunching down the gravel path, she glanced east and saw the razor's edge of light that presaged the dawn. To her surprise she realized at that moment how much she had missed watching the sunrise over those deep green hills.

On her left, a man in a hunting jacket and boots came running around the hedge, cradling a shotgun. No hunter, she thought, but rather a guard. And he was on the lookout for people coming in, not those going out. *Get into character and stick to your role*, she thought.

Affecting a slight stagger, the type that might go with a hangover, she continued three or four steps, and then looked up as if seeing the man for the first time. She froze, lifted a finger to her pursed lips and shushed him. Then she gave him a big smile and a broad wink, and tiptoed on. The "hunter" gave her a conspiratorial smile and let her pass.

Once out of sight, she pulled off her shoes, hiked up her skirts and fell into a light jogging pace. A cooling breeze tossed her hair and tall grass swabbed her feet and ankles with dew. The first birds of morning acknowledged her passing with song. It would be a pleasant dawn run to her uncle's little house.

She could hardly wait to get back to Sean's cottage, set up her room with the darkroom gear she had bought, and develop the film in her camera. Once she knew where O'Ryan kept his money and how much he had, she could direct her two partners to take it away from him.

- 14 -

Every great city has a personality all its own. Over time, any area cluttered with enough humanity takes on human characteristics. Like the grand dame of Europe she is, Paris is flashy, always wearing her best jewelry and charming her visitors with witty stories and a gay smile. Morning to evening, she shows the tourists why she still deserves her singular sobriquet: the City of Lights.

But Morgan was no tourist. He knew the old girl's other face. He had seen her without her wigs and girdle. He was familiar with this town's seamy underside, her sewers and subways. He knew this city as the center of Europe's underworld. He knew the worst and, like a boy with an aging favorite aunt, he loved her anyway.

A light rain fell on his uncovered head as he walked the narrow back streets, at home in the dark. He wondered if he should have stayed at Claudette's instead.

Morgan had taken a taxi to Claudette's apartment after the shooting match. After she didn't respond to his knock he opened the door with the two keys she had given him.

"Hey, baby, did you wait up for me?" he called as he entered. A quick look around told him that he was talking to empty rooms. Nothing was disturbed, and there was no reason to suspect trouble. He opened the closet to see if a coat had been pulled out, or if her day outfit was hanging in its place. No, it looked as if she had not been home since they separated at the Air Show. He figured that she was just staying elsewhere for a while. He realized how much O'Ryan must have spooked her, but knew she would return. Too bad. He had wanted to celebrate his victory with her. Instead he stood his new gun case in the closet.

He had picked up a new toy for himself at the Air Show, a sniper rifle complete with scope. It would sit there for a while, until he was ready to leave town. His immediate course of action was to shower quickly and change clothes. He could have gathered his things and left, but not without saying good-bye. Maybe he should have waited for her to come home but he was too excited by his victory to sit still. Already he was pacing like a caged tiger. He had to get out.

His thoughtful stroll through the city continued until it was nearing dawn and he was listening to the staccato beat of his own shoes on the rain-slicked sidewalk. In black denim trousers and a leather jacket he wandered the streets without purpose or direction. He did it often, knowing it was impossible for him to get lost.

He didn't change his pace when two sets of footsteps were added to his own, but he did change directions. He knew by the sound he was being followed by two large men who were amateurs at it. No problem. He was just in the mood for a good mugging.

He turned several corners, crossing the street whenever his followers got too close. He smiled when he came to a cross street he judged to be a total of twenty-two feet wide. He would not likely find a narrower lane. At the corner he stopped to stare up at the street sign, nailed to the brick wall of a building as was common in France. He could just make it out in the darkness. Rue de la Chat-Qui-Peche.

"Street of the cat who fishes?" he wondered out loud. His French was rudimentary, but he was pretty sure that was it. Or maybe it was the cat that was a fish. It hardly mattered. He walked on, knowing a street this narrow would be crossed by an even narrower alley, where he hoped to find some privacy.

Morgan could almost feel his followers' arrogant overconfidence as he stepped into the dead end passageway. Near the alley's end wall, he turned to face them. Two large lineman types in cheap sweat shirts and slacks stepped forward. Clearly one was East European. His facial structure and hair were unmistakable. The other brute was pure Irish. They moved in unison, with smooth coordination that gave silent evidence that they were not amateurs at this part. He smiled at them, looking forward to a nice, quiet fight to release his tension.

"You boys don't know what you're getting into," he said with a grin, slipping into a relaxed ready stance.

"We know who you are," a voice said from behind the two bruisers. The third man stepped forward between them, pointing a small automatic pistol at Morgan's midsection. "We know who you are and what you're capable of. Nonetheless, we're quite capable of teaching you some manners. You should be more careful who you mess around with. Our boss is not the forgiving type. Now you hold still, and these gentlemen will administer the lesson."

No mention of O'Ryan's name was necessary for Morgan to know who sent these men. He was a little surprised, though. He didn't think the Irishman would be this vindictive.

It seemed unlikely that he could draw his own gun before this shooter blasted him. He doubted he could beat the two punchers very badly before number three ended it with a bullet. Any way you looked at it, it looked like a bad time. Still, he braced for a battle. Maybe he could flip one of the punchers into the gunman and give himself time to get a weapon into play.

While Morgan was formulating a battle plan, he saw a well-dressed man step from the shadows and slide a four inch steel blade into the gunman's kidney. Before the dropped gun clattered to the ground, Morgan leaped right and stamped out with his left heel. Puncher number one yelped and dropped to the asphalt, clutching at his dislocated knee. Number two leaned into a hard right cross but Morgan blocked it cross body, grabbing the puncher's wrist with his own left hand. Morgan pulled the arm forward and the rest of the bulky attacker followed. The big Irishman found himself spun into the wall face first. Then Morgan snapped the arm back, and swept his enemy's feet out from under him. His skull hit the ground with a sickening crunch.

Number one was up on his one good knee just in time for Morgan to deliver a swinging back fist, followed by a straight jab that put the fighter to sleep.

Morgan wasn't even breathing hard. The action had lasted no more than seven seconds.

"Very impressive," the newcomer said. "On the evidence, I'd say you must indeed be Morgan Stark. You are everything she said you were."

He was a tall man but reed thin. He had a long aquiline nose and thin ascetic lips. His easy smile added to an overall impression of classic handsomeness. The knife he wiped on the dead man's shirt was a classic Laguiole, with leg shaped handle and Turkish clip blade. It is the knife of France, subtle and feminine, just as the Bowie is the classic American knife. Only a Frenchman would carry this knife, although this man's accent was almost unnoticeable when he spoke English.

"You have to be Raoul Goulait," Morgan said. "I'd like to know how long you've been following me, but first, shouldn't we be moving on. That is a corpse in front of you."

"So? This is Paris. Who will say anything? I only caught sight of you a few minutes ago. I didn't find you at the air show tonight, but I did meet the young woman, Claudette."

"Ahh, Felicity must have described both of us to you."

"Yes," Raoul said. "I was to meet you at Claudette's flat, but I arrived too late. She thought if you hadn't waited for her to come home, you might be wandering in this neighborhood. I probably spotted you soon after these cretins did. I don't imagine you needed help with this crew, but it seemed the gracious thing to do."

"I appreciate it." Morgan extended his hand.

"Is there anything else I can do to help?" Raoul reached to share a firm handshake with his new ally.

"Well, you could steer me to a place that serves a good cup of coffee at this hour. Then we can talk about friends we have in common and illegal gun shipments you might know about. I'll even pay."

"For the coffee perhaps," Raoul said, leading the way out of the alley. "The information is a courtesy for the lovely friend we have in common."

- *15* -

Chastity Brady had been head teller of this branch of the Bank of Ireland for only two years, but she had spent five years working her way up through the ranks. Her instinct for customers moved her to the window the distinguished gentleman was approaching. To her eye it was obvious that he had spent a pretty penny on that gray suit. He was clean-shaven but for a large bushy mustache. This was a successful man, that was obvious to her, so she knew that he may be there to take care of a major transaction.

*　*　*　*　*

Sean didn't feel like a particular success at that moment. He was most uncomfortable with his part in this scheme, but none of his nervousness showed. Felicity had spent the week convincing him to do it and all weekend coaching him on how. He had to appear confident, even a little arrogant. Her whole plan depended on his not being questioned. It was to be a bank robbery without firing a shot.

"I have a deposit to make," Sean said. "A deposit into a Mister Ian O'Ryan's account." Don't smile, he told himself. *Remember the timing. Felicity said timing was important.*

The teller accepted the preprinted deposit slip. Sean gave her time to read the deposit. Fifteen thousand Irish pounds. She must be expecting an important business transaction. Then he slid the check across the counter.

*　*　*　*　*

Chastity gave the customer a warm smile before

looking down at the check. First she saw that Mister O'Ryan was dealing with an American company. Then she noticed that the check was drawn on a local branch of the Allied Irish Bank. Only then did she notice the amount of the check, forty-five thousand pounds. She patted the bun on the back of her head, pushed her bifocals to the top of the bridge of her nose and craned her head upward to again face her customer.

"Sir, this deposit would require a substantial refund."

"Mister O'Ryan assured my office that this was a substantial institution," Sean said. "Don't you have the funds available?"

"Of course, sir. But, well, was Mister O'Ryan aware of this?"

"Of course," Sean said. He didn't sound angry, just annoyed and a little disappointed. "When he gave me the deposit slip to avoid any confusion, I was skeptical. He had advised us to move our U.K. business to your bank because you are larger than our present bank."

"Well naturally, sir. We do much more commercial business than..."

"But we don't have every normal transaction questioned at our current institution." Sean leaned into the teller's cage and adopted the frown he wore when a parishioner confessed to a mortal sin. "No one questions my business associates' checks when I make previous arrangements with them. I was considering following Mister O'Ryan's advice. I must also consider advising him to move his accounts to my smaller but more personal bank." He held her eyes and did not move.

* * * * *

To fill time, Chastity checked her cash drawer. As head teller, she was as responsible as any bank officer for the institution's success. She knew this was a common enough transaction in every way except the amounts involved. And it was still before noon on Monday, the busiest day for most businessmen. Mister O'Ryan may have intended to call the bank, but instead got involved in some other business. He was an important customer. It would not go well for her if she cost the bank his business. And if she failed to take this deposit he might indeed move his accounts.

Her mind on her career, she looked down at the check again.

"There's no problem, sir," she said. While Sean watched, she did the necessary stamping and initialing of documents. She was too important to need anyone's approval.

* * * * *

Sean controlled his breathing while he placed his small valise on the counter. The teller counted his change into it. Felicity had rehearsed him well that morning. Trembling inside, he replayed her words in his mind. *Don't let your eyes bulge or your jaw drop*, she had said. *Remember, you are accustomed to handling large sums of money. Give the woman a small scale thank you when it's over. Leave at a slow, even pace. Remember, you are not running away.*

As Sean stepped out into the sunlight his car pulled up in front of him. He got in next to his niece who hit the gas as soon as he was seated. Then he heaved a monstrous, shuddering sigh.

"I knew you could do it, Uncle Sean," Felicity said as she pulled the bulky beast of a car out into the light traffic.

"Aye, lass, and I hope the good Lord can forgive me. Lying and stealing in the same day."

"I think the good Lord understands the concept of the greater good," Morgan said from the back seat. "We know O'Ryan was paid most of that money to commit murder and arson, or worse, to corrupt other young men to do it. How can anything you do to prevent that be a sin?"

"That's something I'll have to pray on long and hard," Sean replied. He looked to his right, offering Felicity a grim, troubled expression.

But Felicity was unimpressed. She realized he had already reconciled himself to it. She knew every man on this little island of chronic poverty had developed a pretty pragmatic form of religion.

"You've had a busy day already, haven't you lad?" Sean asked, pointing Felicity to head south on the coast road.

"Yeah, but fun," Morgan said, accepting Sean's valise. While they talked he consolidated Sean's take with his own from earlier that morning. "I met Felicity at Heathrow in London at eight this morning, so she could give me the deposit slips I needed and the bank names and addresses. You know how fast we hustled back here when I was through."

"Tell me lad," Sean asked, leaning back, "were you sweating like mad in those London banks?"

"Nah. Red's a master at this. Her scams never fail. I had complete confidence. Besides, I could always run for it if anything went haywire." Morgan ducked a backhand slap from the driver.

"I just hope the risks you both took turn out to be worth it," Sean said.

"What'd we get, Morgan?" Felicity asked.

"All told, I count a hundred thousand pounds, even. My calculator says that's around a hundred and seventy-two thousand dollars American. Either way, a good chunk of his reserves."

"Good," Felicity said, nodding and smiling. "He can't have enough left to juggle with. He'll have to curtail terrorist activity now. He can't support the payroll." She pulled out around a farm cart and continued. "That'll be enough to attract his financiers' attention. He'll never convince them he was robbed. They'll shut him down."

"I still don't understand," Sean said. "You'd think with his wealth that such a sum would be just a drop in the bucket."

"I understand your confusion, Uncle Sean," Felicity said, slowing to let a dog cross in front of her. He does handle huge sums. But he's already overspent himself. He's taking the operating funds from one operation to finance another. That's what Morgan meant by robbing Peter to pay Paul. All in all, his outgo exceeds his income right now. All we needed to do, you see, was to leave him with too little to juggle with."

"I guess I understand that much," Sean said. "But won't you two be wanted for passing bad checks? Not to mention myself."

"You?" Felicity's laugh was tainted by a slight American lilt. "Nobody could recognize you from the description. Not with that ridiculous mustache. As for us, we're playing a time game here. It'll take six business days for the checks to bounce, be redeposited, and bounce again. Then they'll trace the business back to the States eventually, but you'd be surprised how low a priority this kind of crime gets. And countries don't cooperate with each other very well on this kind of thing."

"Meantime, O'Ryan's accounts are attached for the missing amounts," Morgan said, picking up the narrative. "Of course, when it finally does catch up to us, we'll deny that either of us ever wrote the checks. Eventually, we'll go to civil court and end up paying back the missing amounts. But this will all take weeks to work out. O'Ryan'll be out of business long before then."

"So what's the next step?" Sean asked, lighting his pipe.

"Well, we've got one more big job ahead of us," Felicity said. "And by us, I mean me and Morgan. We need to stop that shipment of weapons from getting into the country. With them he could continue the violence for a while. Without them, he's stopped cold. And he can't afford to replace them now."

"And you think you can separate the man from these guns?"

"Morgan says we can disrupt and abort the deliver," Felicity said.

"I know when they're coming," Morgan said, rolling down his window. "Felicity's friend Raoul told me that much over a cup of coffee last night, but he didn't know the location. I'm hoping somewhere in those records Red photographed we'll find a clue to the place. Then we can shut this creep down for good."

- *16* -

"There's no flavor on this earth as fine in the morning as Dundee Marmalade," Felicity declared. Morgan glared at her out of the corner of his eye. The noise from her crunching on that toasted English muffin was piercing, but while he watched her she wiped orange jelly from the edge of her mouth and he couldn't conceal a smile. Eight by ten photographs of bank records, notes, letters, newspaper clippings and business ledgers covered the table. Across from Morgan, Sean sorted pictures from one pile to another. Morgan did the same.

"If you drip one drop of that stuff on even one of these pages, I will personally make you eat it."

"Uh huh. You and what army, pea brain?"

Morgan snarled. "Keep it up, Red. I think you'll find celluloid to be an acquired taste."

Sean was getting used to them talking to each other this way and had already learned not to interfere. It was harmless byplay and served to vent their frustration. He already sensed that in a crunch, they were ready and willing to die for one another. But he also understood how frustration could make the closest of friends snipe at one another.

It had been a long day for Morgan already. He was out at first light, sighting in his new rifle, setting the zero for long distances. For the last two hours they had looked over these documents. Now all three of them had coffee and the men had finished their breakfasts.

Sean started with one huge stack of pictures. He read each one to himself, translating aloud any Irish idioms, slang or place names into American equivalents whenever possible. Then the sheet went into Morgan's pile. He searched for any coded phrases or terrorist jargon. He highlighted any significant data with a yellow marker.

When a sheet passed to Felicity it got a third close inspection. Then she loaded whatever seemed important into her photographic memory.

Morgan stopped on a particular sheet. Although he held a perfect poker face, Sean noticed that he read it through twice. Then he picked up his mug and tipped its base to the ceiling.

"Say, Felicity, how about a refill? This is a coffee-intensive job."

"Well, boyo, since you asked me so nicely..." She collected his mug and Sean's and headed for the coffee pot, but Sean kept his eyes on Morgan. While she was faced away, Morgan leaned forward. In a smooth double shuffle he took his next page while sliding the other back into Sean's pile. The priest scanned it again, noted what he had overlooked, and put it at the bottom. He looked up in time to see Morgan's eyebrows rise as he stared at his new page.

"Hey Red, I think I've got something."

"Like what?" Felicity asked, returning to look over his shoulder. "It looks like another delivery authorization. See?" She pointed at a line on the sheet. "Hardware. They're never very specific."

"This one's more detailed," Morgan pointed out. "Look here."

"What're those numbers?"

"If I'm not mistaken, this is a longitude and that's a latitude," Morgan said. "You wouldn't use them for normal land travel."

"No. Only for planes or ocean going vessels. Uncle Sean, have you got a map of the island?"

Sean spread a large map of Ireland on the table. Morgan took a moment to orient himself, then dropped the point of his Parker onto a spot on Ireland's south western coast, in County Cork.

"How close is that to the spot?" Sean asked.

"Morgan can hit any place on a map with pinpoint accuracy, Uncle Sean," Felicity said. "If he says so, that *is* the spot. It's a function of his sense of distance and direction."

"You're joking."

"Really spooky, it is," Felicity said. "I've spun him around blindfolded, indoors, and he's pointed to magnetic north as accurately as any compass."

"Okay, so we know where," Morgan said. "This isolated bit of rocky coastline is a smuggler's dream. And thanks to Raoul we know when. Dawn, tomorrow. So now what? There are a dozen places just as good for what they'll be doing. I can probably stop the drop, but alone I'd never keep them from simply moving the goods back out to sea. They'd just come back in another place, at another time."

"Don't worry," Felicity said. "I know people out there who might be persuaded to give us a hand."

"Don't be silly, girl," her uncle said. "Nobody lives out there except..." He paused as worry tightened his lips.

"That's right Uncle Sean, the wanderers. I'm going to pack a change of clothes. If we head out right away I think we can make the connections."

Felicity moved off but Morgan stayed behind. He looked at Sean and his smile faded like the Irish mist.

"Uncle Sean, could I ask a favor?"

"What is it on your mind, lad?" Sean asked, startled by Morgan's serious tone.

"Would you please not tell Felicity about what was in that newspaper article?"

"Oh, yes." Sean nodded. "I see your intentions, son. You want to protect her from a hurt. But you can't keep such a thing from her forever. It just wouldn't be right."

"Not forever," Morgan replied. "I'll tell her. Right after I send Ian O'Ryan to hell."

"Morgan." Felicity's voice came from the other room. "Are you getting packed? We need to get moving if we're to get there today."

- 17 -

To Morgan, it seemed a fantasy landscape where the earth met the moon.

The long drive west had convinced Morgan that all of Ireland looked the same. A huge flat rock covered with a thick green carpet. Some giant prankster had pulled up all the trees and stuck them back into the ground close together in clumps for easy accounting. The dense grassy foliage covered the island like a verdant tablecloth. The Irish cut small holes into it to grow food.

But Sean had dropped them off near the coast in the southwestern corner of Ireland, leaving Morgan and Felicity to walk farther toward the edge. In hiking boots and backpacks filled with camping gear, they invaded this foreign Ireland. It felt different there. This was true desolation. The air was crisper, sharper, and slightly scented by the distinct odor of the ocean.

They stopped on a hilltop, where Morgan could look down on breakers rolling into the coast. The salt spray leaped and clawed at the sky. Here the velvet carpet came to a sudden end, its edges ragged and frayed. It was pulled back away from the jagged edges of the huge rocks that grew up like rotten teeth along the coastline. Here, where the ocean attacked the land, was a natural fury he had not suspected of this fairy tale country. This place was as raw as a panther's snarl, and as barren and dismal as the lunar surface.

Something about the atmosphere prodded the pair to silence. It was as if they didn't want to compete with the crashing surf or the wind that moaned with so human a voice. They hiked nearly two miles following the coastline before the girl made a comment.

"You hear that mournful sound?" Felicity asked,

shifting her rucksack to a more comfortable position on her back. "Years ago, people used to believe that to be the wail of the banshee."

"Sounds just like the blues to me. Your friends choose to live here? I mean on purpose?"

"No one bothers them here," Felicity answered. "All the wanderers really want is to be left alone."

"Well that explains it. I guess we're invading their territory. Whoever's tracking us is real good, and he doesn't want to be seen."

"I picked him up only ten minutes ago," Felicity said. "If we just walk a bit more, I think he'll report us to the camp and they'll send out an official welcoming party." Felicity looked around, staring into a clump of trees where she knew their watcher hid.

*　*　*　*　*

To little Timothy, hiding among the trees, this duo was indeed a mystery. They were outlanders, but they seemed at home here. That alone struck him as strange. Both wore stretch corduroys and good hiking boots. Each wore a twill outing jacket, hers a jade that matched her eyes and set off her brilliant red hair. Their rucksacks were full, but the weight hampered neither of them. They were experienced hikers by all appearances. She had the easy gait of a country girl and the skin and cheekbones of an Irish woman.

The man was dark, not like charcoal, but rather with a deeper tan than the boy had ever seen in his twelve years. And his hair was like black sheep's wool. He carried a long canvas case across his back in addition to the ruck, and binoculars around his neck. He had a powerful stride, a city stride, yet it seemed suited to long distances.

Little Timothy was known to his clan as an excellent observer. He would report these two in full detail to Papa. He would know just what to do.

Austin S. Camacho

*   *   *   *   *

It was late afternoon when horses appeared at the edge of the thin woods. Felicity was sitting on a large rock looking out at the sea. Two of the riders, the more muscular pair, held back a few feet while the oldest of the three walked his stallion forward until he was looking over the girl's shoulder. The wind whipped her long tresses, the horse's mane, and the rider's gray hair.

"Is it really you, girl? Are you the O'Brien girl, the one we called `the mist' back in the old days?"

"Tis I, you old fox," Felicity replied, turning with a smile. "I've missed you, O'Faolain. You and the boys are me kith. And I need you now."

"Young Timothy tells me you're traveling with a black man. Where is he?"

"In the trees," Felicity replied. "Behind you. He's had a gun on you. I couldn't be sure you were still the man in charge hereabouts, and your clan hasn't much of a reputation for hospitality to strangers."

"Behind us? Impossible." O'Faolain turned to shout this joke to his men, but the words caught in his throat. Morgan stepped from the tree line and walked out between the two horsemen, holstering his automatic. He stopped next to O'Faolain, the obvious leader.

"Felicity tells me you people control this part of County Cork. That you hate intruders and that you'll likely help us keep the violence from touching your area. I hope my appearance won't affect that decision."

The two men's eyes locked and O'Faolain stared down for nearly a minute, evaluating. After probing Morgan's eyes, O'Faolain's lined and weathered face split into a wide smile.

"I wondered if she'd ever find a man out there strong enough to be with her. You've got the fire lad and that's for sure. Patrick! Pull this young buck up behind you, I'll

123

take the lass, and we'll head back to camp. After we get a warm meal into them we'll talk about this trouble they've got."

Morgan knew he was behind an excellent horseman as soon as he was mounted. The ride was fast but steady and smooth. Within a few minutes, they broke into a large, mostly flat clearing. Wagons painted in bright, cheerful colors and patterns were scattered about in a haphazard manner, and campfires dotted the area, laid out without any apparent plan.

Morgan had never seen wagons quite like these. They were round, like huge wooden beer kegs laid on their sides. The doors on the backs looked like regular house doors. Near each one stood a few large draught horses. The relaxed demeanor of those big animals spread a peaceful calm over the scene. Children ran, women worked, men smoked and chatted. These people looked just like those he had seen in Dublin, except for the wariness in their eyes. They were just as friendly, but a bit less trusting.

The group dismounted in front of a large central tent. The gray haired man who Morgan marked as the obvious leader strode over to Felicity. They looked at each other for a moment, before he threw his arms around her and gave her a bear hug. They slapped each other on the back and arms several times amidst loud laughter. Then Felicity waved to Morgan to follow and they headed into the tent.

They sat on folded blankets in a rough circle and were served by a very young dark-haired girl. A younger man sat on either side of O'Faolain and five other men filled out the circle, as deferential as any general's staff. O'Faolain took a long drink from his cup and waited long enough to be sure no one else would try to speak before he did. Then he looked at Felicity and said, "From the beginning, girl. What's it about, and what's it got to do with us?"

"You're not so far away that you've lost sight of The

124

Troubles, now are you?" Felicity asked. Then, while they drank ale and ate the now familiar stew, she outlined her uncle's problem. O'Faolain's eyes followed hers as she described the church bombing and how they dealt with the hand grenade thrown into the public house. She quickly outlined O'Ryan's financial situation and how it was his Achilles Heel. Without hesitation she explained their approach to weakening O'Ryan's financial state. Finally, she told him about the weapons O'Ryan was planning to bring onto the coast nearby.

"And that, I take it, is where you'll be needing our help," O'Faolain said. "I see why you want to do this thing, and Lord knows I don't want those horrid weapons to come through my lands anymore than you do. But how in the name of glory are you going to keep the boys from just pulling up and landing somewhere else?"

"That part I'll leave to Morgan," Felicity said. "He's a trained sniper, you see. He'll wait until the boats are ashore, then take out the leaders from a safe place in the rocks." That drove O'Faolain's eyebrows up, and the younger man sitting on his right turned and spat on the ground. Morgan marked him as the danger man in the room. His resemblance to O'Faolain was unmistakable.

This was some kind of council he figured, with all the decision makers in a circle on the ground. He wondered how Felicity fit into this all male group. His question was soon answered.

"Do you know what kind of company you've fallen in with, my lad?" O'Faolain asked Morgan in his lilting accent, which was a little different from Felicity's. "Well, let me tell you. This child wandered out onto the heath and had nearly died of exposure when we found her. Nursed her back to health, I did. Me and me old wife. This girl swore she'd repay us somehow. Well, everyone you save says something like that, don't they?" He smiled around the circle, and all of the older men grinned back.

"Well, it wasn't a year later, we hit some tough times. Now I don't mind telling you, we sometimes makes ours by taking from the rich and giving to the poor, that is, us. Well, this one comes to me and says `I know where there's some good pickings'. Then she sallies on into Dublin one day and comes back with her pockets full. Turns out she's the most talented natural pickpocket the good Lord ever put on this earth. That's how we come to start calling her `the mist'. And that's when I says, `one day, love, you'll get yourself into a bind. When that day comes, you can count on O'Faolain's clan to get you out of it. You're our own kith and kin and that's for sure. And that's how it is."

"Well then, I'll leave you old friends to catch up on things and iron out the details of tomorrow's fun," Morgan said, rising. "I'd like to go check out the territory. Walk the grounds a bit. You understand."

"Indeed I do, lad. Unfamiliar lands do make a body nervous."

Morgan stepped out of the tent into the gathering twilight. He walked a good two hundred yards before turning. He knew who he would be facing, who had followed him to the edge of the clearing. He wanted his follower to be able to speak without his elders overhearing. Morgan guessed that this was the future leader and he wanted him in on the mission. But they would have to come to an understanding.

"What's your name, son?" Morgan asked.

"I'm Danny."

"Danny O'Faolain I take it?" Morgan pressed.

"Yes, as a matter of fact, and I'll be asking the questions."

"Okay. What's on your mind, son?" Morgan leaned against a tree, with his hands in his pockets. He wanted to present the least threatening front possible.

"I want to know what makes you so sure that you can make this incredible rifle shot. And why do you care about what happens here in Eire? You don't look very

Irish to me. And why should my people get involved?"

"You don't want much, do you?" Morgan said with a grin. "Well let me give this a shot. First, you should get involved because it's your turf. And because Felicity O'Brien asked you to. I care because she cares. She's my best friend and I guess that makes me as Irish as I care to be. That's enough for your elders but not enough for you, I see. And that's how it should be." Morgan took a deep breath and looked into the younger man's eyes.

"You don't want your people involved with an amateur. That's fine, because I'm not one. But I'm not a thief either. I'm a professional soldier. I'm a mercenary, and in that business there's an elite class. Planners. Night raiders. And snipers. I'm one of the best. If those crates come up on shore within the range of my rifle I can hit them. But we'll need numbers to stop a whole landing party."

Danny O'Faolain reached to his waist and drew a short dagger. "So, among the elite, are you? Some great fighter from a foreign shore come to save the poor micks, huh? Let's see you prove it." For a moment, Morgan feared he had made a big mistake. With unexpected speed, the tall Irishman flipped the blade into his hand and threw it just to Morgan's left. It thudded home in a young three inch tree fifty feet away. Morgan whistled.

"You ain't bad there, pal," Morgan said, reaching into his right boot. "Of course, trees don't duck or shoot back. However..." His arm blurred, and an instant later, a black blade sprouted out of the tree trunk just a half inch from the Irishman's knife. Morgan turned to Danny O'Faolain. "Satisfied?"

"For now. But I'll be watching tomorrow. I'll be watching you close."

"Yeah, well be up early," Morgan called as the younger O'Faolain walked away. "If the sun's up, I'll already be gone."

- 18 -

There was no way to tell if the mist was moving in from the ocean or out from the land. The cold crept up from the rocks. Morgan stared through his Steiner binoculars out toward a small natural inlet. He sat nestled in a granite formation that nature had cut into sharp angles. This was the nearest cover or concealment to the most likely landing site. He was five hundred fifty yards from his probable target, in the dawn's first light, with a thin mist and a little bit of a tail wind, at a slight elevation from the target area.

"Piece of cake," he said, hoping the lie was convincing.

In truth, these were pretty shoddy conditions under which to attempt the shot of the century. A dozen skeptics surrounded Morgan. The wanderers carried FN-FAL rifles which they had gotten God knows where, plus a few Stens. They were prepared to ride into the midst of the smugglers on horseback, laying down a barrage of fire, hoping to route them in confusion. This, of course, after Morgan took out the smuggler leader and a couple of key men with a few well placed shots.

"It can not be done," Danny O'Faolain said, shaking his head. "It's got to be half a kilometer even after they reach shore."

"Can you do it?" Felicity asked, her voice a little shaky.

"Let's just say it's on the outside edge of possibility," Morgan said with a grim smile. "If I get lucky." He surveyed the area while he unpacked his rifle. A small wooden shack stood not far from shore. That would be their meeting point. Wagons waited nearby, onto which he was sure they would load their cargo. He could let them get closer, but once unpacked he figured they would break out machine guns and maybe even grenade launchers to assure themselves a safe trip. No, the only time to hit them was as soon as they landed.

Morgan had filled his back pack with loose earth. It served as a rest for the barrel of his SSG69 sniping rifle's barrel. The twenty-five inch barrel's tip extended over the edge of the rise Morgan was settling behind in prone position. Morgan loaded five rounds of 7.62 millimeter ammunition into the rotary drum magazine and seated it with a solid slap. He pulled the plastic stock snug into his shoulder, and pressed his cheek tight against it. He tuned out the crowd around him, settling his breathing into a steady pattern. Only then did he take the safety off. He worked the bolt, chambering a round.

He was ready to go to work.

Three tenths of a mile away, a rubber raft slid up to the shoreline. Through the rifle's twenty power scope Morgan watched five black clad men slip into the waist-deep water and drag their boat onto the land. Felicity knelt beside him, watching through the light gathering Steiner Miltary-Marine binoculars. They illuminated shaded areas and never needed focusing. If he missed, she would be able to correct him.

Four rafts were now sliding to the shore. Each carried five men and four or five wooden crates. Morgan relaxed his eyes and let his partner scan for the leaders.

"The head man is third from the right, right now," Felicity said in a low whisper. Morgan never even considered the possibility that she might be wrong. On her way to becoming a top notch thief and con artist, she had trained herself to read body language, eye contact and hand gestures to tell who in a group did the telling, and who the listening. If she said so, this was the man.

Morgan zeroed in on the target and a smile spread across his face. He recognized this man. Morgan had put that face into a wall on a Paris back street not so long ago, and it looked as though Morgan had broken his nose in the process. A gracious fate had placed a man who tried to kill him at the other end of his telescopic sight. This would be a pleasure.

Morgan had sighted the rifle in at four hundred fifty yards. It was the farthest he figured any sane man would try for a man sized target. Here he was, violating one of his own cardinal rules already. Still, in testing this rifle had exhibited almost no windage drift. All he needed to worry about was elevation. He waited for his target to stand still for a moment and settled his crosshairs on the top of the man's head. From this distance, he figured the bullet should impact eighteen or twenty inches down. That would put it at about the tip of the breastbone.

The leader of the smugglers placed his hands on his hips, shouted an order, and struck an arrogant pose. He was smiling, his body facing the small band of raiders on the hill, his head turned to the water. The wind held its breath. Morgan just stopped breathing and squeezed his trigger with the same gentle touch he would use to caress a beautiful woman's most sensitive area.

The blast was deafening and everyone in the wanderer party jumped except Morgan. Loud as it was, the men on the shore could hear no noise at that distance. The target stumbled back three steps, clutched his rib cage, looked around in surprise, and fell over onto his back. One of the others called to him, not yet alarmed.

Right through the lungs, Morgan thought.

Incoming stimuli: first, the mule kick to his right shoulder. The slight ringing in the ears, despite ear plugs. The thunder of horses' hooves as the wanderers charged the smugglers, hollering all the way. The comforting smell of cordite. Then Felicity's voice, more strident than before.

"Number two is to the right about ten feet, standing in

a raft."

Morgan had faith in his partner. She knew the field of vision through the rifle scope was too narrow for him to scan for a target. Also, a moving target, even a slow one, would be impossible to hit at this distance. In the seven tenths of a second it would take for a bullet to reach the shore, it would be easy for a man to move six feet in any direction. She had accounted for all these variables in less time than that, and chosen the best target.

The face he zeroed in on was quite intent. The smuggler was concentrating on his own telescopic sight. No doubt he was locked onto an approaching wanderer. Morgan squeezed the trigger again, and his sight picture went out of focus.

"Low and left," was all Felicity said. Morgan shrugged to loosen his shoulder and looked again. His target must be a pro, he thought. He did not move, even though the heavy bullet had smacked the raft no more than two inches from him. Morgan took a deep breath, held it, and fired again. This time the man at the other end of the scope dropped his rifle and clutched his abdomen. Considering the power of his rifle, Morgan knew his target was dead before he hit the ground.

Half a mile down range, Danny O'Faolain fired his rifle from the saddle with uncommon accuracy. At a full gallop, he hit one out of perhaps three men he fired at. But he knew that was enough to keep the smugglers hopping. Leaderless, they lost precious time looking for someone to tell them what to do. Meanwhile, the mass of Gypsies whooped like wild Indians, picking off the invaders with ease.

Machine gun fire rattled across the tiny bay and two of the wanderers fell from their steeds. A few reined up their horses, intimidated, but the chief's son charged right toward the gunner. The AK-47's barrel swung on line with Danny's chest. The wanderer shouted in defiance and spurred his mount forward. The AK released a long string of bullets, but they were all too high. The smuggler flipped backward and sprawled on the ground.

Morgan dropped his head on his arm. It was a hell of a shot, and just in time. He liked the kid and did not want to see him killed in this silly fight.

"I can't get any more from here," Morgan said. "I'd as likely hit friend as foe with so much movement going on."

"Well then, let's go join the party."

*   *   *   *   *

By the time Morgan and Felicity galloped down to the land's edge, the action was over. Twenty corpses lay on the ground or bobbed in the surf. Most had succumbed to gunshot wounds, a few to knife attacks. The black rafts cluttered the shoreline, looking like punctured inner tubes.

The wanderers scurried about, cleaning the smugglers of their personal knives, guns and currency. They also harvested cigarette lighters, binoculars, watches, anything that might fetch a price on the open market. Morgan had seen and even done this type of scavenging before. It was obvious from her face that Felicity was no stranger to it either. To the victors belong the spoils in this type of situation, but Morgan was interested in a different kind of booty.

He was using a large Bowie knife he had found on the ground to pry one of the crates open when he felt a hard slap on his back.

"That was a rare bit of a romp, eh?" Danny O'Faolain said. The stiletto he held in his right hand was black with blood. "You know, I'm the sort of man what says he's wrong when he's wrong. I want to tell you, you've got the eye of a hawk and no mistake. I wouldn't have believed it if I didn't see it with me own eyes. Never have I seen shooting like that." Danny held out his hand

and Morgan took it. The shake was firm and solid.

"I had my share of luck too," Morgan said. "Now, help me find out what's in this box, will you?" The two pulled on the wooden crate's lid, and others who saw them turned to the crates nearest them. This, it seemed, was where the real treasure would be.

With the squeak of ten-penny nails forced from green wood, the top planks pulled loose. Felicity leaned over to look into the dark box. Morgan noticed birds singing overhead for the first time. He realized they had stayed away since the gun play. Now their song signaled a return to normality. It was a false signal.

Morgan plunged his hand into the crate and pulled loose his prize, wrapped in rags and covered in gun grease. He pulled the rags away revealing the metal object within.

"Sweet mother of mercy," Danny said. "What on earth kind of a gun is this, now?"

What Morgan held aloft bore a vague resemblance to a rifle, but with a too-wide barrel, an oversized tin can jammed into the middle of its plastic butt, and a carrying handle shaped somewhat like a suspension bridge.

"This ten pounds of death, boys and girls, is called the Pancor Jackhammer," Morgan explained. "Thirty inches long, eighteen inch barrel. This, folks, is a submachine gun. This cylinder behind the hand guard is a rotary magazine and chamber."

"And if you don't mind me asking, what's so special about it aside from its bizarre appearance?"

"Well, Danny, this particular machine gun fires twelve gage shotgun shells," Morgan said, scooping up a handful of shells and pushing them into place. "You load your ammo into this ten shot cylinder and you can fire these shotgun shells singly, or at the rate of two hundred forty rounds per minute. That's four in a second, just by holding the trigger down."

To demonstrate, Morgan swung the weapon toward the rocks they had just abandoned and squeezed. A three shot burst pumped forward. A vertical string of explosions rained shattered stone down onto the rocky ground. All eyes were fixed on the devastation.

"One man armed with one of these in an urban environment is more dangerous than a squad with rifles," Morgan said. "He can clean out a house or a narrow street in nothing flat. Our friend O'Ryan is dealing in some very awesome ordnance here."

"Perfect for fighting in the city," Danny added after a low whistle.

"And worse," Felicity said, "unlike ordinary machine guns, the ammunition for this thing is readily available anywhere." She turned and walked toward the shore, and the other two followed. "Looks like there must be four or five dozen of these guns here. There are people up north waiting for these thingies. But I don't think they'll go out and do the dirty deeds O'Ryan requires if he doesn't come through with the firepower. And, you know, his foreign masters will be most unhappy if no terrorist activity takes place."

"That's right," Morgan said, nodding. "And if they ask about what happened to their money, he won't even be able to point to new weapons. They'll never believe somebody just ripped him off. Any way you look at it, this should be the final nail in his coffin."

"Well, we can make sure a use is found for these beauties, aside from shooting at people," Danny said. He signaled his men to load the bodies onto the rafts and drag them into the ocean.

"All but one," Morgan said, checking the gun's weight. "I'll be taking a souvenir."

"They'll make for some exciting hunting," Danny said, sighting down a barrel. "You know, we ought to go on a hunt tomorrow and try these things out."

"Sorry, Danny," Felicity said, watching the gulls circling above. "We have to get back home. My uncle Sean will be worried sick about us."

- 19 -

"Nothing truly funny has been written in America in thirty years," Felicity said through a guffaw. "But every one of Robert Benchley's stories is hilarious."

The long rowboat began to rock with her laughter, and Sean glared at her over his shoulder.

"Child, do you want to scare every one of the fish away?"

Sean sat at the stern of his wooden vessel, his line in the ocean, working at fishing in what even Morgan saw as a studious manner. Sean was a serious fisherman. Flies he tied himself adorned his special fishing hat. A knife, a hook disgorger and pipe tobacco were tucked into their specific pockets in his special fishing vest. His once red tackle box was filled with every imaginable type of bait. He had already flipped four fat whitings into the boat.

"I think you're off base," Morgan said, moving as little as possible. He was lying along the center bench, a folded jacket propping up his head. "Now it's true, the humor of that time stands out. I kind of dig James Thurber myself..."

"You just like looking at the pictures."

"Funny girl," Morgan said. He was a casual fisherman, but appeared to have a natural feel for it. He seemed to choose bait at random and jerked his pole one way or another from time to time. But in three hours of floating on the tide he landed five flapping white fish.

"Always got a kick out of Ogden Nash myself," Sean chipped in.

"Me too," Morgan agreed, "But humor didn't die in nineteen fifty. You need to read some Woody Allen. Not see, mind you. Read. Funny as Thurber, I'm telling you.

Far outshines his movies." Morgan reached into the water, into a net hanging off the side of the boat, and pulled out a bottle of Guinness Stout. He was again moved by how clear and tranquil the ocean seemed here. Joe Montana could throw a touchdown pass to shore from where they were. The water was shallow there and excellent for fishing. He knew there was cod, herring, probably some mackerel around, but why work at relaxing?

After the messy job with the wanderers, Morgan needed to relax, and he knew it was the same for Felicity. They had returned the same night, riding to within a couple of miles of Sean's house in a colorful wagon drawn by four proud stallions. They said long good-byes to old and new friends. Then they enjoyed a special walk together, in a deep silence filled with meaning. Something they could share with each other but could not share with anyone else, that calm time after a caper.

After a good night's sleep, Sean suggested fishing as a way to pass a peaceful day. In an unaccustomed flash of domesticity, Felicity rose early and packed a picnic basket with rolls and cold fried chicken from the night before. Shortly after dawn they grabbed fishing gear and a couple of books and headed out.

Now they floated at anchor over the Irish Sea. Felicity sat curled up with a book in the bow, in a heavy wool sweater. She needed no pole or reel to relax. The morning's light conversation appeared to be enough.

"Got to admit, I'm impressed," Sean said.

"Well, that was out of nowhere," Felicity said. "I'll say thanks, but what did I do?"

"Guess it just struck me how well the two of you can really let go," Sean said. "Even here in Ireland, there aren't many left in this day and age who can appreciate the blue of the sky, the quiet lap of tiny waves or the gentle rolling motions of a small boat. You two are city people, but you still know how to set the fast pace aside and enjoy the smell of fresh salt air."

"Guess you've kept us from getting bored with good conversation," Morgan said.

Sean snapped his rod, but failed to set the hook and some fish lived to swim another day. "That's another thing. In the time we've been out here, we've talked about books, shotguns, old movies, jewelry and Irish poetry. Felicity's always been a reader, but I've got to admit I'm surprised at how well read you are, Morgan."

"Well, as a mercenary soldier I use to end up with a lot of free time on my hands between jobs," Morgan answered. "That was before I hooked up with your niece. Besides, it pays a merc to be knowledgeable, especially about history and geography." He was pulling in his line to check his bait when Felicity made an innocent request.

"Would one of you kind gentlemen please pass me a piece of that chicken?"

There was an eerie silence as each member of the trio glanced at the other two.

"Uncle Sean?"

"I had me tackle box," Sean said.

"I was carrying all this fishing gear," Morgan said, curling one corner of his mouth. "I even had a pole and reel for Felicity that she ain't even using." He turned to glare at the girl. "Your hands were empty."

Felicity managed to stop her blush at her neck. "Well fellows, shall we be heading for the shore? Packed us a really good lunch, I did."

"Photographic memory," Morgan muttered, getting the oars into the water. "You'd think you could remember a little thing like a lunch basket."

"I notice the stout found its way into the boat."

*   *   *   *   *

Fifteen minutes later Morgan was securing the boat to a small pier, whipping half hitches into the nylon line.

137

Sean handed their gear up onto the wharf.

"Shake a leg, fellows," Felicity said. "I'm so hungry my stomach thinks my throat's been cut." She marched off toward the car, parked near the road.

The temperature was in the upper sixties on shore with a gentle breeze that reminded Felicity that the area held some good memories for her. How odd, she thought, that geography affected a town less than its style. Looking around, she realized that Wicklow could easily be mistaken for Kennebunkport, Maine. Same weathered buildings. Same weathered people. Same salt smell, same sound of gulls and boat motors. And lobster pots are lobster pots the world over. Perhaps all fishing towns were really the same. Maybe the people in all fishing communities were in a way related.

* * * * *

"'Tis a fine day the Lord's given us for fishing," Sean called out to a group of men passing on their way to the shore. Some yards behind Felicity, he and Morgan meandered toward the road. Morgan only nodded while Sean waved to these hearty fishermen, some professionals there to make a living, some sportsmen like himself. The smiles that split those lined faces were comforting because they were genuine.

Sean's smile faded when his gaze fell on Morgan again. The black man's head snapped up, as if he was listening to a faraway voice. Sean felt a chill run up his spine, although he didn't know why. He followed Morgan's gaze as it focused ahead, toward the road.

"What is it, lad? You look like you've just seen a will o' the wisp."

"Something's wrong," Morgan said, not turning. "Felicity's in danger." Then he was off at a sprint, moving faster than any man Sean had ever seen.

* * * * *

Icy sweat slid down Morgan's back as he ran. His breath came in ragged gasps. The nine millimeter tucked into his waistband rubbed his hip raw. It was no pocket pistol, but under the bulky sweater it wasn't too conspicuous.

When he reached Felicity she was scanning the area with worried eyes. She stood in a slight crouch, fingers extended. He imagined he could see her ears perked up like a cat's.

"You feel it?"

"Yes," Morgan replied. "But so vague. No direction. Not really a danger signal, but..." His right hand slid under his sweater at the sound of an approaching automobile. The two adventurers formed a still life study in tension as a bulky gray Mercedes limousine rolled toward them. The driver, a nondescript man in full livery, looked through them. Then the single passenger in the back seat glanced out the window.

Ian O'Ryan's eyes locked onto Morgan's with a strength that threatened to bore through the back of his head. In the four seconds it took for the vehicle to pass, one could see a burst of rapid fire connections, calculations and conjectures pass over the intense leonine face. O'Ryan's face clouded over, his bushy red eyebrows arching until they almost touched. Blood flushed into the already florid face, and one expected to hear a roar issue forth from behind the tinted window glass. As the car slid past, Morgan's hands dropped to his side.

"Well, we're blown now."

"That him?" Felicity asked.

"That's him. And we're made."

"Afraid so," Felicity said. "Your presence here after the air show is way too much of a coincidence."

"And I'm sure he knows by now it was a black man who emptied his London account."

"He might even know about the deposit slips by now,"

Felicity said, shaking her head. "And the red headed night visitor. It was stupid of us to hang around."

"Agreed. But now what..." Morgan was interrupted by the sound of an engine over torqued. The limousine roared toward them in reverse. They stood their ground as the car's brakes locked and it skidded to a halt in front of them. When the rear window powered down, Felicity found herself eye to eye with perhaps the most electric presence she had ever encountered.

The wavy red mane, the broad shoulders, even the tan eyes with flecks of red in them, none of these was the answer in itself. Something about his aura was overpowering. Her heart hummed in her throat, her knees weakened and without thinking, she licked her lips. When he smiled she felt waves of pure sexual energy flowing out of him, washing over her. Then he spoke, and it was the voice of a lion in human form.

"Mister Stark, aren't you going to introduce me to your charming companion? No matter. My dear, I am Ian O'Ryan."

O'Ryan's gaze never left Felicity, and she felt quite naked before him. Morgan was also looking at her, looking worried. Could he see she was captivated?

"Mister Stark and I met in Paris recently," O'Ryan said, not waiting for Morgan to speak. "He travels a great deal. I've heard he's been visiting in England lately. And I imagine he's also been touring our little island. All the way down to the southern coast."

"Mister Stark is quite the adventurer," Felicity said, recovering from the spell. "That's what I like about him. We're partners, and I go by Felicity O'Brien." Behind her, Sean approached. From the way his pace slowed she knew he must recognize the car's occupant. And it was just as clear that he was recognized as well.

"Ah, Father Sullivan. I might have known you'd be somehow connected to this pair."

"Get away from me niece, you grinning devil," Sean said.

"Let's not be unpleasant, boyo," O'Ryan said. "I was just about to invite the young lady and her adventurous friend to a little fox hunt tomorrow."

"I don't think we can make it." Morgan leaned on the limousine's roof, bringing himself within striking distance. The big Irishman did not react, the significance of which was not lost on Felicity, and she could see that it was not lost on Morgan either.

"What do you say, girl. I'd have thought you the type of lass who loved to live dangerously. Besides, if you refuse my hospitality, I'll just have to ask your kind uncle to join me later." He looked up into Morgan's deep brown eyes. There was no doubt of the meaning of his words.

"We wouldn't dream of disappointing you." Felicity said. She kept her voice even while waving her uncle to silence. "I think we ought to keep this between the three of us. Don't you agree?"

"Oh, absolutely. Let's keep non-players off the green. My estate at seven a.m. I think you know the way." The window slid up. O'Ryan tapped his chauffeur on the shoulder with a gold headed cane and in response he popped the clutch. Tires squealed and in seconds the big gray automobile was in the distance. Silence hung in the air until the dust settled and the car was out of sight. Sean was the one who broke the stillness.

"You can't go."

"We have to, Uncle Sean," Felicity said with an affectionate smile. "You heard him. We could run, but you couldn't hide. You wouldn't hide."

"You're bloody well right I wouldn't. I'm not afraid of that snake."

"And that's why we'll be at this hunt tomorrow morning," Morgan said.

"Oh you can be sure it's to be a hunt you're going to, all right. Only it's you two who's to be the prey this time, and that's for sure."

Both Felicity and Morgan nodded their heads.

- 20 -

At six fifty-four in the morning Felicity drove her uncle's ancient green Volvo around the huge building known as Orion House and parked it amidst the Mercedes, Jaguars and Peugeots. Morgan still could not believe people drove around there indifferent to things like cracked windshields. His elbow hung out the passenger side window for the entire drive. Thanks to one of O'Ryan's helpers, he did not have to roll it down.

They disembarked, and Morgan stood for a moment, taking in the massive Georgian structure which served as his present enemy's home. It made him think of *Gone with the Wind*.

"A huge monument to the man's mammoth ego," he said. "I knew he was nuts. I mean the man tried to have me killed because I embarrassed him. I just never dreamed the scale of his delusion."

"Let's just keep in mind," Felicity said, "that he may be a lunatic, but he's a dangerous lunatic."

"Lunatics usually are."

A man with the look of a bar room bouncer walked toward them across the sward. He was dressed in traditional fox hunting gear. His red blazer's sleeves and shoulders were being stretched to their limits. As he drew closer Morgan did a subtle double take. The man was familiar, like the ghost of an old acquaintance.

"You must be Miss O'Brien and eh...Mister Stark, eh?" The man's enunciation was unnatural, almost eerie in its clarity.

"That's us," Morgan said. He and Felicity had considered and rejected the idea of wearing fox hunting clothes, opting instead for corduroy pants and blazers.

"We will be riding to hounds in ten minutes. Please

follow me." They walked into the nearby field. The grass was short, the ground soft and springy. It only took fifty yards for Morgan's curiosity to get the better of him.

"What's your name, pal?"

"Liam, sir," the guard returned. "Liam McCallister."

"Have we met somewhere?"

"No sir," Liam answered. Then he stopped and turned to make eye contact. "I understand you met my brother in Paris. And I believe you may have seen him again after that."

The image rushed into Morgan's mind unbidden. He last saw that face, with a few subtle differences, at the other end of a telescopic sight. Liam was even bigger than his brother had been. As they came upon the field Morgan wondered if he would have to kill this man too.

"It's like a picture from one of my childhood storybooks," Felicity said under her breath. The mist rose up from the moist earth. Thin, wispy clouds hung above, whipped by a high wind into a skeletal form, like the bleached white rib cage you see in desert pictures. An omen, she wondered?

"Ah, the fire haired light of this morning's hunt has arrived." O'Ryan sat his stallion like a prince. He controlled the animal like an extension of his own legs. Staring down at Felicity, he was dripping charm. Felicity's breath caught in her throat. Perhaps because of her earlier story book thoughts, his broad smile under the hat brim somehow made her think of the wolf in Little Red Riding Hood.

She could see in his eyes that O'Ryan was appraising her, maybe just the way that wolf would. If so, then he saw a Red Riding Hood in slacks so tight they might have been sewn around her, displaying the excellent curve of her hips; riding boots with heels that brought her legs into perfect tension; a jacket that was a perfect fit at her shoulders but could not close in front because of her chest; and a long red mane as fiery, though not as unruly as his own. He might see her as an exciting possible conquest, but would that make him forget she was sent from the enemy camp?

"Benson has your horse, and Mister Stark's," O'Ryan said. "Would you like to see the fox?"

"Only one fox here worth seeing," Morgan said, giving Felicity's rump a playful slap. "Want a leg up, Red?"

"I can handle it," Felicity said, blushing even though she knew none of the Irish natives got the joke. She swung up into the saddle with a natural rider's easy grace. Morgan mounted his steed in a somewhat less graceful movement, and they followed O'Ryan at a trot. Felicity pulled close to Morgan and spoke in a low tone.

"The field will be moving erratically, so stay sharp."

His brows pushed together. "The field will move?"

"Sorry," Felicity said. "The field is also what they call the pack of riders chasing the animal." She pulled her horse closer to Morgan and lowered her voice even further. "and thanks, pal."

"For what?" Morgan asked in an equally low tone.

"Breaking the spell. This guy warps my thinking, but I'm straight now."

O'Ryan waved them toward him. "Here he is, my friends, and isn't he a beauty?" The two newcomers pulled their horses over to the small cage and stared down. The skittish creature kept glancing around, as if in a desperate search for an escape route. For no reason she could tell, Felicity was sure it was a vixen, a female. Her fur was long and a bright rust red. Her black legs stood out in stark contrast to the white fur of her underbelly. She was maybe two feet long, with the white tipped tail adding another foot or so. She pricked up her pointed ears, giving the impression of alertness.

The woman on horseback identified with the small but defiant caged creature. She suspected that, once released, it would never be caught again.

"I offer you the privilege of releasing the animal and starting the hunt," O'Ryan said, beaming like a gracious host. Felicity slid from her saddle and knelt next to the small cage. Having never been caged herself, she looked into the fox's eyes for insight. She saw no hatred there, or rage or even sorrow. The creature's entire being was focused on escape. Felicity slipped the latch and lifted the wire gate. The inmate sprang from its cell, and vanished in seconds into the sparse woods.

"Bon chance," Felicity whispered. "Go with God."

"Now the sport begins. Loose the hounds!" O'Ryan said in a harsh roar. His horse reared, his red mane flew, and he waved a short shotgun over his head. For a moment, Felicity could see the image of that other Orion, the legendary hunter. Then the dogs rushed past and all the riders followed them. Felicity looked down to see they each had a gun in a leather scabbard by their saddle. Twenty dogs and half a dozen guns. It seemed to her an awful lot of firepower for one small fox.

Felicity stayed in the middle of the field as they chased their wily quarry across the countryside, over a fence and through a stand of short trees. She stayed in the middle of the field but she noticed that they were leaving Morgan behind. She considered him an adequate amateur but it was clear that she and the other horsemen there outclassed him. The other riders, except for her partner, whooped and hollered, exhibiting the same blood lust the hounds showed.

About ten minutes into the chase, the trail led over a ditch that proved wider than it appeared at a distance. Morgan's horse balked at the jump and it required some effort to regain control. O'Ryan came crashing up behind him and, grinning, slapped Morgan's mount hard on its rump with his riding crop as he passed. He seemed paralyzed with laughter as Morgan's steed bolted off. Verbal commands and hauling on the reins had no effect. He was headed into a dense thicket at a full gallop.

Felicity, fifty yards away, saw the action out of the corner of her eye. She dug her heels into her mount and was charging toward Morgan almost before his horse bolted.

Morgan knew she saw him but pulled his focus away from her. He couldn't slow his spooked beast, but by yanking hard to one side, he managed to avoid one tall tree in his path. Then he was moving like a train at full steam toward an overhanging limb certain to split his skull, although the horse would slide under it. Jumping at this speed would likely cost him a sprained ankle or worse, but his options seemed limited. He clenched his teeth and tensed for the dive.

He saw a small pale hand with polished nails grasp his reins before he realized he could hear a second set of hooves beside him. Felicity murmured comforting Gaelic words to Morgan's steed and the two animals veered off to the left. A moment later they slowed to a trot and shortly after, came to a stop. Morgan dismounted and wiped his brow with his sleeve.

"Thanks, Red," he said. "You saved me some lumps for sure. Your friend Ian's got a pretty strange sense of humor."

"My friend?" Felicity replied. "Like hell. I'm here rooting for the fox. Come on, let's go find the field."

"We're already in the field."

She slapped his shoulder, stifling a laugh. "All right then, let's go find that gang of riders chasing the fox. Come on." She turned her horse and Morgan shook his head. He grabbed the reins again, but as he put his foot into the stirrup, he froze.

"Hold up a minute." While Felicity sat in wonder, Morgan released his horse, took a dozen paces to a small stream and squatted down on his haunches. He could sense her fascination as she stepped over next to him.

"He's been by here," Morgan said. "Look." He watched her green eyes.

"Oh my. I didn't see anything at all at first. But then, as if by magic, those tiny paw prints just appeared in the turf."

"You just didn't know what you were looking for."

"Nonsense," Felicity said. "I had to stare to see them, but you spotted them a dozen yards away."

"It's just training," Morgan said. "Now get the horses, girl. Let's follow."

He may not be much of a horseman, but Morgan considered himself a natural tracker. He knew that if hunting dogs were tracking him, he would follow a stream and move in the direction of the wind. He assumed a fox would do the same.

They stalked in silence for fifteen minutes. The forest was thin and the morning sun beamed in like a spotlight with a yellow gel on it. The air was so sharp and clean it burned the nose, and each step they took released the scent of clover. Crickets and birds harmonized in an impromptu chorale. The atmosphere was soothing, almost hypnotic. The stream dove underground and again Morgan was following almost invisible tracks.

At the edge of a clearing, they saw him. The fox looked over his, or probably her shoulder, sharp snout sniffing the air, sensing no danger. Felicity smiled at the kindred spirit and waved the animal away. With a flip of its bushy tail, it hopped off. Beyond where the fox had stood, lay what looked like a large puddle.

"The spring must resurface right here," Felicity said. "Let's give the horses a cool drink."

"Wait!" Morgan shouted, but it was too late. Felicity had already seen what he spotted a second sooner, a human form face down in the water. The body's arms and legs were on dry land, but the rest was in the pool. Dressed in brown trousers and a green flannel shirt he blended in with the environment. The man had been big: big shoulders, big head, big hands. Even at a distance Morgan could see red specks in the thin brown hair.

Felicity's scream echoed across the glen, even as Morgan sprinted to the body. A finger pressed against its throat proved it was too late for a rescue. Morgan got a firm grip on the corpse's collar and heaved. The mud sucked at the body, then made a kissing sound and let go. After a quick look, Morgan let the man settle back into the pool of water. A shotgun had done its grisly work on that face at close range. Felicity did not need to see this.

"It's him, isn't it?" she asked, her eye clenched tight.

"Yup."

The other riders galloped to them, homing in on the girl's scream. O'Ryan rode in a slow circle around the clearing before dismounting. He stood at the dead man's feet and removed his cap.

"Poor Max. Looks like we've had a hunting accident, eh?"

"Hunting accident my ass," Morgan said. "The man's stone cold. He's been dead for hours."

"Well, you're smart, for a soldier," O'Ryan said, his fists on his hips. "Now how can we know which of these shotguns, well, missed the fox?"

"Well there's no way to know, is there?" Morgan asked, reaching to his horse. "But I'll bet my life it couldn't have been either of ours." He snatched his scatter gun from its scabbard and every male fox hunter followed suit except O'Ryan. Morgan pumped the weapon, pointed it skyward and pulled the trigger. There was the loud click of a hammer falling on an empty chamber. "Didn't think you'd have the guts to trust us with that kind of ammo."

"And can you blame me, lad?" O'Ryan said in a sudden, vicious shout. "You two come at me out of the blue. No declarations of war for you, laddie-buck. Just move in and attack. You've cost me a great deal, you two have. Money. An important delivery, I suspect. Several good workers. A trusted employee there in the bog. Well, the money and the goods I'll have to replace. I'll have to get me some new helpers on the payroll. And once a man betrays me..."

"He never did," Felicity said through clenched teeth.

"His only crime..."

"Was stupidity, dear lady," O'Ryan said, cutting her off by slicing the air with the edge of his hand. "More than I can tolerate."

Felicity O'Brien was shaking with rage. She could not believe that big, harmless, lovable dope was lying dead and disgraced because of this big toothed beast. A single tear slid down her left cheek. Involuntary spasms opened and closed her fists. Her hatred leaped out at O'Ryan like a living thing. When she spoke, her words were as hard and cold as ice crystals.

"I thank God he put me in the right place at the right time to bring you down, O'Ryan. You're not a hunter. You're an animal. The most vicious inhuman beast on this earth."

"All hunters are animals, lass," O'Ryan replied. His tone was cool now, on the downhill slide from the manic high. "And you hurt me, but you certainly haven't stopped me anyhow. It ain't over. In three weeks I'll be winning the grand prix at Francorchamps. By having some trusted agents wager what little I have left on the obvious winner I'll be able to recover from me recent setbacks. It'll take me a year to rebuild me fortune, but this'll keep me in business. You see, girl, I can't be stopped."

"Want to prove that?" Morgan asked. "Want to end this right now?" He stood, hands loose at his sides, staring into Ian O'Ryan's eyes. The black man had a genuine hard look, and there was steel in his voice. Three shotgun barrels pointed in Morgan's direction, yet a brief look of doubt passed over O'Ryan's face. It lasted only a second before he recovered his arrogance.

"No need, lad. You and the wench can go in peace. There lies me retribution." O'Ryan pointed at Max Grogan's body. "I calls us even up now."

-21-

Felicity paced in her way, which means she walked in aimless circular patterns around the lawn, patterns which always seemed to bring her back to the door. She held her elbows as she walked, as if to hold the tension in. Morgan sat with his feet up in a lawn chair.

Sean had brought a straight backed chair out from the kitchen. He sat in front of his house watching his two visitors, fearing an explosion of violence any minute. He had felt their anger when they returned, only moments ago. While Morgan related the morning's events, Sean's feelings went from worry through horror, rage, fear and grief. Now he sat numb, hoping "the kids" as he now thought of them, would not do anything rash.

"First, we need some answers," Felicity told no one in particular. "Why didn't he kill us right then and there?"

"No need," Morgan answered. "Besides, he knew I had a pistol under this blazer, and that I'd have made quite a mess before I went down. Maybe even got lucky and nailed him."

"You hurt him, lad," Sean said. "He told you so. And now he's hurt you. This morning was just to show you his power. Can't you just let it lie? Go home before you, or me niece gets hurt worse?"

Morgan looked at Sean with something akin to shock. A glance at Felicity told him she felt the same. Sean probably thought this was his fight and not really theirs. Felicity's mouth opened and closed, as if she couldn't formulate her answer, didn't know how to explain what to her were such obvious feelings. It was a tough concept to verbalize. For her at least, but not for Morgan.

"Father Sullivan, do you like western movies?" Morgan asked.

"Why yes, but..."

"Have you ever seen `The Magnificent Seven'?" Morgan continued.

"Sure I have. Why do you ask?"

"Remember James Coburn's part?" Morgan asked.

"I suppose."

"Well I'm like that guy." Morgan looked him dead in the eye with a straight face and said, "Nobody hands me my own gun and tells me to ride on."

Felicity's tension broke and she could not repress a giggle. In the time it took her to recover enough to take a deep breath, she remembered Steve McQueen's response.

"I've got nothing better to do," she said in the same dull tone. Morgan had expected her to know it, and rewarded her with a broad smile. It took Sean a moment to catch up.

"Well, that out of the way, what do we need to know next?" Morgan asked.

"I need more information," Felicity said, staring into the sky. "The next question is, what is Francorchamps?"

"Not, what," Morgan said, crossing his legs. "Where? Francorchamps is a town in Belgium. In that town is a race course, generally called Spa-Francorchamps. Auto racing is the big thing there, but they do motorcycles too. Three weeks or so from today there's a major motorcycle grand prix. I'm sure O'Ryan intends to win this race and lay enough side bets to get back on his feet."

"So we've still got him," Felicity said with a wry smile. "All we have to do is see to it that he loses that race."

"And just how do you plan to do that?" Sean asked, lighting his pipe. "He's known to be the best."

"And he's feared by every other biker on the circuit," Morgan added, heading for the door. "He's known for his ruthless tactics, doing anything for a win."

"Okay, let's look at our alternatives," Felicity said. "Perhaps we can get him barred from the race somehow."

"Not likely girl," Sean said. A ring of smoke began to circle his head. "It's a bit late to be putting in protests and the like. You can be sure he'll have all the legal rigmarole nailed down tight."

"Probably right, Uncle." Felicity picked up a small stone and began tossing it like a coin. "So what else? Sabotage his cycle maybe?"

"Sounds easier than it is." Morgan returned carrying a case of stout bottles. "First we'd have to find out where he keeps his bike. Or bikes. Then, of course, he'll have security. There isn't much time to locate and identify the target, examine and breach his security, and then put the fix on the bike."

"Oh, I think I can get to the machine."

"Even if you can, Red," Morgan went on as he handed her a stout, "can you doctor a high tech motorcycle so an expert would start a race with it, yet the thing would break down later?"

Felicity took a long drink before answering. "I'm not a mechanic. And you're not a thief. So what does that leave?"

"Could you interfere with the race while it's going on, maybe?" Sean asked, opening a bottle for himself.

"That'd likely get us in Dutch with the police," Felicity said, finishing her stout. "It won't help anything for us to end up in the hoosegow. They'd just start the race over anyway. No, he's got to be beaten without disrupting the whole event. What else is there?"

"I enter the race," Morgan said with grim finality, and tipped his bottle up.

"Have you raced motorcycles before, lad?"

"Once or twice."

"Well, you could sign up I imagine, but where'll you get a motorbike?" Sean asked, reaching for a second bottle. "Those thingies are kind of specialized, it seems to me."

"True," Morgan said. "It's the best plan I think, but

we'd never find a 500 CC racing class bike on such short notice." He drained his bottle and let the last drops linger on his tongue. The stout was dark and thick, much like the problem they were wading through.

"Wait!" Felicity spun toward Morgan, her face alight with inspiration. "I bet I know where we can get a racing class motorcycle in short order." She was in the door before the men realized a decision had been made.

*   *   *   *   *

The Empire State Building was the first great skyscraper. Erected in nineteen thirty-one, it remained the world's tallest building for nearly forty years, until the World Trade Center rose up at the southern tip of Manhattan Island and outreached it by a hundred feet. Soon the Sears Tower in Chicago overtook it, but still the most prestigious businesses on the East Coast flocked to the Trade Center's Twin Towers until they disappeared in 2001.

Not long ago the Seagrave Corporation occupied five floors of a building that stood in the shadow of the World Trade Center "ground zero" and predated even the Empire State, but was considered a skyscraper when it was erected. The closely held corporation was recently forced to relocate to a pair of suites in a gleaming steel tower farther uptown. Under new management, the Seagrave Corporation earned its profits through commodities trading, international real estate development and operating an import-export business.

The chairwoman of the board and the company's matriarch was Marlene Seagrave. Blonde and blue eyed, she was a beauty queen a dozen or so years ago. Then she married a cruel, manipulative man named Adrian Seagrave. He used money as a tool, and often as a blunt instrument. It gave him the power to use people, and she let him use her. She never recognized the strength of her own will until after her husband's death. He died trying to kill Morgan Stark and Felicity O'Brien. And they came close to death saving her life in the fire that destroyed the entire building the company occupied then.

The sudden change in her life did not crush her as she first expected it. Finding herself with an incredible amount of wealth and power, Marlene flowered after Adrian's passing. She took control of the corporation and kept it moving to new levels of growth. And her husband's final enemies became for her, two new friends. While she helped them establish their new business, they helped her establish her new identity and self confidence. So, when her secretary buzzed her in her private office with an international telephone call from a woman who identified herself as "the redhead," she took it right away, even though she had just gotten in.

"Felicity, it's been too long. How are you? Where are you? Is this call business or pleasure?"

"I'm fine. I'm in Ireland. And I'm afraid it's business, Marlene." Felicity never liked to soft pedal a favor.

"Well kid, I figure you don't call trans-Atlantic for nothing. And you don't owe me any explanations, never do. Just tell me what you need."

"Well, okay. A racing quality motorcycle."

"I beg your pardon?" Marlene said, as if she was not sure she had heard Felicity correctly.

"Morgan needs to be in a race. You run a major corporation and I figured you'd sponsor a racer or two."

Marlene slid off her heels and rested one leg on her low desk. "You know, we do sponsor a NASCAR racer," she said. "There's a racing yacht too. Don't know if there's a motorcycle flying our banner. Is this a rush type thing?"

"I'm afraid so. The race is in three weeks."

"Sure glad you guys don't make impulsive decisions," Marlene said. "I was thinking of taking some vacation time in a couple of weeks. Listen, I'll check on this motorcycle thing. Can I call you back?"

"Marlene, you're the best. Let me give you this number. Call anytime. I'll be here. And...thanks, pal."

"Anytime, kid."

*   *   *   *   *

The sun had broken through while Felicity was inside, so she was squinting when she stepped out. Morgan was nowhere in sight. Her uncle waved her in the direction of the ruins. She smiled and wandered off.

Felicity walked without any real direction at first. Relaxing her own mind, she let the sensation creep into her head in gradual increments. Soon she could feel the subtle tug of another mind. She drifted off to one side, toward her partner. Since her childhood wandering those very hills, Felicity could always sense danger approaching. She was accustomed to it. But this psychic link with Morgan was still new to her.

She was not reading his mind, of course, she just seemed to know where he was. She could follow some unknown signal like a homing beacon right to him. If his emotions were intense, she could feel them too. Sometimes, she even experienced his sensory input, felt what he felt, heard or smelled what he did. It was that discovery that both cemented their friendship and barred a sexual relationship.

She walked up behind him, but she knew he was aware of her presence. In fact, he must have known she was coming for five minutes. He stood with his hands on his hips, staring out over a slight rise in the ground.

"What are you up to?" Felicity asked.

"Just scouting the perimeter. Trying to see where an attack would come from."

"No alarms, no trip wires?" Felicity asked.

"For what? I always know when they're coming. I just want to see from where."

"I called Marlene," Felicity said after a moment. "She's calling back but I think she can get us a bike."

"Great," Morgan said. "I want to stay by the house today anyway. Noticed a pretty nice chess set in the living room. Let's go back and find out what kind of a chess player your old uncle is."

As they strolled back across the meadow, an unaccustomed chill crawled up Felicity's back and she felt the urge to take Morgan's arm.

"Hey, pal."

"Yeah?" Morgan slowed his tread to match her usual walking pace. She could tell from his voice that he could feel her apprehension.

"If we can get a bike, and if we get you signed up, and if we can get there in time..."

"Yes?"

"Do you think you can beat him?"

"No," he said.

"No?"

Morgan grinned and shook his head. "Red, he's an experienced professional racer. I can't beat him. Then again, I don't have to."

"Huh? But I thought we agreed..."

"Red, I don't need to win. I just need to make sure he loses."

"Oh."

* * * * *

Felicity awoke five seconds before the telephone rang. She knew her location and the time without conscious thought. Location: her uncle's living room couch. The time: midnight plus ten minutes. Memories of the day rushed back on her. She shopped at the local market with Morgan, after which they spent half the day collaborating on dinner. She taught him the right way to make Irish stew, with layers of potato, onion and mutton boiled in a big iron pot.

Then she settled down to watch an extended chess tournament, still surprised at Morgan's talent for the tactical strategy involved. He compared it to warfare. She dozed off on the sofa and the men must have left her there when they went to bed. The bell rang, and Felicity answered it on the first ring.

"You're not anxious or anything?" Marlene Seagrave said. "Sorry about the hour, but I just got home and I had dialed before I realized the time difference."

"Not a problem," Felicity said, swinging her feet to the floor and sitting up straight. "We crime stoppers never sleep. So, what's the scoop?"

"Good news all around, dearie," Marlene said. "First, the Seagrave Corporation does indeed sponsor a motorcycle team. The rider's name is Jacques Martens. I understand that he has an excellent motorcycle, state of the art, and he's already entered in the Grand Prix at Spa-Francorchamps."

"That's great, Marlene. Is he any good?"

"Hasn't won a race in three years," Marlene said. Her laugh floated across the phone lines, delayed for a second, and Felicity missed a couple of words. Marlene repeated. "I told you it was all good news. I've arranged to have the bike in the race representing my company, but the rider's name is changed."

"You're a living doll."

"I owe you my life," Marlene said. "This is nothing..."

"I told you never to say that again. We agreed..."

"You're right, I'm sorry," Marlene said, then paused for a moment. "I'll be there too."

"In Belgium?"

"Sure," Marlene said. "I told you I was due for a little vacation. I'll do a couple of days in Paris, then hop over to the race. I wouldn't miss Morgan representing us. By the way, is he asleep?"

"Afraid so. Want me to wake him?"

"No, no. Just tell him to be prepared to win when I get there."

After settling all the details of where, when and how, Felicity hung up and sat in the dark for a while. She stared at the chess set across the room. Things were going according to plan. In fact, they had no right to expect things to be this smooth. Yet, she had a bad feeling about this scenario. Bad for Morgan. She felt a sudden urge to go to her partner and cuddle him.

She had been close to Morgan in that way before, deriving comfort from his massive arms, but in a platonic way, despite his being the sexiest man she knew. If she went to the bedroom now, he would understand and welcome her in. When she fell asleep, he would move to the couch. It was a comforting thought, but she knew she wouldn't move from the sofa. If she went to Morgan the way she had imagined, he would know she did not have her usual level of confidence. She would rather keep that to herself as long as possible.

Besides, her uncle would never understand.

- 22 -

The trio flew into Paris by way of London in the middle of the night. The population in the Airport at that hour didn't qualify as a crowd. They moved through them and outside with unexpected ease. At the curb, Sean was surprised to find a black BMW fighting with the taxis for space at the exit. Morgan smiled, showing how pleased he was with the driver. The young woman at the wheel popped the trunk and opened her door enough to set one foot on the pavement and stand.

"Felicity, Uncle Sean, this is Claudette Christophe, the pearl of the quarter," Morgan said. "Claudette, Felicity O'Brien and her uncle Sean Sullivan. Now that we're all old friends, let's get moving." Morgan and Sean loaded the luggage and Morgan reached for the passenger side door."

"You should let the girl sit in front," Claudette said.

"That ain't no lady, that's my partner," Morgan said. "You're the girl." Perhaps to make a point, Morgan pulled the back door open and smiled at Felicity. She stood still, ignoring him. For a long moment the two women locked eyes, trying to evaluate each other's face. Sean was a keen observer of human ways. He knew that a man may need body language, posture, speech pattern, even a sample of someone's philosophy to make a judgment. But a woman, a good woman, could see all there was to any other woman in her face. The long tense stare ended with two smiles. Then Felicity nodded, gave an address on the south side of Paris and got into the back seat. Sean slid in beside her, Morgan settled into the front seat, and Claudette pulled her car into traffic.

Sean's eyes flicked to Morgan. If he noticed the

tension he gave no sign. He conversed with all the passengers during the drive to Felicity's apartment, riding with his hand on Claudette's knee. When they arrived, all four climbed out of the car. Morgan held Claudette close.

"Appreciate the lift, beautiful. Coming in for coffee, or a drink?"

"Please do come in for a while," Felicity hastened to add.

"I regret I must decline," Claudette said. "I'll need my rest for tomorrow's work, and Morgan is bad for my concentration. And he has trouble concentrating on more than one woman at a time." Her eyes roved Felicity from her ankles up. Sean guessed she was comparing her own figure to Felicity's, and finding herself wanting.

"I'll show you who I'm concentrating on." Morgan pressed a lingering kiss onto Claudette's mouth. She looked at the priest with embarrassment, and drove away at a tire-spinning speed.

As soon as they were inside the door, Felicity said, "Charming girl, obviously highly intelligent, and quite beautiful. How does she keep herself so nice and slender?"

Felicity continued on to her bedroom but Sean stopped just inside the door, stunned to see that this apartment was identical to the one he visited in California. It was beginning to sink in that Felicity was indeed quite wealthy. And with that understanding came another realization. She would never have been content in his world.

* * * * *

"Hey, The Sea Hawk's coming on, and it looks like it's in English," Morgan called. "Want to watch it?" A half hour and three cups of tea after their arrival, the travelers were getting settled in.

"Sounds like a good way to relax myself into sleep mode." Felicity was gathering snacks in the kitchen, wearing a blue silk robe that seemed a little big on her. Morgan sat bare-chested and barefoot on the couch. Sean was already snoring in the guest room,.

Felicity was carrying a tray into the living room when she heard the numbered buttons on her cipher lock being punched and saw the doorknob beginning to turn.

When Raoul Goulait pushed the door open, he found himself staring into a gun barrel held by a very grim looking black man.

"A do not disturb sign would have done, my good man," Raoul said. "If I'm interrupting something..." Before he could finish his sentence, Felicity leaped to the front door.

"Darling, I wasn't expecting you until morning."

"Your famous sense of time is slipping, sweet," the Frenchman said with a dashing smile. "This far after midnight, it is morning. And Paris, like New York, never sleeps." Felicity smiled, and apologized for Morgan's trigger nerves with a long deep kiss. Morgan turned his attention back to the television set.

"I have the papers you need," Raoul said when he came up for air. "These should ensure you free passage throughout Europe, even with the special items your partner likes to carry. I thought, Cherie, that we could retire and enjoy the waning hours of the night in the way we both like best."

"I can't tonight, silly." Felicity watched his face drop, and followed his eyes over to the sofa. "No, you green-eyed dope. There's nothing but business between Morgan and me. I told you. But my uncle's here. I'm not sleeping with anyone with him under the same roof."

"Ah. That explains why you're wearing my robe," Raoul said. "I know you don't own one. Good thing I visit as often as I do."

"You know anytime I'm on the continent you're welcome in my home, and my bed. But not this time. It's kind of a special case."

"I understand ma'amselle," Raoul said with a feigned sigh. "There will be another time, yes?"

*   *   *   *   *

Morgan was almost always the first to rise, so it was a surprise to open his eyes to the sound of a gas stove lighting. He sat up and looked over the back of the sofa to see Felicity in the same silk robe, pulling things from the refrigerator. He stretched, swung his bare feet to the floor and padded into the kitchen. Felicity's unbrushed hair appeared to be clinging to her head in fear, and her lost expression made her look like a little girl standing in daddy's bathrobe.

"What you up to, Red?"

Felicity kept moving, sitting milk and a carton of eggs on the counter, and then reaching on tiptoe to pull a glass bowl from a cabinet. "I figured I'd make us some breakfast before we go. Do you think that pan is hot enough yet?"

Morgan turned down the heat under the pan filled with blackening butter, shook his head, and turned to grip her shoulders. "Slow down little princess. Those eggs will cook up fine if you relax a bit. And if you don't set yourself on fire." Felicity tried to reach for an egg but Morgan refused to release her until he had rolled up one sleeve, then the other, past her elbows.

"Now how else can I help?" Morgan asked.

"Do you know how to make a hollandaise?"

"Nope. I don't care, and neither does Uncle Sean. He's a simple guy, and so am I. Make us something easy while I go get him up."

So it was that the trio enjoyed a modest breakfast of scrambled eggs and toast. Then they climbed into Felicity's Paris car, a Mercedes Benz 450SL convertible, for the three hour drive to the race course. Morgan sat beside Felicity and opened a map. She stared for a moment, memorizing her route, and pulled into the brisk Parisian traffic

"You know, I've never ridden in a Mercedes Benz," Sean said from the back seat.

"Actually, it only looks like a normal Mercedes," Felicity said. "It's really an AMG Hammer. Car's so responsive the company makes you go to a special seminar to learn how to handle it."

"Things ain't always what they seem," Morgan said. "That goes for people just as much as cars. So don't be surprised if the Belgians turn out to be a surprise. Where they live makes them weird people."

"Why's that?" Sean asked.

"Oh, no." Felicity muttered under her breath as she pulled the car up onto the autoroute. "More philosophy."

"You might expect Belgians to be kind of like the Irish," Morgan said, making a point of ignoring Felicity. "After all, Belgium's temperature norms are about the same as Ireland's, and both countries do border on the same ocean. The difference in latitude is nominal. But still, there's this basic difference in climate. I mean, they can't get that steady hanging mist in this country, like they've got over in Ireland. That romantic fog they've always got in the U.K.? It can't survive here. Know why?"

"All right, lad, I'll bite," Sean said. "Tell us why."

"It's because it never goes forty-eight hours in this place without raining. I'm convinced the weather has a real affect on the people here."

"I see they're not shy about driving," Sean said. "Do they have speed limits here?"

"It's a hundred ten kilometers on the autoroutes, Uncle Sean, but drivers here pretty much ignore it. Not to worry. This baby can do almost three times that."

"Yeah, and she's not afraid to push it," Morgan said.

The highway segment of the trip was smooth and uneventful. In the province of Liege, they branched off the main road, heading for the twin cities of Spa and

Francorchamps. In minutes they were navigating streets as narrow and twisted as a politician's man. Morgan picked up his narrative as if he had never left the subject.

"Look around Uncle Sean, and you'll see what I mean. The Irishman's full of life, you know. When he's had too much beer, he's as likely to burst into song as anything else. Belgians are hard and grim. They drink their beer in gloomy little places. And they get a lot of their emotional release from driving too fast on these twisted, narrow streets. You can see how all the buildings are brick here, and usually painted gray. Not like the colorfully painted homes and thatch cottages you've got in Ireland."

A family on the street caught his attention. "Look at those guys. People don't dress colorfully here, or even speak colorfully. They're not bad people, or rude like the French. Just dull." Morgan turned to face Sean to finalize his point. "It's got to be the rain." He was stunned to see his adopted uncle riding with his eyes clamped shut. His hands were folded in an attitude of prayer. Morgan wondered if he had been that way the whole trip.

*　*　*　*　*

Following Morgan's directions they arrived at the race course without an accident or a ticket. After showing passes, the three travelers strolled down to the pit area. Morgan caught the familiar smells of grease, engine exhaust and spilled gasoline. He spotted four mechanics in white uniform overalls and another man sitting to the side. He was short and slight but wiry, like a jockey. His hair was jet black, his nose long and upturned. When he saw the visitors, he snapped to his feet and rushed forward, hand outstretched. Morgan took the hand and found the shake firm. Small fingers threatened to cut into Morgan's hands.

"Ah, you must be Mister Stark. And this would be Miss O'Brien and Mister Sullivan. I am Jacques Marten. You will call me Jacques. We have an excellent crew assembled and I am told by our employer that we are to extend to you every courtesy. I assure you..."

"Calm down, pal," Morgan said. "And please, call me Morgan." He was sure Martens considered him some eccentric friend of the wealthy Mrs. Seagrave. Some bored rich fellow fulfilling a fantasy of riding in a motorcycle grand prix. Or maybe he figured Morgan to be a journalist like that George Plimpton guy who would write about the experience. Well no harm there, but for a pit crew to work well they would need strong communication. That would require an informal atmosphere.

"My friends and I are new at this," Morgan said. "We've got a lot to do, and I've got a lot to learn in a short time. The first thing we need to do is meet everybody. Then I'd like to meet the bike, and maybe take her for a tour of the track. Okay?"

"We will help all we can, but I am the only one here who speaks English. My team is French and Belgian."

"Not a problem, Jacques," Morgan said, smiling and shaking his shoulder. "I learned a certain amount of pidgin French in Vietnam, and Felicity here is fluent in the language."

Introductions were made in short order. Felicity impressed the mechanics with her agility in their language. Sean became intrigued by the power tools and special equipment involved. The team seemed positive and pleasant enough, an easy group to work with. Amid the growing camaraderie, Morgan asked where he could change and walked into the back rest area to suit up.

Morgan was happy to find a custom made black leather racing outfit waiting for him there. He was anxious to try the bike out. As he stripped, Felicity followed him and closed the door. There was no change in his actions. Their bodies held no secrets for each other.

"That was an amusing speech you made in the car on our way here," Felicity said. "How do you know so much about this little country? Been here a lot?"

"I've made a lot of money here," Morgan replied, wriggling into tight leather pants with peculiar knee pads. "I was a diplomat for a little while."

"A diplomat? You?"

"Yes, Red, a diplomat," Morgan said, pulling on protective boots. "For more than one third world country, I'll have you know. It was part of my fee for merc work, sort of a perk for services rendered. It came in mighty handy because, armed with that diplomatic immunity, I was able to sell my signature at the bottom of end user certificates."

"That's got something to do with arms sales, right?"

"Right the first time," Morgan said, pulling on and zipping the leather jacket. "If I signed the certificate that would testify that the little country I represented was the actual end user of those weapons. That paper made the manufacturer, the shipper and the dealer all look legit. For my signature and handling the logistics with Fabrique Nationale, the local arms manufacturer, I made big money with little risk."

"All for buying in some country's name? How much can there be in that?"

"It set me up for life," he replied, dragging on heavy leather gauntlets. "The last purchase I brokered was for fifteen million dollars worth of FN/FAL's for one small African country building an army to fight the commies. My commission was twelve and a half percent of that. Expenses involved in the delivery ate up nearly half of it, but I still did okay."

Felicity chuckled. "I'm sure. You'll have to tell me that whole story some day."

"Sure, Red. But right now, let's go meet my new bike."

When Morgan strolled out to the motorcycle, Jacques fell in behind him. They stopped and stared together at the machine, which was painted a deep reflective black with vivid, vibrant orange and blue stripes. The yellow number seven on the sides was echoed by another under the windshield. The name "Seagrave" stretched across the body in big white letters. "Michelin" and "Champion" stood in smaller letters on the rear of the gas tank.

Morgan raised a thoughtful eyebrow. In his view this thing was neither fish nor foul, that is, neither Yamaha nor Honda. He knew that neither Harley Davidson nor Triumph ever appeared on these tracks. The bike had a longer wheelbase than any five hundred cc grand prix machine he had ever seen. And the front suspension looked more like a car's MacPherson strut than the usual telescopic forks on motorcycles.

"It's an Elf," Jacques said, interrupting Morgan's thoughts.

"A what?"

"We bought it from the Elf petroleum company," Jacques said. "Honda is working with the design also."

"I see," Morgan said, pulling on his helmet and climbing aboard the beast. "Anything I should know before I take a couple of laps?"

"Just remember you're holding a hundred and fifty horsepower with no fork up front. You can't steer through corners. You'll have to use the lean angle. Lean deep."

Morgan shook his head, saluted, and fired the bike up. For the first time he considered the course he was about to tackle. This track was almost seven kilometers of gradients wandering up and down. That meant a little more than four miles of very fast course ending with the long straightaway coming out of Les Combes down into Eau Rouge, considered by many to be the sharpest bend in motor racing. It was a beautiful course, slipping through the forests of the Ardennes. At that moment, it looked like an amusement park laid out just for him.

Morgan roared out onto the track with a smooth burst of power, cruising to warm up the tires and attune himself to the bike. Carburetion seemed clean and he liked the cycle's acceleration. The vibrations soon smoothed to nothing as Morgan tuned out everything except the track. As always on a racing bike, sound became a steady state for Morgan, soon imitating silence very well. The air was crisp to the taste. He settled in, got comfortable and started to become one with the machine.

On the third lap, Morgan decided to test the motorcycle's limits on the long straightaway. Opening up the throttle all the way, he wound the long Elf up to just under one hundred eighty miles per hour. She gave a triumphant roar. Machine and rider felt good. It was coming back to him faster than he had dared hope. Despite the wind blast tearing at him, Morgan decided he could hold one hundred ten going into the next turn. He heaved the bike over hard and extended his right knee, prepared for it to brush the ground.

At the apex of the turn the steering jerked in a violent reaction and for a moment Morgan imagined himself rolling with his cycle across the center grass. Had he overdone it, he wondered? He managed to right the bike in time, looping far out on the track. In a race, that would cost him a place or two. He cursed himself for steering too much, and not leaning enough. He knew he had to listen to the man who had been riding that bike, and to remember it was not like anything he had ever been on before.

At the end of the third lap, Morgan pulled into the pit. The entire ten man crew greeted him, but only Jacques and Felicity walked right up to the motorcycle.

"How's it feel?" Felicity asked when Morgan pulled his helmet off.

"You mean how does the bike feel or how does it feel to nearly wipe out the first time on it?"

"I want to know how you feel on the bike," Jacques said. "Can you adjust to the handling?"

"Jacques we've got a lot of work to do to get me up to speed. I'm having a little trouble changing directions. The steering's set real heavy."

"It is good that you can feel the motorcycle's quirks," Jacques said, with a smile. "I do run the steering heavy. That's so I can set the steering damper very light. I want to feel what the tires are doing without any, er...distortion. Is that the right word?"

"Sure," Morgan said, dismounting. "We'd better find all the little things about this monster that can kill me, and find them quick. And we'll need to set up a training schedule for me. I'll need my edges honed if I'm to stop O'Ryan from winning this race."

After a long silence, Jacques said "I suggest you stay away from Ian O'Ryan on the track. I've raced against him. Accidents happen around that man. That's why he's sometimes called `the widow maker' by other racers."

- 23 -

During the next three weeks, Morgan became a part of his race team and his motorcycle. The team took rooms in a modest nearby boarding house. Morgan altered his diet, stressing seafood and vegetables but refusing alcohol, even the famous Belgian beer. Every morning started as they had in Ireland, with push-ups, sit-ups and a run. He spent his days riding, or working on the bike, making small but crucial adjustments. He spent his evenings talking about the bike, the race, and his opponents, trying to absorb all he could about the upcoming event.

At first Felicity observed this routine from a distance, knowing that Morgan had pretty much tuned her and her uncle out. After a couple of days she decided to drive to Brussels. She returned late in the afternoon with several books and an idea. At the end of day three she waited in Morgan's room for him to return from a hot bath. She was sure she was a pleasant surprise, but his expression asked why she was there.

"I've been searching for a way to help you win this race," she told him. "The only thing I could think of was to reduce the tension and relax you. Get naked and lie down."

"I beg your pardon?" Morgan clutched at the towel which was his only garment.

"Relax. I got some manuals and I've been studying up on massage. I plan to give you a good rub down every night."

They both chuckled and Morgan stretched out face down to let her get to work. She started high and worked her way slowly downward. After just a couple of minutes Morgan gave a surprised "Humph."

"What did I do?"

"Nothing bad," Morgan said, moving his mouth as little as possible. "You had a good touch on my neck, light but firm. The really nice surprise was that you've got the strength to work my back muscles. You didn't get all this from just reading some books, Red. You're obviously a natural. And it's just what I need after a day on that bike."

Felicity grunted and continued. She focused on the big latissimus dorsi that supported his spine and had held him erect for several hours on his motorcycle that day. In a few minutes she worked up a sweat herself, but she could feel the muscles loosening at last. She wondered if it was enough. Then the thought popped into her head that Morgan did indeed have a strong back, and she new somebody who no doubt appreciated that.

"You know I was kidding around when you came in," she said. "But I was wondering. Do you want me to try to find Claudette tomorrow? I mean, I'm sure she'd be happy to help you to relax in the more traditional way."

Morgan looked too calm to laugh, but he did manage a smile. "No thanks. I know it's outmoded thinking, but when I'm really training up for something I avoid sex. I think I can convert that energy and the thin line of tension into something useful on the track. Claudette knows it too. That's why she didn't stick around."

* * * * *

On the morning of day four Felicity awoke a little late and a little sore. She took a longer than usual shower, easing her weary shoulder and back muscles. When she stepped out into another gray morning she began to wonder if the weather was affecting her the way Morgan thought it affected the local residents. When she reached the track she found her uncle already there. He was sitting alone in the bleacher seats, watching

Morgan circle the track. She climbed up behind him and stood with her hands on his shoulders.

"I hate to say it, but I'm getting bored," she said without preamble. "You?"

"Mostly, I feel kind of guilty," Sean said.

"Goes with being Catholic."

Sean shot a damning look over his shoulder. "Don't start, girl. What I mean is, I feel this is all for me, and I shouldn't have gotten you involved in the first place. But, aside from that, you're right. There's nothing here for an old man like me."

"I believe I have the solution to our mutual problem." She dropped a map over his shoulders into his lap. "I've scheduled a little day trip for us. That ought to keep us busy." She didn't mention her other agenda. She thought it was also a perfect opportunity for her to get closer to her only living relative.

They began with a short but pleasant drive to the ancient abbey of Stavelot, just a few miles south of Spa-Francorchamps. Sean knew well the castles and ancient churches of Ireland and England, but this was something new and different to him.

In this unique setting, they also toured the "museum of the circuit." It showed the history of the track at Spa-Francorchamps with eighty race cars, motorbikes and other vehicles.

That success behind them, Felicity and Sean were soon following the winding roads with ease, exploring the lovely Ardennes Mountains. They became real tourists, learning a new country with plenty of time to spare.

Felicity gravitated to stores, but shopping was not a pleasant experience for Sean. She found some factory outlets in Liege which offered beautiful crystal and lace, but her uncle made such a scene, she had to leave empty handed. He was still grumbling when they sat down at a corner tavern for a snack.

"I don't understand how that man could believe any of

that bottle glass he sold could compare to fine Irish crystal."

"Is that what all this is about?" Felicity could not contain her laughter. "Uncle Sean, those pieces right in front of you were Waterford."

A waiter brought menus, saving Sean the embarrassment of answering her, but he could not hide the color creeping up his cheeks. This time Felicity stifled her laughter. She could feel herself slipping into her childhood habit of teasing her uncle as he struggled with the menu.

"I assume that you'll have no trouble finding something you like, Uncle Sean," she said in a serious, schoolteacher tone. "A priest's background in Latin should make these French phrases quite simple."

"Young miss, you can laugh at this poor old man all you want. I'll be happy to order if you don't mind us eating roast beef with chocolate sauce or the like."

Felicity ordered in smooth, casual French, and as the waitress walked away she said, "You know, this country is known for some rather unique cuisine. For example, horse meat is quite popular here."

"I'm sure," Sean said, squirming in his seat.

"Of course, I'm sure you'd prefer some of their richer delicacies, such as rabbit in plum sauce."

She stopped as the waitress returned with two glasses of local beer. She had ordered Morgan's recommendation, Stella Artois, not the more popular Jupiler, which Morgan told her was less flavorful. The beer was followed by a pair of sandwiches.

"Here you are, Uncle Sean. Coq Monsieur."

Sean seemed delighted by the choice. "What is this you've ordered? It looks to be a grilled ham and cheese sandwich."

After lunch he left the restaurant chanting "Coq Monsieur, Coq Monsieur" as if he thought if he could just remember it, he would never run the risk of getting one of those other horrible things Felicity had mentioned.

Days flew past as niece and uncle toured the countryside. Morgan commented that Felicity's new fascination with souvenir shops and theme parks seemed out of character, but her nightly reports as she administered his massage seemed to be the outlet they both needed as the race grew near.

The final outing was to the caves at Remouchamps. Said to hold the world's largest underground lake, the caves descend to a natural walkway that follows the water's edge. The walls are so high, no end can be seen. Once inside, they knew the ground was above them, but the darkness gave the illusion of a starless sky.

The pair wandered alone, isolated in their private universe. The huge cave seemed to demand silence. Each turn opened to a new vista of rock shelves, all lighted to enhance their vivid colors. The air seemed alive, but not with the sharp odor of stagnant water. Instead this was the brisk smell one catches beside a rushing stream. It was comfortable and cool like all caves, a little over sixty degrees.

All this raw beauty entranced her, and from all appearances her uncle as well. They stopped on one of the ledges, staring at the vast expanse facing them.

Felicity looked up, at the beads of stone cascading from the highest edge. It's called flowrock, but she saw it as a falling blanket of pearls. Threads of amber twined the beads like fine gold chains woven with magical delicacy. Every few feet a small cluster of quartz burst from this pearl blanket. To Felicity's eyes they were the perfect diamond accents. She couldn't guess what her uncle was seeing in the majesty of their surroundings until he broke the silence.

"This is why I am a priest." His words were barely a whisper, yet they seemed to come from every corner of the cavern. Felicity studied her uncle. He was taking in every inch, absorbing every shape and color. When

Felicity placed her hand over his it was a tentative yet loving gesture.

"Why'd you run off and leave me, lass?" Sean had not moved his eyes. He continued staring at the rock walls. Felicity looked out over the water lapping at the stones and breathed a long, deep sigh.

"I never left you, Uncle Sean. When I left Glendalough, you were all I took with me. I carried your laugh and your brogue and the smell of your pipe tobacco everywhere. When I did something you didn't like, you scolded me. When I was alone and scared, you held me. Until Morgan came along, you were all I had."

Sean looked at her now, his face showing his lack of understanding.

"I had to leave what you represented to me. Ireland, your beloved Ireland, that kills people because of their religion, made no sense to me. I watched my parents die on our way to church. Then they sent me to you. I grew up saying my prayers and doing catechisms. And I'd sit at mass on Sunday and look at the altar boys. I knew half of them were involved in the killing, one way or another, running errands for the Provos or fouling wells or something to cause trouble, and still they stood there in their white robes, looking all innocent."

A thick anger began to well up in Felicity. The pressure of her hand increased on Sean's. He must have felt it but still he did not speak. Instead he turned his hand to grasp hers.

"Every time you stood at the altar, you were one of them," Felicity said. "One of the reasons my parents died. But, at one o'clock on Sunday, you were Uncle Sean again. It was just too much for me."

Sean watched his niece's green eyes flare, then a veil dropped and all her pain and anger went back to their safe place, deep in her mind. Sean cleared his throat.

"Felicity, I cannot change the past with a few words. If I tell you that you should have come to me, we both know those to be wasted words. Children never see that as an answer. What you're saying makes a great deal of sense to me. I hurt you by not seeing your pain." He turned her to him and rested his hands on her elbows. "The ignorance of the radicals killed your parents, not the Catholic Church. I'll not apologize for my calling, or my church. I am a servant of God. I cannot condone your running away or the life you've led..."

He paused, staring into those eyes he remembered so well. This was the tear stained face of the little girl they brought him all those years ago. His voice caught in his throat.

"You've become a beautiful woman who is everything I could hope for. I admit that your relationship with Morgan confused me, but I think he's given you an inner peace you could never have found if you'd stayed with me. I'm praying that now that we're together again we can build a new family and bury those old ghosts. Both our ghosts."

- 24 -

Morgan could feel the ghosts around him in the darkness. He was communing with the spirits of his predecessors, the creators of the object before him. The object of his meditations.

He sat cross-legged on the garage's cement floor, bare-chested and barefoot. His hands rested on his knees and his eyes were closed. His breathing was slow and even.

It would have embarrassed him if anyone saw him like this. The lotus posture, like meditation itself, just never seemed a very masculine activity to him. Yet, he could not deny what he learned those long years ago in the east. That a man could unite with a weapon or an inanimate object and it made a difference. So, the night before the race, he sat meditating on the Elf motorcycle. In a sense he was feeling every inch of the machine, opening his mind, letting the spirits of the bike's creators teach him all he should know about it. Many Westerners might think it was nonsense, but he knew it would maximize his chances for success tomorrow.

The door behind him opened without disturbing his danger instincts. He let his mind float down from the world of the ghosts to the more solid plane of reality. When he turned his head, the movement in the dark startled the newcomer.

"Pardon, monsieur," Jacques said. "I did not know anyone was here so late. I only came by to...to say good-bye to her." It took Morgan a moment to realize who "she" was. He stood up, and rested a hand on Jacques' shoulder.

"I'm only going to do this once," Morgan said, smiling. "I told you, I'm not here to take your place. After tomorrow it's your bike again. And with my blessings. She's a beauty and like nothing I've ever seen, but I'll be lucky if she doesn't kill me tomorrow."

"You are an unusual American," Jacques said, walking around to the other side of the motorcycle. "I've watched you during the rides and after. You realize, as few of your countrymen do, that a machine like this has a soul. A soul breathed into it by its designers, and its builders, and the mechanics who have worked on her. You should see that once you ride her in a race, she won't be mine anymore." He ran his hand over the gas tank with touching sensitivity.

"You needn't worry, my friend." Morgan stepped over to him as he talked. "Once you've had her on the track again, she'll be all yours. And I can make sure Madame Seagrave keeps backing you until you turn your beauty into a winner. Eh?"

Morgan's head whipped around as if he heard something. But no sound had gotten his attention. Instead he had gotten a warning signal of imminent danger. He didn't know why, but his peculiar instincts were never to be denied or ignored. He signaled Jacques to kneel in the dark and wait.

Two long minutes later, the door edged open a few inches. A man, clad all in black including a ski mask, slid into the room. He held a small pistol in his right hand. He slid to the side, unaware of the men already in the room as far as Morgan could tell. Behind him, another intruder in identical gear entered in a crouch. He carried a tool box which he set down in front of the motorcycle. He maintained silence as he opened it and picked out a wrench.

A saboteur, Morgan thought. Did this mean O'Ryan knew who his opposition was? Or was he just putting the fix in on a few of the other riders? Maybe he was just going after the new guys, the ones he didn't know. Either way, Morgan was sure this midnight mechanic must have been sent by O'Ryan. And if he was good enough to alter the brake pressure, the transmission or the steering damper, a rider could die finding out his bike had been readjusted.

As the wrench moved toward the machine, Jacques popped up from behind it. He had murder in his eyes but, Morgan thought he also saw a smile in the gloom.

"Ne touche pas, monsieur," the Frenchman said, planting a solid left on the ski masked jaw. The man at the door pointed his weapon, but Morgan's hand clamped on his wrist and jerked up. There was an ear splitting blast in the small enclosed garage and the flash blinded Morgan for a moment. The gunman got in a couple of punches to his midsection. Then the two of them tumbled to the floor, wrestling over the gun.

Morgan could hear Jacques locked in a fist fight, and the sound of running feet. At least four more men came in. These guys had brought heavy backup. Jacques was being overpowered and Morgan could not shake his enemy's grip on his gun. He heard Jacques take a couple of hard blows. A quick look up showed two men holding the French rider, working him over.

Then the door flew open, lights came on, and a bellow like the roar of a wounded bear filled the room. Sean rushed in and smashed one of the black suited invaders in the face with a crushing right. He went down and stayed down. Two of the others released Jacques to trade punches with Sean, but the trading was not even. Sean still moved like a boxer, and each punch had telling effect. It was now four against two on that side of the room. From the look of things, just the kind of brawl Sean loved.

Just as Morgan managed to get his feet up between himself and his personal foe, Felicity appeared. She smacked a spanner against the gunman's wrist and the pistol hit the floor. Morgan's body snapped straight like a band of spring steel, sending the man on top of him flying the length of the room. He hit the wall like a broken doll. Before his body could even slide to the floor, Morgan was amidst the pack surrounding Sean.

Now it was three against four, and the battle wasn't close to even. Jacques turned out to be a decent scrapper, but either Sean or Morgan would probably have been too much for the remaining four attackers. Together they had no trouble sending them scurrying, like roaches when the lights come on. The home team came to an unspoken agreement not to give chase, but stood in the doorway, breaking into uncontrolled laughter.

"Come on back when you want some more," Sean shouted. "And bring your cowardly boss with you. We'll be teaching him the same lesson." Then they locked up the garage and headed back to their hotel. On their way, Sean put an arm around Morgan's shoulders and asked again, "Are you sure you're not just a wee bit Irish, lad?"

* * * * *

In Morgan's room, Felicity got to play Florence Nightingale. There were bruised knuckles all around, plus a split French lip, a cut over an Irish eye and a powder burned black cheek. No one in the room minded these minor injuries because they knew they had sent the other men home looking a lot worse. Morgan looked up at Felicity as she pressed an icepack against his face.

"Well, we know he's desperate and playing for keeps," he said. "I'm a little worried about this now."

"You need to rest for tomorrow's race," Felicity said. "I'll go down and set up an alarm system around the garage. I can wire it to ring here and give any uninvited visitors a good solid electrical charge."

"I doubt they'll be back tonight," Morgan said. "But I can expect some trouble during the race. And more important, I'm worried about after the race. Win or lose it won't be over for O'Ryan."

"We can take care of ourselves, lad," Sean said through a grin. "Sure and they know it now."

"Yeah, but it's getting crowded here," Morgan said. "You're a hell of a scrapper, Uncle, but you're not a professional at this. Ian O'Ryan is. There's also Jacques now. Claudette'll be here for the race tomorrow and Marlene Seagrave too. Too many targets. As soon as you guys are gone I'm calling in some backup from the States."

"We've got somebody good on the payroll," Felicity said.

"I'm sure we're thinking alike. Now finish wrapping these guys up so I can get some rest. I've got a race to ride tomorrow and I'll need everything I've got to take out that Irish assassin."

- 25 -

From the grandstand, the motorcycles looked like toys laid out on a driveway to Felicity. They were lined up like checkers on the asphalt, so no one was right in front of or beside anyone else. The collective engine sounds formed a wave of guttural white noise. The crowd, in a gay mood, generated its own blur of sound. The colorful outfits of the audience were a disordered reflection of the riders' leather suits in bright reds and greens and whites.

Except for the one rider in black. It was the only way to identify Morgan. All the helmets had smoked glass, making every rider a faceless ornament worn by a motorcycle. Felicity looked around at her uncle and her friends, old and new. Marlene had made it to the race, and Claudette sat beside her. They were all smiles. They sensed the tension, the anticipation in the air. But did they sense the danger?

It was a perfect day for a race. There was almost no breeze. As usual in Belgium, cloud cover prevented any glare, and there was a threat of rain later in the day. It was sixty degrees with low humidity.

Down on the track, the motorcycle between Morgan's knees purred like a contented kitten. He inhaled the slightest smell of oil from the invisible exhaust of the field. They were ten bikes across, and six rows deep. Each rider was part of this intricate design, yet each was in his own world with his bike.

Morgan looked around, taking in the entire field of competitors. There, to his right and just behind him, stood a black Ducati. Gregorio Lavilla took the British Superbike Championship on a very similar machine in 2005. The rider would have been unmistakable even without "Widow Maker" lettered on the back of his bike, and "Orion the Hunter" gracing the side. Morgan was again impressed by the man's stature. He was a solid mass of brute power.

If last night's attack was random, Morgan still had the advantage of surprise. It would be foolish to give it away. But then, he considered, it's not a duel if only one person knows about it. He waved to the other rider behind his opaque face shield and pointed at the front of his own bike.

"Look Ma, no forks," he said, and laughed. He saw realization dawn in his target's body language. Now he was sure that O'Ryan knew he was there. Now it was a duel.

Then the flag came down, motors snarled into life and Morgan found himself fighting to be part of a race. Running this course alone was one thing. Sharing it with sixty daredevil world class competitors was a very different experience. He remembered that the Belgian Grand Prix was where records got set.

The mass of steel settled into a line at the track's inside edge coming into the second lap and Morgan was unaware of anyone else's position. *Only about ninety laps to go*, he thought. He was still somewhere near the middle of the pack, which seemed almost like a miracle to him, doing one hundred eighty miles per hour on the long straightaway. He heard the crowd cheer as he passed the grandstand. He dropped it down to one hundred ten as he went into the first deep turn, laying his knee pad on the ground. He heaved the bike over and it told him right away that it was the wrong move. The handlebars tried to jump out of his hands and he almost didn't recover control.

Less input on the handlebars, Morgan told himself, and settled back into the line of riders. Two bikes passed him on that turn. One of them had to be O'Ryan on his way to the finish line. Morgan set his sights on staying with the "widow maker"or two slots behind him at most. O'Ryan had forgotten him, he hoped, and would focus on the race. He had to believe every man on the track wanted to win.

*   *   *   *   *

After watching the motorcycles circle the track for fifteen minutes, Felicity was exhausted, dripping with perspiration in the cool air. She felt much of what Morgan felt. Her limbs were tense, her pulse thudding as if she were running a marathon. Did Morgan know? Probably not. His attention would have to be focused well beyond any awareness of her. He would see nothing but the track, his gauges, and the other motorcycles.

Felicity was, in fact, impressed. Everyone down there understood defensive driving, and there was not even a hint of an accident. The machines moved around one another in smooth, predictable patterns. Deep and fast was the only way to take a curve. Morgan was holding his own. She managed to track him and O'Ryan. She knew her partner's objective. If he could, Morgan would get in front of O'Ryan and just slow down, appearing to lose control. But that knowledge did little to ease the tension. After just one hour she wondered how a man could complete, let alone win, such a race. Already time was losing all meaning.

When it hit, it hit with concussive force. She knew her partner was in great danger, and that danger was not coming from the track. Her uncle screamed, and that was when she knew her nails were digging into his hand. She tipped back her black fedora, raised Morgan's binoculars and scanned, not the track, but the street and the field beyond. She didn't know what she was looking for, but she would know it when she saw it.

There in the trees. Almost invisible. She had no doubt. That glare. It was a rifle barrel. Felicity thought, *could O'Ryan be this stupid?*

"Come on, Uncle," she said. "We've got to get to the car. Now!" Pushing past spectators Felicity thanked the Lord she was not wearing a skirt that day. She was ready for action in lightweight pearl gray slacks and a loose cotton sweater. Her suede walking boots were low enough to be fine on the gravel on the way to the car. She was in the driver's seat and had the engine roaring before Sean quite got his door closed on the other side.

"Hang on, Uncle Sean," she said through clenched teeth as she threw the sedan into gear. From the way his head snapped back she knew Sean was unprepared for the takeoff. He had seen her drive, she realized, but had never seen the serious driving of which she was capable. It took her just five seconds to get the car up to sixty miles per hour. The AMG Hammer, as she had told him, was no Mercedes Benz. The builders used the Mercedes body because it was the only one that could take the stresses the car would be subjected to. She had handed over a Mercedes and a hundred and twenty thousand dollars for the conversion. On a test track she had pushed this machine up to one hundred eighty-six miles per hour and even at that speed it handled better than anything else on the road. She would reach the gunman in no time.

*   *   *   *   *

On the track, Morgan made his first serious run at O'Ryan's lead. They were riding in line. O'Ryan slid out from the center just a bit and Morgan saw his opening. He gunned the throttle and burst forward. In sixth gear at nearly twelve thousand rpm he was pushing one hundred seventy five miles per hour too near the curve, and O'Ryan was dropping in toward the edge. Morgan could see himself pushed off the edge into the center grass. That would end the race for him. He knew his bike gave him only one advantage. He had stability on the brakes and he would have to push it to the limit.

The crowd was on its feet when Morgan locked up his brakes. The back wheel jumped almost two inches off the deck but with cool efficiency, O'Ryan slid past in front of him. There was no contact and they were both still in the race.

*   *   *   *   *

The tree was small, the ground fairly level. Up among the leaves, Sean could see the barrel pointed toward the riders. Felicity drove straight toward the tree as if her life depended on it. Sean said a silent prayer when he realized she was not slowing down. The last minute fishtail tore up turf and weeds. The impact smacked Sean's head against the dashboard. The left quarter panel flexed in as the car bounced back from the trunk. A man wearing jeans and a golf shirt crashed to earth, stunned. Felicity was out of the car and leaping. She snatched up the rifle and pointed it at the fallen man.

"Go ahead, missy," the gunman said, his face crinkling in a smile. "It's just an air gun with rubber bullets."

"Just enough though, isn't it?" Felicity said. "No one would hear the quiet pop of this toy, but the bullet would slap the tire right out from under a motorcyclist in a deep curve."

"Very perceptive," he said, standing to brush himself off. "I'm afraid you'll never get to Timothy, though. He's clear on the other side of the track."

"Where?" Felicity asked.

"Screw you." As the words left his lips, a rough hand fell on the man's shoulder and spun him around into a devastating right hook. On his back, his eyes looked out of focus but Sean was pretty sure the gunman could see him well enough.

"Where?" was all the priest said.

"I can't tell you."

"I think you can," Sean said. He lifted the man by his collar and smacked his head into the tree. "Now."

The man pointed at a random pile of unused hay bales halfway around the track on a rise to the side of the race area. Again Felicity could just make out a gun barrel.

"The bastard really hedges his bets," she said. Then she grabbed her hat, planted her right knee in the sniper's crotch, and sprinted for her car.

"You'll have to drive, Uncle," Felicity said. "I'll have to hop out fast to stop that guy before the next turn."

Sean didn't argue, but pushed in behind the wheel and pulled away from the tree as soon as Felicity was inside. His driving wasn't pretty, but then, she knew that this car's handling was more sensitive than any other machine on the street. Felicity had attended a special seminar when she picked it up from the factory to teach her how to drive it. In Sean's hands it was a bucking bronco out of the old west, diving left and shooting right at the slightest touch of the steering wheel. He managed to man handle the beast in the right direction, barely keeping it under control.

The shortest way to Timothy's position was driving clockwise around the outside of the track. Felicity had switched seats because the passenger side faced the race. She could see the second gunman nested in the hay bales. He looked relaxed and comfortable there, with his rifle in a good supported position. On this curve he could fire one pellet at the right time to knock Morgan's bike out from under him. Morgan and his machine would roll off into the center of the track and O'Ryan could concentrate on winning the race.

Felicity popped her door latch as they approached their target. She hoped he would not hear them over the sound of the motorcycles but she saw him freeze in place for a second and new she would not be so lucky. The shooter spun around to face her as the big gray car rolled toward him. The passenger side door was already open. As the car thundered past, Felicity dived from it. She landed on the shooter like a swarm of hornets, scratching, spitting and cursing. He screamed at the onslaught and struggled to his feet. She grabbed at the rifle, somehow causing it to fire into the air. He swung he rifle's butt at her head but she ducked it, dropping into a deep crouch and gripped both his trouser cuffs. Before he knew what was happening, Felicity stood up, yanking his feet out from under him. He went over the bales backward, tumbling down the hill toward the racetrack.

Felicity collapsed on the hay bales, out of breath, praying she had done enough, soon enough, to keep Morgan alive.

*   *   *   *   *

Morgan had lost ground when O'Ryan cut him off, but he would not stay back. In that last deep turn he was forced to lay the fairing on the deck in order to stay on, and he took the corner at one hundred thirty miles per hour, but he passed another rider in the process. Now he rode on the Irishman's tail again, waiting for an opening. He would haunt O'Ryan, keeping his mind off the finish line because he knew Morgan was in his slipstream.

On the straightaway, O'Ryan shook a slim squib out of his glove. Only a superhuman rider or a fool would take his hand off the clutch at this velocity. O'Ryan did it, just for a second, long enough to squeeze hard on the pellet in his hand. He slowed, and for an instant Morgan was passing him on the inside. Then a thin jet of oil squirted from O'Ryan's glove. It splattered Morgan's face shield. O'Ryan roared away from his now blinded nemesis.

The greasy smear on Morgan's helmet was just enough to cloud his vision. He had fractions of a second to make a decision. Wiping his visor would only smear it worse. If he pulled over to clean it, he lost. If he slowed to a safe speed, he lost. If he tried to continue the race blinded as he was, he lost. But there had to be a winning alternative. There always is.

And Morgan found it. He would have to do what O'Ryan had done. He would have to do something only a fool or a superhuman rider would even attempt.

In the grandstand, Claudette jumped to her feet with her hands over her mouth. Marlene gasped and her gasp was taken up by the entire crowd. The crazy black rider had flipped his visor up. He was riding with his face exposed.

On his bike, Morgan knew that O'Ryan would assume he had dropped off, but he could not turn to see him. Morgan crouched low, trying to use the tiny windshield for protection. For racing purposes he liked it low and out of the way, but now he could not get behind it. He glanced up and down, seeing just enough to continue. His eyes watered from the wind blast and he could not escape it. He had to fly by instinct.

Morgan chose a course that seemed almost impossible, even to him. He would rely on his senses to tell him when he got too close to another rider or too close to falling. It was a radical use of his mysterious danger sense. He had no idea if it would work, but he knew this bike like a brother and was one with it. He could feel the road as if his feet were touching it, instead of wheels. He had a hundred and fifty horsepower between his knees and he milked it all at once.

"Come on," Morgan said, talking aloud to his mechanical steed. "You're the quirkiest motorcycle ever to circle a track and you've got something to prove too. Are you going to let an Irishman on a Japanese bike beat you? Come on. Give me the power and I'll take you out in style."

Morgan's stunt had given him an unanticipated edge. Other riders were giving him a wide berth, since it was obvious that only an idiot would stay on the track with his visor up. Morgan dived into the straightaway two lengths behind the "widow maker" and moved to the outside. His tires whined under him and he realized a slight sprinkle had started.

Fine, Morgan thought. *Let's just make this as impossible as it can be.* He was almost even with O'Ryan's bike as they approached the far end hairpin curve, La Source, just before the pits. Morgan wondered if anyone could see him coming or could guess what he planned to do. If so, he suspected that they were praying he would not try it.

He was wrong. Two hundred yards away, Felicity O'Brien stood up in front of the hay bales and shouted, "Take him out. Now!"

At the apex of the curve, the track was banked almost sixty degrees. Morgan leaned into it and let the Elf's radical steering setup take over. The motorcycle dived into the center, spearheading toward O'Ryan's front fork. Halfway there he realized the Irishman was accelerating out of the turn. His knee was on the deck and he was pulling away. Morgan yanked the handlebars and smoothed his path. He would pass behind the hunter's bike.

No!

The Elf fell into the inside lane for just an instant. Its front tire made the slightest contact with O'Ryan's rear wheel, nicking it, tread to tread. Leaning as he was, it was just enough. O'Ryan spun out, and rolled across the grass on the inside. Morgan's world went crazy and he was spun high into the air.

Tuck and roll, like they taught you in jump school. Pull in your arms, idiot! Pull up your knees.

His back hit the ground first, the leather taking the friction. Then his head smacked down, the helmet jarring his brain. Now everything was spinning. Then the world was still, but he was spinning. He wanted to throw up, but refused to. Then someone was shaking him.

"Where does it hurt?" the medic asked.

"Nowhere. Everywhere. Got to sit up. Where's O'Ryan?" The medic pushed him down, but he popped back up. There, only fifty yards away, sat O'Ryan. The medic by him was slapping his own ankle, signaling the area of O'Ryan's injury. That ankle was the least of his worries, Morgan knew. His chance of winning the race was over. There was no recovering the money he needed now. With two good legs he could not have run far enough or fast enough to escape this failure.

O'Ryan flipped his visor up and glared at Morgan. Wondering if he understood American hand signals, Morgan leaned over on his left arm, raised his right, and pointed his middle finger into the air in Ian O'Ryan's direction.

- 26 -

When Sean traveled to Paris on a rare vacation years ago, he had stood on that very spot, staring up at the magnificence of the cathedral known as Notre Dame. He was overwhelmed by the majesty of the historic structure. He viewed it with reverence. It never occurred to him back then that there might be a restaurant across from it.

"My compliments, my dear," Marlene Seagrave said, holding Sean's arm as the small group entered. "Tour D'Argent is one of the finest restaurants in the world. The height of French haute cuisine. When did you make these reservations?"

"The day we arrived on the continent," Felicity replied, easing Morgan between herself and Claudette using only smooth body language. The Maitres D' ushered them into the elevator, which looked to Morgan like an eighteenth century sedan chair.

Upstairs they were directed to their table. Even there, at the height of continental fashion, they attracted attention. Felicity, stately and aloof, strode through the room in a knee length dress. The skirt was black with a slit in the back that drew every man's attention to her long legs. The top half was white and sleeveless. Her hair hung long and flowing.

Two steps away, Claudette Christophe swept across the floor, a black pearl, icicle cool in a skin tight, mini length, sleeveless, backless, gold lame sheath.

Morgan beamed like the kid escorting the home coming queen to the prom. He seated both ladies, before sitting between them. He was pouring wine for all before he realized what he was doing.

"Felicity, dear, why is there already wine on our

table?" he asked. "Not just here, but open."

"I called ahead and ordered for everyone," she smiled. Claudette gave her a brief icy stare that everyone saw but Morgan ignored. "I wanted to save the men the hassle of trying to order from the French menu and I do know the cuisine here. At the same time I had them open the Beaujolais to let it breathe before we drank it."

"You've thought of everything, dear," Marlene said. Her hair was up in a chignon and her black coat dress looked more expensive than it needed to be. Her makeup was applied with an artist's touch. One would have to look hard to see any age difference between her and the other two women.

"So, lad, how does it feel to have the race behind you?" Sean asked. "You come out of it all with nothing but cuts and bruises."

"I credit that to protective clothing and a good helmet," Morgan answered. "The bad news is, our boy O'Ryan ended up with nothing but a sprained ankle."

"Haven't we grilled Morgan enough?" Felicity asked. "I thought the setting here would be enough to hold your attention."

"Actually, I've hardly noticed the restaurant, child," Sean said. "The view of the Seine's got me. At this height, it's just magical to look down at the barges drifting along. Indeed, the beauty of God is in even the simplest things."

Morgan was not as comfortable as Sean. He stuck a finger in his collar and twisted, trying to loosen it a little. He reflected that he was paying a price for this fine company. He had let Felicity dress him in a three piece suit, a glen plaid suit at that. The shirt was a kind of windowpane plaid in some pastel color. Worst of all, he was wearing a tie. A red tie. In fact, kind of a pinkish color. He resented Sean getting away with wearing his priest's black suit. That collar meant never having to wear a tie.

"Relax, darling," Claudette whispered, leaning close and rubbing his thigh under the table. "You'll feel better after you eat something. And I promise I'll get you out of those clothes just as soon as possible."

A waiter appeared and set a variety of containers on their table. The women reached for silverware but the men moved with reluctance.

"Eat," Felicity said. "It's cold lobster."

"Sorry," Morgan said, reaching into the appetizer. "Didn't recognize it without the shell." Morgan munched a piece, but didn't go near the strange goo that came with it. Sean, it seemed, was numb to embarrassment after a week traveling with Felicity, so he didn't hesitate to speak up.

"All right. Just what is that sauce?"

"It's called lagardere," Marlene said. "It's delicious. This lovely place has spent four hundred years, perfecting its sauces."

"Taste it, Uncle," Felicity said, leaning toward him. "All it is, is mayonnaise with some herbs and stuff mixed in."

"You have a way of making the finest things sound so common," Claudette said, but after Felicity's remark, Morgan tried it. She was right. It was good.

"I must say, this is the way to spend a vacation," Marlene said when the entree arrived, duckling bourdaloue with lemon. "I haven't had such a time in quite a while. An exciting race, and a landmark meal with the best of friends."

"Yes, too bad it has to come to an end," Morgan said. "We're taking Uncle Sean to the States with us right away. Can't hang around here too long. Until our boy Ian's taken care of by his old friends, we'll have to be real careful."

"So you're taking off with her, are you?" Claudette asked. "Another hit and run visit." Her voice was low, but her tone was not soft.

"Once we get things straight," Morgan said, "I'll be back to set things right here with the race team. And I'll need a place to stay."

"What if I am busy when you get back?"

"Then you'll un-busy," Morgan said.

"Ain't love grand?" Marlene asked, and everyone laughed.

*   *   *   *   *

Before dessert, the ladies excused themselves to powder their noses. When they were out of sight Morgan leaned over to Sean.

"Well, how'd you enjoy the duck dinner. Excuse me. Duckling."

"To tell the truth, it seemed a bit greasy to me lad. All in all, I prefer your turkey. One of the best things about America, I'm thinking."

"I'm with you there, Uncle Sean," Morgan said. "But, the place is nice and quiet, and the girls are loving it."

The women returned just in time for the flambéed peaches. At last Morgan was about to really enjoy something when the Maitres D' stepped up to their table. He stood close to Felicity and addressed her in a soft tone.

"Mademoiselle, there seems to be a small problem. Somehow, your automobile alarm has begun to sound. May we ask you to come downstairs and deactivate it?"

"We'd better both go," Morgan said, standing. He didn't think anyone could have arranged any trouble this soon, but it was better to be safe.

*   *   *   *   *

Morgan and Felicity rode the elevator to the ground floor and walked to the outdoor parking area. It was a beautiful night, the sky filled with stars and a gentle cool breeze rustling the tree tops. Paris had a background noise all its own that said people had places to go and were in a hurry to get there. Morgan stood near the car with arms folded while Felicity got in and turned off the alarm.

"Do you think someone was fooling around with the car," Felicity asked, "or did another patron just bump up against the door?"

"Who knows?" Morgan replied. "Either way, no harm done. I'm probably just being paranoid."

"You carrying?" Felicity asked on the way back to the restaurant.

"Of course."

"You are paranoid," Felicity said, her eyes laughing at him. She took his arm and hugged herself to him. It had been a long twisted path from her uncle asking for help in her office to the final nail in Ian O'Ryan's coffin just hours ago. She felt a little funny about dragging her only real friend into it all. Now she just wanted to feel close to him for a little while. Then she remembered the people waiting for them.

"She's jealous of me, you know."

"What are you talking about?" Morgan asked.

"Claudette thinks I'm the competition."

"Now you're being paranoid," Morgan said. "She knows the score between us. Maybe she just knows there's a space in me you can reach that nobody else can."

That comment put Felicity in a pensive mood but as they stepped into the exotic elevator, she adjusted her smile and released Morgan's arm. His expression also became more serious. They stepped out of the elevator as business partners. When they reached the table, only two people were there to greet them.

"Where's Marlene?" Felicity asked.

"Got a message," Claudette said. "Business. Right after you left."

Morgan waved the nearest waiter over. "Did you see Madame go to the telephone?"

"Yes sir," the waiter replied. "Then another gentleman escorted her to the elevator."

In that instant, the world changed for them. Felicity swallowed hard, but it was Morgan who spoke.

"Damn! Caught us napping." He took three seconds to think, then locked eyes with Felicity. "Wait three minutes and then follow me. Once you've got my direction, call the police. Stay with Uncle Sean at all times. And don't follow too close." With that he left.

* * * * *

On the street, Morgan asked himself how he could have been so stupid. Did he really think it would take O'Ryan more than a couple of hours to organize his revenge? Did he think the man rational enough to concern himself with saving his own hide? No, Morgan reminded himself, this guy was a loony tune. He would want to hurt Morgan even more than he wanted to live, and he would not want to wait.

"Over here," a voice called, and Morgan turned toward it. The man stood under a street light. He had the cold eyes of a street killer, the kind that come twelve for a dime in any European capitol. "Follow me," he said when Morgan came within range, and the two walked off. After four twisted blocks they came to a narrow alley. Inside, five men stood framed by the harsh light of the street lamp at Morgan's back. He recognized three of them from Orion House. The others, like his guide, were local talent. Marlene Seagrave stood against the left wall. Morgan's mouth set in a grim line.

"You've got me. Now you let the woman go, or it's a blood bath right here and now."

"We don't want the girl," the biggest Irishman said. "She was just the bait."

"Do you remember the way?" Morgan asked Marlene. She nodded her head. "Then go back to the restaurant. Tell Felicity where we are. We'll be gone by then. Tell her not to change plans. Got it? Good. Go."

Marlene scrambled away as quickly as she could.

Two of the hoods pointed guns at Morgan but nobody spoke until the clicking of her heels was lost in the night. The big man spoke first.

"Now, you take off the coat."

"Liam, isn't it?" Morgan asked as he obeyed. "Liam McCallister. We met at Orion House. I think I met your brother in an alley not far from here," Morgan raised his hands without being told. One of the gunmen came close to Morgan's side. From behind him, another man removed the pistol and big knife from their holsters. He carried no other weapons this night, because some idiot convinced him that combat boots were not acceptable in a fancy restaurant, and dress shoes could not hold his other two knives.

"Aye, I remember you," Liam said. "I wish me brother could be here to see you in our keep. Now we've got a car to put you in, and then we'll take you to the boss."

"Meaning O'Ryan, right?" Morgan asked with a smirk that flashed arrogance. "Didn't he tell you? I'm the reason your brother can't be here. He was trying to smuggle guns into your country so I put a bullet through his thick head on the Irish coast. I kind of thought you'd want to discuss that issue before we went to talk to O'Ryan. I mean, come on, don't you want to take a shot?"

"The boss said take him straight in," one of the other Irishmen said, but Morgan knew it didn't matter. He watched rage grow in McCallister's face until it was almost purple and the whites showed all around his eyes. He wanted to take care of this himself. And if a scrap started now, Morgan had a chance to escape. Even if he didn't he could prolong the action there until the police showed up.

- 27 -

Claudette, Sean and Felicity reached the street just in time to see Morgan turn a corner. Felicity hated letting him go off alone, but she knew he had the best idea of how to handle this situation. Their partnership had no real leader. When a situation came up, whichever of them was best qualified to deal with it just took the lead. She had to trust his instincts on this, just as she would trust her own.

"Claudette, could I get you to please go back inside and call the police?" Felicity asked.

"We're not going to just let him go off to the slaughter?"

"He knows what he's doing, lass," Sean said. "From what I've seen in the last few days, I pity the ones who try to take him anywhere he doesn't want to go."

"Well, you two can call the police and sit and wait," Claudette said in a sharp, accusatory tone. "It sounds to me like he's made a bad choice of friends. And partners, if that's what you are. I'm going after him."

Tossing her head, Claudette started across the street with all the haste that her clinging dress would allow. Felicity shook her head and turned to tell her uncle something. As her head moved, something caught her eye. It was a reflection of some type from the roof to the right across the way. Was that the glint of steel?

"How could I be so stupid?" Felicity said under her breath. It seemed obvious that O'Ryan knew them as a team. He would want revenge on both of them. He wouldn't take the chance that one could escape just because they split up. Did she really believe he would be so disorganized as to lead one of them away and not leave a trap for the other? And would his revenge not be more thorough if their friends suffered also?

All this flashed through her head in an instant. She might embarrass herself if she took the wrong action, but what was that against a life? Before Sean knew what was happening, Felicity had kicked off her shoes and was sprinting after Claudette. The Haitian girl was almost under the corner street lamp when the redhead hit her cross body. The two women landed in a tangle of long limbs.

Claudette already had a fist balled and aimed at Felicity's head when they heard a sound like a loud cough and a spider web crack grew on the windshield of the car they were leaning against. Felicity looked up and the sound repeated itself. A hole appeared in the car's fender, two inches from her head. Claudette screeched in terror, which seemed normal for a person who realizes that someone is shooting at them. A moment later it must have dawned on her that that Felicity had saved her.

"Merci," Claudette said. "I guess I owe you my life."

"Thank me after we're out of this," Felicity answered. She knew they were on a bull's-eye, as surely as if they were a pair of ducks chatting with a decoy. There was no way for them to get to better cover. And long before any gendarmes could arrive the sniper on the roof would hit one of them, or worse, hit the gas tank of the car they were hiding behind. It would go up and take them with it. Worst of all, if she died who would get after Morgan to save him from that madman who set the traps they had fallen into?

- 28 -

Morgan stepped further into the alley and put his fists up. Everyone shifted positions so that three men stood behind him, including both gunmen. Good. He needed them close together.

McCallister roared like a maddened bull and charged. Morgan ducked under a roundhouse right and snapped two jabs into McCallister's face. This guy would be no trouble if Morgan could keep the other five out of it. Liam put a left and then a right into Morgan's upraised guard. Morgan feinted with his left, then crouched and lifted a right hook into Liam's stomach.

"Is that all you got?" the big Irishman asked. He put it all behind a hard right hand that caught Morgan on the point of his chin. Morgan flew back with the impact, harder than anyone in the alley expected. He crashed into one of the gunmen, sending a pistol sailing through the air.

"Hold him," McCallister said. The former gun holder grabbed Morgan's left arm and one of the others grabbed his right. Liam stepped in and smashed his jaw with a left. The follow-up right almost took Morgan's head off. He clenched his teeth against the next punch. When it came he yanked his arms into his chest and snapped free of the two men holding him. Now he would see what the competition was.

One of the thugs put an arm around his throat. Morgan pulled him into a shoulder throw that landed him on the only man with a gun out. Now it was a fight.

Morgan dived into the center of the group, knowing he had to use their numbers against them. An edge of the hand chop to the throat put one Irishman down until further notice. He blocked a clumsy punch and snapped a middle knuckle into a Frenchman's temple. He wouldn't be getting up. A stamp kick to the knee took another out of the fight.

That quickly it became a one on one battle. McCallister saw it all, and now had doubts. Then he spotted Morgan's knife where one of his men had dropped it, and snatched it up.

"This is a fine blade, boy," McCallister said. "Let's see if it'll carve you up." He held the knife like a seasoned fighter. The seven inch blade made small circles out in front of him, waiting to slash Morgan's stomach. In response, Morgan unbuckled his belt and pulled it from his slacks. He wrapped each end around a hand and stood with it taut in front of him.

"Come on with it." Morgan said it softly, smiling. "I think it's about time we ended this." The pair circled, until Morgan's back was to the rear of the alley. McCallister slashed at his midsection, but he stepped back out of the way. The second slash made Morgan leap back to avoid the blade. Now he stood just inches in front of the wall. This would have to be it.

Sensing victory, Liam McCallister lunged forward. The point of Morgan's Randall Model number one fighting knife arced toward its owner's navel. Morgan's left fist rose, snapping his belt taut and almost vertical. The belt hit the outside of McCallister's wrist and his arm was slipped past Morgan's body, to Morgan's right.

Morgan took a long step forward with his right foot. Now the two men were almost back to back and the belt slipped naturally around McCallister 's throat, over Morgan's right shoulder. Morgan crouched and snapped his hips upward. McCallister teetered on the fulcrum of Morgan's back and then flipped through the air. He landed with a thump, face down in front of Morgan, who quickly turned as he planted his right knee high on Liam's back.

"Say hello to your brother for me," Morgan said. Then he whipped his head back and heaved with all his strength. The belt slid up to Liam's jaw, and there was a loud crack from the man's neck.

Morgan closed his eyes for an instant when he snapped Liam's spine. When he opened them, he saw a man in the darkness across the alley pointing a gun at him. Morgan had flipped another man into this one, but he appeared to have shaken the cobwebs out of his brain while Morgan was busy killing McCallister. He would have come to, to see his partners scattered around the alley and maybe in time to see McCallister flying over Morgan's back. No doubt he would have concluded that Morgan was too dangerous to take prisoner. That meant Morgan would need to move fast to stay alive. He braced for a sprint out of the alley to the street. There he could lose himself. He stood and launched himself forward.

And his foot slipped.

Damn these slippery soled dress shoes, Morgan thought as his foot went out from under him. He heard a snub nosed pistol's blast, felt a thirty-eight caliber punch in his left thigh. He fell as the gunman stirred his nearest partner, the one Morgan had thrown. While he held the gun on Morgan, the other man dived on Morgan's back. Morgan felt a cosh or blackjack smack against his head. He managed to bring an elbow up into the hitter's gut before the second blow. Then he lay still.

*   *   *   *   *

His head still pounding, thug rolled off Morgan's back, dropping his blackjack beside him.

"This guy's got to have the hardest head in the world," the assailant said. "Let's get the others and get out of here."

"I don't know," the gunman said. "I think everybody else is dead."

"I ain't," a voice called from the side. "I think the bastard broke my knee. I'd like to kill him now, but the boss wants him alive. You two pick him up and get him in the car, then help me in. Nobody else is in any condition to follow."

Leaving their three friends where they lay, the two who brought Morgan down carried him to a van, and then returned to help their injured partner to it. Their tires squealed as the van shot off into the night. The fight and the escape all took place before any of the local citizens felt the need to call the police.

- *29* -

Sean prayed for deliverance for himself and the two women across the street. They were pinned down by a sniper on the roof of a nearby building, while he stood helpless in the doorway of the restaurant they had just left. He knew it was just a matter of time before the gunman got the range and killed them both if not for some intervention.

*   *   *   *   *

Above, on the roof in question, two men lay prone at the edge. One held binoculars focused on two women hiding behind a car. The other looked through the scope of a long bolt action rifle. The rifle was on a bipod, evidence that they had had plenty of time to set up their ambush. They figured by now the black man was en route to their boss O'Ryan for a special punishment. They simply needed to dispatch the girl, and if convenient, her three friends. So they decided to just delay these two girls until the third came into view.

"There she is," the spotter said when Marlene Seagrave rounded the last corner. She was out of breath, but when she saw the other two on the ground she tried to run to them. She was slow, though, and an excellent target. Killing her would bring the other two skirts into view for sure. The sniper was certain he would not miss again.

"Not very sporting, gentlemen," a voice said behind the killers. It was a voice as cool as a tomb and just about as comforting. The spotter spun, reaching for the gun in his shoulder holster. The newcomer put a nine millimeter slug between his eyes. The other man leaped to his feet and dived at the tall man.

*　*　*　*　*

"Get down!" Felicity shouted as Marlene came into view. Marlene must have heard her words but missed intent because instead of diving for cover she bent as low as she comfortably could and kept walking until she reached the car the other two were lying beside. Felicity was surprised she made it alive.

"What's going on?" Marlene asked.

"I'm not sure any more," Felicity said. She looked up toward the spot where the sniper had been just in time to see a human form separate from the roof. As he dropped she followed him with her eyes and tracked him by his screaming all the way to the street.

"The danger seems to be over," Felicity said, standing. She walked, unhurried, to where the fallen man lay. She stared down at his face frozen in fear. One of his legs was bent up under him, and she had no doubt that he was quite dead. She didn't recognize him. A local hire, she assumed, of O'Ryan's. One way or another, she and Morgan were certainly to blame for a serious depletion of his work force.

A small crowd began to gather around the corpse. Sean stood close to Felicity, and Marlene clung to her hand. Claudette stood by the priest muttering something low in French. Sean may have mistaken it for a prayer, but Felicity knew Claudette was commending the dead man's soul to hell.

"Are you all right?"

Felicity knew that smooth, accentless voice. She turned and stared into the tall man's ice blue eyes. He wore a light blue suit, perhaps the only type he ever wore. He did not smile, he rarely did, but she was glad to see him.

"Paul. Where did you come from?" Felicity asked. "Are you responsible for this?"

"Mister Stark called me about twenty-four hours ago. He told me you might be in some danger. He was right. And yes, I am responsible."

Felicity rested a hand against Paul's arm and smiled. "Well, don't misunderstand. I certainly am glad to see you, and you do have a knack for taking direct action at the right time, but didn't you see Morgan come out?"

"Yes."

"Couldn't you see he was walking into a trap?" she asked.

"Of course."

"Well then, why didn't you follow him?" Felicity asked, looking up into his eyes. "He might be dead now."

"Mister Stark's orders were to watch you," Paul said. He turned as he heard a siren approaching. "I should not be on hand for the police to question. I'll be at your apartment when you're finished talking to them. Good night." Paul faded into the crowd, and Felicity knew it was no use looking for him. The ability to disappear was one of his strengths. As she watched the police approaching she felt a tug on her sleeve.

"Who was that spook?" Claudette asked.

Marlene stepped close to answer. "Paul used to work for my husband. He was a loyal employee who did, er, odd jobs."

"Now he works for Stark and O'Brien," Felicity said. "Morgan uses him for courier work, mostly. He's totally professional and can be trusted with anything. He just saved our lives. But there will be no mention of him to these gentlemen." Felicity pointed at the police cars pulling up and smiled as the irony hit her. "You know, all my life I've been grateful for this universal truth, until today."

"And just what truth would that be?" Sean asked.

"The fact that the police, without exception, arrive on the scene too late."

- 30 -

Despite the pounding at the back of his skull, Morgan kept his eyes closed after he regained consciousness. He wanted to get a feel for his situation before he faced it.

He was seated, naked but for his underwear. He could feel a bandage around his left thigh. The front of his body was dripping with sweat. The wetness did not give him any hope of sliding out of the wire holding his wrists to the wooden chair's arms. In fact, the moisture caused his wrists to chafe painfully. The wires holding his ankles to the heavy chair's front legs cut into him in the same way.

As perspiration dripped from his bowed head to his legs, he realized the heat was coming from in front of him. The smell of a wood fire told him that he was facing a fireplace. It accentuated the acrid taste in his mouth. He fought to keep his dinner in its place. Nausea, he knew, was not unusual after being knocked unconscious.

His ears brought him three messages. First, the crackling in front of him confirmed the fireplace. From his left came the sound of sea gulls, and waves crashing, but no voices. That put him on a deserted area of coastline. The only other sound in the room was the rhythmic click of boot heels. Someone was pacing in the room. It was not hard to guess who that impatient person was.

Morgan let his eyes slide open and looked up. Staring into Ian O'Ryan's red flecked, hate filled eyes, Morgan found that not all the perspiration on his brow was due to the heat.

"At last," O'Ryan said. "The hunter has captured his

elusive quarry. It's about time you were awake. The sun's well up." He stood framed by the glow of the fire behind him in riding pants and boots, bare-chested. The same matted hair that stood on his shoulders rose up again on his forearms. His body also glistened with sweat and for the first time Morgan could sense the aura of power Felicity had felt before. His florid face gleamed with rage. Morgan forced calm into his voice.

"So?" Morgan asked. "You haven't killed me yet?"

"Killed you?" O'Ryan screeched the words, his brogue so thick Morgan could barely understand him. "You haven't suffered yet. Not half. You cost me the race, me fortune, and me position with the people I work with, bucko. Now me backers, they're going to think I embezzled their money. They'll think I misused me funds. Me career's over and me life's in jeopardy to boot. You're going to hurt for that, you bastard, you're going to hurt bad. But before I hurt you, I want to know, I got to know. Why?"

"Well, it's like this," Morgan said, looking into those fevered eyes. "You tried to hurt a man who couldn't really defend himself against a guy like you. And he happened to be my adopted uncle. See, that little Irish village matters to him. We never moved against you until you tried to blow him up. By the way, where are we now? There's nothing like this in Glendalough."

"You like me little chateau?" O'Ryan's pacing took him near a window. "We're on a wee island off the French coast. Rather isolated. Nice beaches. Spectacular view. And plenty of privacy. A suitable final resting place. Perhaps I'll feed you to the lobsters."

"I still don't get it," Morgan said. "You plan to talk my ears off, or torture me just for fun, or what?"

"Oh, no, this is business, lad," O'Ryan said through a too-big grin, "and it'll be you who's doing the talking soon. You're going to give me something to barter for me life with, lad. A bit of information."

"What do I know that's worth anything to you?"

"Did you expect me to be buying that malarkey about adopted kith and kin?" O'Ryan spat out the window. "Nobody takes a risk like that as a favor, boy. You're working for somebody, and I mean to know who. MI-5? The American CIA? Interpol, maybe? No matter. All such outfits got secrets. You know some of them, and I'll know them too soon."

"Look, this is stupid," Morgan said. "I don't know shit that could be of use to you. Why don't you just give me a shot of pentathol or something and satisfy yourself of the truth?"

"Why?" O'Ryan said, stepping close. "Cause the old fashioned way is so much more bloody fun." The right cross came out of nowhere and lifted Morgan an inch off the chair. Blue spots danced in front of his eyes. O'Ryan was as strong as a draft horse. If this was today's menu, Morgan had already had enough. He heaved himself forward with everything he had and tipped the chair maybe an inch forward. A fist like a five pound ham rocked him back. O'Ryan laughed, a big booming guffaw.

"Now that chair, that's an antique, it is. Solid oak and must weigh as much as you do. You can't shake it, lad. Just sit tight and take your lumps." This time Morgan saw it coming and tensed for it. Still, that piston-like right arm pumped a blow into his stomach that forced the breath out of him.

"Anytime you'd like to talk about your bosses," O'Ryan said, "we can quit this."

"S'matter, ugly?" Morgan slurred through thick lips. "You tired already?" O'Ryan's bellow of rage shook the house, and three more hammering punches sent Morgan spinning into oblivion.

- 31 -

A hot breeze whipped into the alley, flipping Felicity's hair. She knelt to survey the damage. The inventory included a crushed larynx. One temple caved in. The big man with a broken neck. Yep, she had no doubt.

"It's Morgan's work all right," she said, looking up. "It must have been one hell of a war."

It had taken nearly five hours and three telephone calls to straighten things out with the gendarmes. She and her friends had endured a frustrating round of questioning before breaking free from the local investigators. On their way back to her car Marlene pulled her aside.

"I can get us back to where they jumped Morgan. Maybe it's not too late."

"It's temping Marlene, it really is, but the locals would follow us, and if there was anything there they'd block us from seeing any evidence that might help us find him."

"Then what do we do?" Claudette asked, joining the other two girls. "We can't just abandon him. He could be in terrible danger. Every minute counts."

Frustrated, Felicity turned to Claudette with a palm raised to quiet Sean on one side and Marlene on the other. "Look, I know what you're all thinking but here's the facts. Either he's dead or he isn't. And we all know that Morgan's a damned hard fellow to kill. If I can get at the last place where Marlene saw him I might be able to trace his movements. But going there now won't help us. I need a minute to think and we need a base of operations where we know trouble isn't waiting for us."

Without a second's hesitation, Claudette said, "Father Sullivan and Mrs. Seagrave, please follow me to my car. Miss O'Brien, you bring your car around behind mine and follow me to my flat. Now, what else?"

"I think that does it right now."

"Good," Claudette said, raising one index finger so her nail hung in the spot exactly between her eyes and Felicity's. "I have money, information and connections. We use what is needed and we do whatever we must. We find my man and we bring him back whole. Comprendez-vous?"

"Je comprend," Felicity said. Then she sprinted to her car and fired it up. She new Claudette didn't quite trust her but very much wanted to. And her mention of their resources had jogged a useful memory. She had connections, but perhaps not the right ones. Felicity might. As she drove she picked up her car phone and pushed buttons for a number she shouldn't have. The voice on the other end claimed to be the night operator for an export company.

"Are you recording?" Felicity asked.

"I beg your pardon?"

"Just tape it and trace it, kid. My name is Felicity O'Brien. You've got a field agent who was in Ireland recently who uses Mr. Grey as his cover name. He contacted me, and he could have a security problem if I don't hear from him in the next hour or so. Pass the message."

Grey had called her back before they reached Claudette's apartment. He was surprised that she had known how to reach him, and more surprised that she chose to. She laid out the situation as well as she dared on an unsecured line. She asked if he could influence the Paris police to grant her even limited access to what she knew would be a crime scene soon. Grey turned out to be more influential than she expected. He called the Deuxieme Bureau, French Intelligence. When that organization reached the Parisian Gendarmerie, problems seemed to vanish. She received a phone call from a very polite inspector who made it clear that she could have anything she wanted and apologized for the trouble. Felicity asked that the scene of the kidnapping, once discovered, remain untouched until thirty minutes after dawn.

She had come on the scene at first light with Marlene, Claudette and her Uncle in tow. When she parked, Paul appeared in his signature light blue suit and opened the door. She had refused to look surprised. He stood guard at the alley's entrance while she examined the bodies there. She wore a white linen skirt, but beneath it, a black leotard and tights showed off the perfect symmetry of her legs while she knelt by a body. She wore black, crepe soled shoes and a wide green ribbon held her hair in place. For her, this was not casual attire but rather, her working clothes.

"If Morgan was dead he'd be here," she said, while she walked back to the sidewalk. "If he escaped, we'd have heard from him. So they must have hauled him away."

"Yes," Paul said, "but to where?"

Felicity did not have the answer. In the past, her psychic link with him allowed her to home in on Morgan but she was getting nothing now. He must be too far away. She would have to rely on her wits. She had nothing to go on, except maybe these corpses.

"These two are from Eire," she said to herself.

"How can you know?" Paul asked.

"It's obvious," she said. "Just from their faces, the shape of their heads, their clothes. And look at this one's shoes." She was crouching on her haunches again. "That's not street dirt. This is rocky soil. In fact, it looks like beach sand. It even has a salty smell. He must have been on the coast recently. A beach. Or an island. A nice, lonely island to hold his captive. Hold him, or..."

Felicity shook her head to clear it, spun and ran past Paul out of the alley. She stopped at the curb and stared into the gutter. She had to stay in control.

Shadows were long and deep in the first light. But the black smear she saw on the street was not a shadow. It was tire tracks. Someone had left in such a hurry, they literally burned rubber. The marks pointed due west. A deception? No, they were in too much of a hurry to take off on an evasive course.

"So we know which way they went," she said, again to the air.

"That's some help," Claudette said.

"Still with us?" Felicity asked

"I won't leave without knowing what happened to Morgan." Claudette's voice was strained, almost choked off. Felicity looked at her and saw that her eyes were brimming with moisture. She was not conscious of chewing her lower lip. Felicity had to reach out to her. She stepped close.

"You do care about him, don't you?" she said in a voice low enough that no one else could hear. Claudette's head rolled forward, so their foreheads touched. She shivered, but refused to sniffle.

"We may not be your idea of a couple, but..." Claudette seemed lost for words for a second, then said "I guess we have an unusual relationship."

"Yeah." Felicity's smile was soft. "Us too. But it's not like yours. In a way I envy you." During a moment of stillness, the two women stood in their own private world. Then Felicity said, "Claudette, you're the only one here who knows France. How far is the coast from here, going west?"

"You'd go northwest to get to the ocean from here, maybe a hundred and fifty kilometers," Claudette replied, stepping back. "Due west, it's more like two hundred fifty kilometers to la cote D'emeraude."

"The what?" The shock in Felicity's voice made everyone turn to her.

"La cote D'emeraude. That's what the locals call it," Claudette said. "In English, the Emerald Coast." Right then Felicity knew, with a sudden leap of intuition, that

that was it. Ian O'Ryan, with his immense ego, would find the one place in this country that sounded Irish and settle in there. He would think it appropriate to kill Morgan there.

"This emerald coast, is it quiet?" Felicity asked.

"It's fairly well populated," Claudette answered, "but there are several small islands in the gulf of Saint Malo. They can be pretty isolated."

"It has to be," Felicity said. Then she looked around. Claudette, Sean, and even Marlene looked anxious for some action. They looked like a posse in an old Western movie, eager to get on the trail. Things were getting too crowded. She knew that, as O'Ryan said weeks ago, she needed to get the non-players off the green. She pulled her uncle aside. "Uncle Sean," she said, "I need to ask a favor. I know you want to help, but I can't do what I have to do with all these amateurs hanging about. It was a mistake bringing everyone here. Would you please get a taxi and take the girls back to Claudette's place? I still don't think my flat is safe."

"Can't the police handle this?" Sean asked. "He could kill you too."

"Me too?" Felicity said. "Morgan's not dead, Uncle. Oh, that's not what you meant, is it? I can see it in your eyes."

"No, child," Sean looked close to tears himself, and she knew it wasn't for Morgan. "He begged me not to tell you, but now, well, he might not be able to."

"Uncle Sean, talk sense"

"It was when the boy and me went through O'Ryan's newspaper clippings." Sean looked at the street between his shoes. "We saw...them." Felicity's brows knit together in confusion for a second. Then it flashed into her mind as if she could read her uncle's thoughts.

"Momma and Papa. It's them, isn't it?"

"They were the victims of his first bomb," Sean said, hanging his head. Her mind rushed back into the past, then hurtled forward, back to the present danger. Her eyes bulged and she forgot to breathe until her ribs ached. Of course. Morgan must have seen the clipping. He saw it and hid it from her. He wanted to kill O'Ryan, to give her that, O'Ryan's death, as payment for her parents' death. Now he might be added to O'Ryan's score instead.

She pulled her keys from her small purse and handed them to Sean. She whispered her button lock's number combination, gave him a peck on the cheek and a fierce hug. Then she slapped Paul on the arm and sprinted for the car. He jumped in after her, but had not quite closed the door before the car squealed away from the curb.

"Where to, Miss O'Brien?" Paul asked, watching the others recede in the side mirror.

"That-a-way," she replied. "The coast. An island maybe. I'll know when I get there." Paul nodded, maintaining his deadpan expression. They rode in silence, while Felicity got her bearings. She found herself on an autoroute pointed at Cherbourg. She slid into the fast lane and opened the throttle. When she tore into a long straightaway, Paul glanced at the speedometer.

"Almost three hundred kilometers per hour," he said. "That will give us the coast in not much over an hour."

"Surprised to see a Mercedes moving this fast?"

"A little," Paul said. "But I've learned not to take things at face value. You are obviously a competent driver." He settled back and relaxed, which Felicity found oddly gratifying.

Felicity drove with grim determination and total concentration. Her knuckles were white on the wheel, her teeth bared. She was glad she was driving away from the sun, so she could keep the hammer down without fear of being blinded. At these speeds she chose not to turn on any music so they traveled in silence, which began to eat at her after a while. Instead of words coming from the passenger side she heard metal clicking and glanced over at her seat mate. Paul had his gun apart on a handkerchief on his lap, apparently cleaning it.

"You are the quietest man I've ever seen," she said.

"Yes ma'am."

"That looks a little like Morgan's gun," she said.

"At a quick glance I suppose," Paul said in a neutral tone that made her observation neither a good one or a mistake. "Mister Stark carries a Browning Hi-power. I use a Sig-Sauer Model P-226. A shade lighter. Two more rounds in the magazine."

"Uh-huh," she nodded. "I recognize it. You know when I met you, you were pointing that thing in my face. Of course, you kept your friends from doing nasty things to me, and you dumped me out of the vehicle when you could have killed me. I appreciate all that, I guess. But still..."

"Still, no one likes having a gun pointed in their face. I understand."

"How do you feel about working for Morgan and me?" Felicity asked.

"I respect Mister Stark. You need to work for someone you respect. And you saved my life. I owe you loyalty. It is good to work for someone you can be loyal to."

"Do you have any family Paul?" Felicity asked, going into a racing turn and downshifting.

"None." Paul reassembled his gun and holstered it. There was a pause, where normally Felicity would expect the other person to pick up the conversation. Then she sighed.

"Has anyone ever told you, you talk too much?" she asked. There was another pause while Paul appeared to consider her question before giving his answer.

"No."

Felicity chuckled, and Paul even gave a small smile.

- 32 -

Morgan's eyes fluttered open. An incredibly loud, cheap alarm clock seemed to be going off in the back of his head. As he looked up, O'Ryan strode across the room and whipped his knuckles around in a back hand slap that twisted Morgan's neck around to the breaking point. He held his head down and watched tiny red drops hitting his bare legs. Blood was dripping from his nose and mouth. He looked up again, to see his torturer drinking from a carafe of water. When he spoke, Morgan's voice held a raspy croaking sound.

"You'd better kill me," Morgan said, "or sure as hell I'll kill you."

"Now, now, lad," O'Ryan said, smiling with those oversized teeth. "You're in no position to threaten. Once you tell me who it is you work for and some of their secrets, I'll end this quick and painless."

Morgan looked at the stairs to his right at the far end of the house. Was anyone else here? Someone he could appeal to?

"You're as stupid as you look," Morgan said. "You and your people should be running, hiding, saving your own necks from whoever you got your money from. You can bet they're not too happy with you right now."

"No need to be so loud, my stubborn friend." O'Ryan stepped in and with a casual movement smashed a left hook into Morgan's ribs. "There's no one else about. Just you and me."

Morgan glanced out the open windows on his left, and this time, O'Ryan guessed his thoughts.

"The island's small, lad, and all mine. There's no one about for miles. You might just as well talk to me and let us end this."

"I'm talking, but you ain't listening," Morgan said through his teeth. "I work for me." This brought a hard right to the jaw, which Morgan rolled with as best he could.

"Haven't you learned anything you fool?" O'Ryan screamed so close to Morgan that he felt drops of spittle against his face. Morgan mouthed words. O'Ryan picked up the carafe and poured water on Morgan's upturned face. Opening his mouth, he managed to swallow enough to make his voice function again. His face burned from several small cuts. Moving his mouth hurt, but his fighting heart would not let him stay quiet.

"Sure. I've learned a lot from this, you ignorant Mick, but you don't have the guts to hear it." That remark halted a punch in mid-swing.

"Like what, nigger?"

Morgan took a deep breath. It always came to that, didn't it?

"I'll tell you what," Morgan said. "I learned what the difference really is between a terrorist and a mercenary."

"Well that's obvious," O'Ryan said. "Your kind works for money. Me and mine work for a cause."

"Bullshit," Morgan said. "You're only in trouble now because the money stopped. And when the money stopped, the terrorist activity stopped. The only real difference is, your kind doesn't play by any kind of rules."

O'Ryan rocked with laughter. "Rules? What kind of rules can killers follow? We're hunters boy, the both of us. Just the same."

"You're wrong, Ian," Morgan said. "Not the same. You hunt like a rabid wolf. Anything in your path dies. Every merc I ever met worth a damn followed the same code. There's things you just don't do." He spat blood on the floor and continued. "You don't work for commies. You don't attack your own country. You never betray a cause. And the highest point of honor, you don't make war on noncombatants."

"Honor!" O'Ryan shouted. "That's a word children use. It ain't about honor. It's about power, bucko. My kind gets it. Your kind gets this." The next punch rocked Morgan back and chipped a tooth.

"You might think that makes you king shit the stinking wonder," Morgan said, his speech slurred, "but it won't get shit out of me. Including respect. Especially respect. I'm still the man you had to tie up to beat. You don't have the guts to cut me loose and face me man to man. And in my last act on earth, I'll spit in your face."

O'Ryan roared with anger. His eyes were white rimmed saucers and a trail of spittle dripped from the edge of his mouth. His rage filled the room, but Morgan's stare cut right through it to O'Ryan's heart. Morgan was beaten, but he was not defeated, and O'Ryan could not stand that. His rage burst from him in one tremendous left cross that turned Morgan and the chair around toward the window. Now, O'Ryan was shrieking.

** "I'll get it all out of you, lad," O'Ryan said. "I'll make you talk and then you'll be begging me to let you die." Morgan's head pulsed with pain as he turned it to follow O'Ryan's movements. His neck ached with the twisting and his mind was numb and spongy. Through the haze he saw O'Ryan reach around to the fireplace. He lifted a poker from it, and Morgan could see its tip glowing white hot. Even the upcurved side point, used for turning wood, glowed. It must have been in the fire all morning. Now O'Ryan stalked toward him with this fearsome weapon. As O'Ryan came around to block the sunlight coming in through the window Morgan's mouth became dry, but he would not break eye contact with his enemy.

"Now, big man, let us hear your courage," O'Ryan said through clenched teeth. He pressed the poker's point against Morgan's right shoulder. Morgan's entire body contracted, arching backward in agony. He screamed louder than he believed he could, and his body shuddered with pain. He smelled the broiled flesh inches from his face and prayed for unconsciousness to take him.

- 33 -

Felicity drove to the coast road, then along the coast of the gulf for a short time. She stopped when she sighted a fisherman with a small motorboat. She leaped from the car, very agitated, displaying a nervous jerkiness she seldom felt and never let anyone see.

"He's out there," she said, pacing in circles, trying to sound rational and pointing to the sea. "He's out there, I can feel it. Oh, God, we can't be too late."

Then she ran down to the rugged, rocky beach. It looked almost identical to the coast where just days earlier she watched Morgan make an impossible rifle shot, then repeat it. She ran to the fisherman and told him in French she needed his boat. Then she pulled out his hand and laid a twenty franc note into it. When he gave her a quizzical look she added another bill, and then another, and kept going. After each one, she looked into his eyes. At a certain point he closed his hand and waved her to the boat. She bounded in, and it was all Paul could do to follow. In seconds they were buzzing out to sea.

The motor was small and relatively quiet. Felicity sat in the front of the boat, as if smelling the sea air for direction. The vessel was a little less than ten feet long, and they were in rough water for such a small craft. Both riders were getting wet, but Felicity didn't care and from all appearances neither did Paul. Felicity pointed after a time and Paul turned left. She turned to see that they were beyond sight of shore, then swiveled back to turn her face into the sharp scent of the salt spray. They were four or five miles out when she pointed another small course correction. After a few minutes of silent sailing, she turned to him.

"I know where he is, you know."

Paul nodded.

"You believe me?"

"Yes," Paul said.

"Why?"

"Because you're sure," he replied. At that moment they heard a scream, like that of a man being flayed alive. It chilled Felicity to her bones. Did her companion feel it? If so, it didn't show on his face. Still, he steered toward the source of the sound without being told.

They were within a quarter mile of the island when they heard the scream. Three minutes later, Paul docked the boat on the end of the beach away from the only chateau. He stepped into the water to pull the boat about halfway up onto the beach. Then he drew his pistol and marched toward the small house with sure, measured tread. His face betrayed a hint of surprise when Felicity stepped in front of him.

"You stay here," she said. "I go."

"No."

"Yes," Felicity said, looking into those icy eyes. "I know how to do this. I'll get up there and get the layout. You wait five minutes, then follow. Make noise. When the bad guys come looking for you, lay low. I'll get to Morgan and get him out. Once I've got him out of the house, then you handle it any way you want. Okay?"

After a pause, Paul said, "Yes, ma'am." He looked at his watch. She turned and sprinted toward the chateau. The ground was the same rocky soil she had taken from a dead man's shoes in a Paris alley. It supported a few trees separated by a thick scrub growth. A sparse grass covered the ground on three sides of the chateau. The house itself was small and unassuming, hand built of stone in a bygone era. It stood two stories high on the crest of a small hill. Felicity figured it for no more than eight or ten rooms.

She circled to the back of the chateau and surveyed the area. Not a sign of life, or a pulse of danger within.

O'Ryan must have assumed no one could find Morgan. Well, she was certain that he would regret that bonehead move before too long.

Still not quite confident, Felicity walked up to the back of the house. This was just too easy. The stones offered convenient hand and foot holds. In less than three minutes she clambered up the wall and slid into an open window. After crouching on the hallway floor for a full minute she made a slow, painstaking exploration of the upper level, to convince herself there really was no one there.

The heat inside was oppressive, stifling. She stepped to the stairwell. It was like walking into a chimney flu. Just a few steps down she could see the lower room around a corner on the flight of stairs. She was looking at a fireplace which, for some unknown reason, was lit. That wall was all she could see. She could hear the heavy panting of a haggard voice. No, closer listening told her there were two men down there, both with labored breathing.

Out of habit, Felicity strung a wire across the stairs, a precaution to slow down any pursuers. Then she crept downward on her belly, one step at a time, like a cobra exploring a new rabbit warren. She froze when a choking cough verified for her that one of the men was Morgan. Then she saw a hand covered with red hair reach for the handle of a poker that lay in the fire. It was Ian O'Ryan, she knew, and she could only imagine one use for the red hot end of that vicious looking implement. She crept down until she was staring between the uprights supporting the banister, looking at O'Ryan's naked hairy back.

O'Ryan grabbed Morgan's knee and yanked him around so that he faced the fireplace, giving Felicity a three-quarter view of his face that wrenched her heart. He looked dazed, on the very edge of consciousness, but he reacted to the heat approaching his face. Only his left eye would open. He focused it on O'Ryan who sneered down at him.

"You've got two bloody great welts there, lad," O'Ryan said. "Your shoulders'll make you pretty easy to identify, and I'm betting that's not good in your line of work. Don't you get it yet? You're nothing but a wee bairn to me. Why don't you do yourself a favor and talk?"

"I'll talk..." Morgan gasped, coughed up a blob of blood, and continued. "I'll talk...to you...when we meet again...in hell."

"Now, that's no attitude," O'Ryan said with a sick chuckle. "Let's see what happens when this hot poker slides up against your neck, eh?"

"No!" Felicity's shout from the stairs made O'Ryan spin as if a ghost had tapped him on the shoulder. "Stand away from him, you great bloody bastard." As she got to her feet she knew the tempting sight she presented. Here stood a mere slip of a girl, alone, unarmed, with nothing but her teeth and nails to fight with.

"What a pleasant surprise," O'Ryan said. "Now, lad, you'll have to watch the girl die before you go." O'Ryan darted forward, and Felicity sprang back up the stairs. O'Ryan swung the poker in a wide arc, cleaving her shadow, but missing her flesh. Felicity danced up steps, a spirit barely in touch with the ground. O'Ryan swung the poker back around as he stumbled forward. The hot point glanced off the banister, leaving a black mark.

When the girl reached the top of the stairs she turned. O'Ryan jumped up three steps to reach her and, to her horror, jumped her wire. He lunged forward, holding the poker like a flaming sword. For the first time Felicity's fear surfaced. She twisted, and the point jabbed past her right breast to stick in the wall at the top of the stairs.

Felicity wished briefly that Paul was less obedient as she kicked at O'Ryan's left ankle. He bellowed his pain and rage as the sprained ankle gave way and she slid past him. If she could reach the bottom of the stairs and lead O'Ryan outside, she could count on Paul to finish the job.

On the ground floor, Morgan was forcing himself to take deep breaths. His bruised ribs were killing him but he had to clear his head. He was not aware of anyone else in the chateau until O'Ryan ran up the stairs. Now he looked up, anticipating their return. The newcomer was Felicity. He could feel it. If she got down the stairs first he would shout to her. If she was fast she might free one of his hands before O'Ryan caught up. That would give him a chance.

Morgan saw Felicity leaping down from the turn in the stairs. She sailed over the last ten steps and landed on all fours. A quick leap took her past him to the door. He understood her thinking, but it was the wrong choice. The door was secured with a bolt, a chain and a key lock. She had no time to open them all. She turned, near panic. O'Ryan was stomping down behind her. Frantic, Morgan tried to tip the chair so that he could at least get in O'Ryan's way, but his efforts were useless. He had no strength, and there was no time.

But then O'Ryan's right foot caught on something. It had to be the wire Felicity always strung across stairs. He stumbled, and his left ankle, twice injured, gave way. He collapsed, open mouthed, at the foot of the stairs. There was a brief, "No!" just before the thump of the body hitting the floor. Felicity raised her hand to her mouth in horror. O'Ryan's final scream was oddly silent. When he pushed himself up on his hands, Morgan could see he had fallen on the poker. The wicked curved edge was a red hot spear which slid into his chest when he landed on it. The point was just long enough to pierce his heart. The pain must have been intense, but he never looked at the poker. He turned his head to look at Morgan. O'Ryan's face displayed more puzzlement than pain or anger. A drop of blood leaked around the wound in his chest, hissing into steam.

When O'Ryan collapsed to the floor, Morgan felt the

gorge rise in his throat. To his last second, Ian O'Ryan never understood how he could lose, or even why he was wrong.

Morgan had only a dim awareness of the pressure easing on his ankles, and then his wrists. He never felt the tiny tender kisses on his head and cheeks. He barely heard the constant outpouring of anguished words from Felicity. The phrase "Look what he's done to you" got through his muddled head, and he wondered how he would be able to do that. He was just aware of his limbs being free when the door was kicked open and Paul walked in.

Paul looked first at the body on the floor, then at Morgan in the chair with Felicity behind him. He looked down at his gun and slid it into its shoulder holster.

"How do I look?" Morgan asked him through swollen lips.

"Bad." Paul made a quick visual evaluation of Morgan's injuries, and then cast a quick glanced at Felicity.

Morgan saw the suffering on Felicity's face that Paul must have seen. He guessed that Felicity had never seen a man really beaten before. Through the slits of his eyes he watched Paul walk over to O'Ryan and turn him over. He looked at the wound and felt the neck for a pulse. Pointless. When he looked up Morgan saw a ghost of emotion pass across his face. Felicity was almost hysterical. Would Paul know what to say to break through to her?

"Miss O'Brien," Paul said, keeping his voice casual, "Mister Stark cannot get out of here alone. You have to help him to the boat. I'll take care of this mess. Please, miss. If the police have spoken to your uncle or your friends we may only be moments ahead of them." Morgan knew better and he knew that Paul had no more respect for police promptness than he did. But his short speech had the right effect.

Felicity knew the police could not possibly be on their

trail, but being spoken to like an amateur reminded her that she couldn't stand there acting like one. Shaking herself into action, she untwisted the wires holding Morgan to the chair. Trying not to look at the awful burns on each shoulder, or the purple around his ribs, or his face at all, Felicity helped Morgan to his feet and the two stumbled out of the chateau.

The sun hit them like a search beacon, scorching their eyes. Pulling one of Morgan's arms around her shoulders, Felicity wondered how Paul would handle the body. Morgan was regaining a little strength, and it seemed that he guessed her thoughts.

"He's a professional, Red," Morgan said. "He'll handle it. You come by boat?"

"Yeah."

"Get me to it," Morgan said. "I won't ask how you found me."

"It's a long story," Felicity said, tripping over some scrub grass. "You know, you're heavy." Like a pair of drunken sailors, they staggered to the water's edge where Morgan slumped into the small boat. He looked at the sky and dipped one hand into the water. He mumbled words Felicity could just make out.

"It's a beautiful day out. That sun feels great on my skin. Thank you for saving my life." Then he passed out.

- 34 -

Morgan slid his eyes slowly open. Felicity sat dozing in the awkward visitor's chair, but she was holding his hand when he awoke. Before getting her attention, he tried a deep breath. It still hurt like hell, but it was getting better. Actually, he hurt all over. The beating and burns aside, he was still sore from the race, the fall that ended the race, the bullet wound, and the fight before it.

The room was all white--the sheets, the walls, the ceiling, even the curtains. Outside the two big windows behind Felicity lay a well kept lawn. The bed was comfortable, and he saw rather than felt an intravenous drip going into his right arm.

"At the risk of being trite, where am I?" he asked, startling his partner awake.

"Hi. Welcome back to the land of the living."

"It's good to be back," he said. "Where am I?"

Felicity squeezed his hand and smiled into his face. "A small private hospital in the south of France. Very small. Very private."

"How long?" Morgan asked. His throat was dry. He pulled himself into a seated position, and noticed he was wearing silk pajamas. He found water on his bedside table, and poured himself a glass.

"Just about forty-eight hours. In and out of consciousness. You were on some heavy drugs while they worked on you." She paused, and Morgan knew there was some important unfinished business she wanted to clear away in a hurry. "Morgan, I know about O'Ryan and my parents."

"I'm sorry now I didn't tell you," he replied, then drained his water glass.

"Wonder if the dreams will stop now," Felicity said, as if she were talking to herself. Then, to Morgan, "Is this empty feeling vengeance for my parents' death?"

Morgan let most of a minute go by, just watching the pain in her deep green eyes. Finally, he said, "You didn't kill him, you know."

Felicity stared out the window. A bird out there was scolding her mate. They were sailing in tandem toward their nest. She turned back to look deeply into Morgan's eyes, trying to see all the way to the bottom line.

"You're concerned about me," she said at last. "You're afraid that killing him would affect me somehow."

Morgan's face was stern, rigid. "Killing a man always affects you. Nobody comes away clean from that. Sometimes, if you do it enough times, a callous can form around your heart, but it always affects you. I don't want that happening to you."

"Don't worry," she said. "I know it was a freak accident. But I'm not sorry about it. And if it hadn't happened, I'd have wanted you or Paul or someone to do it anyway."

While holding that thought in his mind Morgan realized how close and restrictive the room felt. He noted the light, pastel blue sun dress Felicity wore and the sunshine outside, and assumed the weather was perfect. He hoped her soul was still as light as it was a week ago.

"Well, can I get out of this bed?"

"I hope so," Felicity said. "There's a crowd of people waiting for you outside."

Morgan buzzed for a nurse. When he looked toward the door he saw Paul standing next to it. Morgan did not doubt that he had been standing there for two days. He waved the man to his bedside.

"Guess I should say thanks," Morgan said.

"You called for backup. Hope I did the right thing."

"You did exactly right," Morgan said. Before he could

say another word, Claudette flew into the room. She wrapped her arms tightly around him, burying her face in his neck. He thought he felt water on his back.

"Okay, doll, you must have got me into this place," Morgan said. "How long am I going to be here?"

"Just until tomorrow, lover," Claudette said, kissing him. "After that we can relax for a week while they wait for the swelling to go down. Then you'll be back for the plastic work. They do the best here. Your teeth will be perfect and there won't be a scar on your face when they're through. Or you shoulders. Or your leg. Actually, they've quite a lot of work to do."

A nurse who was a perfect Elle Macpherson look alike brought a wheelchair. With a deft body check, Paul replaced her. With Claudette and Felicity's help he got Morgan into the chair. Paul pushed it slowly while Felicity pushed the wheeled I.V. pole. Claudette held his hand as if she thought he might disappear if she lost her grip on him. As they rolled down the long antiseptic halls, Morgan's mind spun at high speed. As his system shook the numbing anesthetics, the questions came pouring out.

"Hey, Red. Have you talked to Grey?"

"Yesterday," Felicity said. "He assures me I have no criminal record anywhere in Europe. There's no problem with regard to the bounced checks because as it turns out, Mister O'Ryan's estate made a contribution to my uncle's church in exactly that amount. He said thank you, and that he never met us."

"Dynamite. Now, have you talked to Fox?"

"This morning," Felicity said. "She's terrified of running the place much longer alone but I told her she could handle it. We're wanted for security on a rock concert. I told her to turn it down. We got a response to my proposal on security for a new office building. That's a go as soon as we get home. There's a bonded courier job that Paul can handle when he gets back tomorrow. We provided a driver and bodyguard to some diplomat or other. You're wanted to outfit a military group in...am I pronouncing this right? Djibouti?"

"Right. Little country near Ethiopia. I'd have to do that one personally."

"Then they'll have to get someone else," Felicity said. At the end of the hall they faced a wide glass door which Felicity reached to push open. As her hand touched the handle, Morgan felt Felicity's nails dig into his shoulder. A heartbeat later his nervous system jangled up his spine and his drug slowed senses brought him the feel, the scent of danger.

"Paul! Back inside," he said, but there was no movement. He twisted around to see a short, squat man behind Paul pressing a slim automatic into his back.

"Out," the stranger said, in an accent Morgan couldn't place. He stared up into Claudette's deep brown eyes and saw terror there. His mind was searching for options but Paul's grunt interrupted him. The gunman had jammed the barrel into Paul's back, but Paul was looking down at Morgan, unmoving. With Claudette and Felicity in danger, their options were narrowed to zero, so Morgan nodded toward the door and Paul moved forward.

They stepped through the wide door into brilliant sunshine. Morgan was assailed by the scent of lilacs. The heat hit him like a living thing and he began to sweat under the tape wrapped around his ribs. They moved across the wide lawn toward a round white table with a huge umbrella over it and four people sitting around it.

Marlene looked as if she could not catch her breath. Sean trembled with rage. Raoul stared at the man standing beside him, probably watching for an opening. The fourth man wore a white suit and felt hat, just like the two men standing at either side of the table. But while they held guns, the seated man's hands were empty. That marked him as the leader.

When the seated man stood he proved to be taller

than his helpers. He walked to Morgan and smiled down into his face.

"You, my battered friend, have interfered with our cause recently, or so I understand."

"So who the hell are you?" Morgan asked.

"You can call me Youssef in your last minutes," the tall man said while sliding a slim pistol out of his waistband. It was an old Russian Tokarev, Morgan saw.

"They have security here," Claudette said in a small voice.

"Not anymore," Youssef said. His complexion was swarthy and rough, and he smiled with only the left side of his mouth.

"A raghead," Morgan said with disgust. "What the hell are you doing here?"

Youssef's eyes flared as he shoved the muzzle of his gun within inches of Morgan's face. "We know you for the blood thirsty counter revolutionary you are, Stark. You are a murdering enemy of our cause. It is only to be decided if these others are to die with you."

Morgan had stopped breathing when the pistol appeared. This man was irrational, Morgan thought. He could go off at any time, and so could that gun. Ignoring the tube down which death could rush at any second, he focused on Youssef's eyes, his own eyes narrowing to slits.

"If you plan to hurt one of those people at that table over there, you'd better kill me now."

Youssef's laugh was high, and his black, oily hair flipped back when his head snapped up. "You are arrogant, black dog. But yes, you have killed many while they have killed none. You are the enemy. You have interfered with our brothers who struggle in Ireland. So, you die."

Youssef's pistol centered between Morgan's eyes. Morgan stared straight ahead, his teeth bared. No weapons. Not even the strength to stand. This was no way to die. His pulse quickened and his legs tensed. If he dived forward, maybe he could give Paul a chance to act.

Beside him, Felicity broke into a high, nervous laugh. "This is about O'Ryan?" she asked. "The boy was robbing you blind."

Youssef's gun swiveled to cover her. "You know this?" He stalked forward, the pistol thrust forward at arm's length. Felicity stumbled back, tripped, and fell onto her side. "How do you know this?" His left arm cocked back to slap Felicity, but Paul intercepted it. Youssef's right arm swept around, creasing Paul's skull with his gun's barrel. As Paul fell away, Youssef sighted down his gun at Paul's head.

"Stop it," Morgan said. "We know O'Ryan was embezzling your funds because we saw the way he lived, asshole." Youssef turned to face him. "And when we went to rob him, we saw how much money he had," Morgan continued. "He was living like a king on all that dough you boys sent him."

Youssef's dark face flushed almost purple. He wrapped his hands into Morgan's pajama top, lifting him out of the wheelchair. "Where is he?" he bellowed into Morgan's face.

"If you're one of bin Laden's boys, or whoever's running the whole al Queda deal these days, you must have known what he was doing," Morgan said. "The one thing Osama understood was the finance end of terror. That's the real reason you're on The Continent, ain't it? I'm just a convenient stopover. Shit, we did you a favor boy."

Tight lipped, Youssef dropped Morgan back into the chair. "Where is he? Where is O'Ryan?"

"Paul?" Morgan looked over at his friend, who had regained his feet.

"At the bottom of the Atlantic," Paul said. "Apparent fishing accident. May never be found."

Felicity took a deep breath and let it out slowly as a new silence settled over the lawn. Morgan and Youssef seemed to share a spotlight, the center of the action. Felicity regained her feet, to stand at the edge of that imaginary spotlight, watching a frozen diorama within it. At that tense moment she had no trouble reading the Arab's face. He was weighing his options, she knew, comparing risk against possible gain.

A slight breeze chilled her a bit, making her aware of how much sweat covered her body right then. And she wasn't even the one under the gun. Youssef was thinking too long, she thought, and every second brought Morgan closer to death. He was sweating too, and probably in pain. She didn't think they could not fight their way out of this one. But if Youssef was not completely irrational, then maybe, just maybe, she could help him make the right decision.

"Do they speak English?" Felicity asked, pointing at the men guarding the table and the gunman behind Morgan. Youssef looked up at her, his face twisted with contempt, and made a noise that sounded like "Feh." She took that to mean no.

"Okay, look. I think poking around Ireland would have been risky for you," Felicity said in what she hoped was a calm, reasonable voice. "We spared you that. But hanging around here, that's just as dicey. Besides, my partner here is out of the counterterrorism business. So there's nothing to be gained by killing him. And by now, somebody inside must have gathered their wits enough to call the police. You start killing people, they'll shut Europe down. Getting out's going to be tough."

Youssef was staring into Felicity's face now, but his gun was still pointed between Morgan's eyes. She knew he could go either way.

"She's right," Morgan said, regaining Youssef's attention. "So how about this? You walk now, and nobody comes looking for you. I tell the cops this was a private argument. You go home and tell your boss you did O'Ryan. Everybody's happy."

Felicity thought they might be getting through to

Youssef, but he dived forward, his gun shoved against Morgan's throat. Breath froze in the pit of Felicity's stomach. It's over, she thought. We've lost.

"Why should I believe anything you say, black dog?" An invisible fist crushed Felicity's ribs as Youssef's eyes bored into Morgan's from just inches away. But despite her fear, her heart leaped with pride to see Morgan meet the Arab's eyes with a fierce energy.

"Because I'm a professional," Morgan said with a contemptuous sneer. "Look it up."

Trembling, Felicity watched Youssef's finger tense on the Tokarev's trigger, then ease away from it. He snapped back as suddenly as he had darted forward and repeated his high, squealing laugh. Then he rattled off a series of orders in Farsi too fast for her to follow. His men gathered behind the round lawn table. Youssef turned as if to go, but spun back around, landing a back hand blow to Morgan's swollen face, hard enough to drop him out of the chair.

"For past crimes, black dog," he said, then spit on Morgan and trotted off to join his men. In seconds they had disappeared into the woods.

Claudette was on her knees in an instant, cradling Morgan, trying to sit him up. Her tears flowed freely. Paul drew his pistol, but did not pursue the Arabs. Felicity was thankful for that, and when she found Morgan's eyes she saw he felt the same way. Then she knelt and helped Claudette get Morgan back into the chair.

"Is it over now?" Felicity asked.

"Now, I think it is," Morgan said. "All over but the healing. Claudette, you got any empty space at your place? I think I need a vacation."

THE END

Author's Bio

Austin S. Camacho is a public affairs specialist for the Department of Defense. America's military people overseas know him because for more than a decade his radio and television news reports were transmitted to them daily on the American Forces Network.

He was born in New York City but grew up in Saratoga Springs, New York. He majored in psychology at Union College in Schenectady, New York. Dwindling finances and escalating costs brought his college days to an end after three years. He enlisted in the Army as a weapons repairman but soon moved into a more appropriate field. The Army trained him to be a broadcast journalist. Disc jockey time alternated with news writing, video camera and editing work, public affairs assignments and news anchor duties.

During his years as a soldier, Austin lived in Missouri, California, Maryland, Georgia and Belgium. While enlisted he finished his Bachelor's Degree at night and started his Master's, and rose to the rank of Sergeant First Class. In his spare time, he began writing adventure and mystery novels set in some of the exotic places he'd visited.

After leaving the Army he continued to write military news for the Defense Department as a civilian. Today he handles media relations and writes articles for the DoD's Deployment Health Support Directorate. He has settled in northern Virginia with his wife Denise.

Austin is a voracious reader of just about any kind of nonfiction, plus mysteries, adventures and thrillers. When he isn't working or reading, he's writing.

Keep up with all of Austin S. Camacho's latest
accomplishments at
www.ascamacho.com

Also by
AUSTIN S. CAMACHO

The Payback Assignment

Meet Morgan Stark and Felicity O'Brien
A Mercenary and a Jewel Thief –
Many find them a deadly combination...

Morgan Stark, a black mercenary soldier, is stranded in the Central American nation of Belize after a raid goes wrong.

Felicity O'Brien, an Irish jewel thief, is stranded in the jungle south of Mexico after doing a job for an American client.

When these two meet, they learn they've been double-crossed by the same man: Adrian Seagrave, a ruthless businessman maintaining his respectability by having others do his dirty work.

Morgan and Felicity become friends and partners while following their common enemy's trail. They become even closer when they find they share a peculiar psychic link, allowing them to sense danger approaching themselves, or each other.

But their extrasensory abilities and fighting skills are tested to their limits against Seagrave's soldiers-for-hire and Monk, his giant simian bodyguard. A series of battles from California to New York lead to a final confrontation with Seagrave's army of hired killers in a skyscraper engulfed by flames.

LaVergne, TN USA
01 October 2009
159593LV00001B/15/A